# Ski Bum

To Jim –
Here's to Park City
1982-83. Think snow!

Colin Clancy

**Ordering Information:**

Special discounts available for **book clubs, corporations, associations**.
For details, contact the publisher at director@vanvelzerpress.com.

The characters and events in this book are fictitious. Any similarity to real persons, living or dead, is coincidental and not intended by the author.

Cover & Chapter Art by Colin Clancy

**Paperback ISBN: 978-1-954253-27-8**
**Hardback ISBN: 978-1-954253-28-5**
**eBook ISBN: 978-1-954253-29-2**

Library of Congress Control Number Available from Publisher

**Printed in the United States of America**
FSC-certified paper when possible

Van Velzer Press
3792 W. Creek Road
Brandon, Vermont 05733
(802) 247-6797

VanVelzerPress.com

*For Amy*

"We all felt good and we felt healthy ... You could not be upset about anything on a day like that."

~ Ernest Hemingway, *The Sun Also Rises*

"… we walked three abreast in the cobblestone street, drunk and laughing and talking like men who knew they would separate at dawn and travel to the far corners of the earth."

~ Hunter S. Thompson, *The Rum Diary*

# 1

I woke to the house shaking like the whole damned thing was about to collapse. The bell had been clanging for half a minute, spitting distance from my second story window, but I'd learned to sleep through it. I raised a middle finger, hoping one of the Amtrak passengers, westbound for Chicago, might catch a glimpse. If I slept a bit longer, took a shower, brewed a pot of coffee, I could've been standing naked in the window sipping a cup in time for the Detroit-bound train. But I was already late for my exam.

The walk to campus took longer than normal, the sidewalks covered in slop snow. When I showed up to the lecture hall, jeans soaked to the knees, people filled about every seat already shading in Scantron bubbles. I took a test copy from the TA and excused myself into the middle of a row. The class was something like Communications Theory, some bullshit gen-ed for juniors who hadn't picked a major yet, and my answers to the multiple-choice questions were either common sense or complete guesses. None of it mattered—I was flunking out anyway.

That night my buddies threw me a going away party, a bash with kegs on ice in the bathtub and the hallway full of people drinking from plastic cups.

"You got balls, man," my roommate said as we stood outside barefoot after our sixth beer pong win in a row, escaping the hot cramped house for a minute. "Just packing up and leaving, becoming a ski bum."

"I need to change things up for a while," I said, which couldn't have been truer. My whole life and everything in it felt stagnant. "Not too late for you to come with. Plenty of jobs out there."

He pondered for a moment, arms crossed, shivering a little in the cold. The sleet turned to fat, wet snowflakes that coated the driveway white but melted as they landed on my forearms. "Nah," he said. "I wish, man. But I can't do it."

"Why not? Everyone here always talks about doing big things. Let's actually do something this time."

I could tell he took my comments as a sort of jab, which they kind of were.

"I wish, man," he said.

* * *

I had trouble sleeping and woke before the train, a little hungover but itching to get out. I grabbed my backpack and tiptoed across sleeping bodies in the hallway to the door. I'd already packed my rusted-out Cherokee—a couple duffel bags in the back and two pairs of skis on the roof-rack. I popped in a Bob Seger CD, whipped a shitty in the wet snow, and headed west in the grey, pre-dawn light.

# 2

The employee housing lobby looked like a college dorm except everyone wore ski clothes, mostly young people but not everybody. A guy and a girl in long underwear played pool while others sat on couches playing video games on a big screen. A bald white dude played ping pong excitedly with a Latin-looking guy while a crowd gathered around them. The South American scored a point, and they both yelled in Spanish.

Ten minutes later, room key issued, I carried as much of my shit as I could down the seventh-floor hallway looking for my room. I opened the door to 716 to find the bald dude from the lobby standing there in nothing but boxers.

"Who the hell are you, and what are you doing in my room?" he shouted.

"Sorry," I said, backing out the door. "Sorry."

The guy giggled like a child. "Relax," he said. "I'm just giving you shit. They told me I'd be getting a roommate today."

He grabbed the duffel bag off my shoulder and dragged it into the tiny room. A half-dozen snowboards lined the cinder block walls and a pile of gear concealed a small desk. A down sleeping bag covered the top bunk and a pile of clothes the bottom, a few trail maps taped to the wall the room's only decorations.

"Bill," the guy said as he shoveled the clothes from the bottom bunk into an empty duffel. "Welcome to the Block."

"Jimmy," I said. "Why's it called the Block?"

"Look around you. Looks like a cell block."

# COLIN CLANCY

Beyond the window the massive mountain disappeared into a thick cloud of falling snow, an unreal sight for a Midwest kid who'd never been west before. Below us people loaded a quad chairlift that went on forever up the slope and disappeared over a ridgeline. If the window had been open I could have thrown a snowball and hit people in the lift line.

"This view, man," I said.

"Can't beat it," he agreed. "You look like you've never seen a mountain before."

"Not a real one. I'm from Michigan."

"No way, man. I'm a Wisconsin boy. Right across the lake."

I stared out for a good minute before lounging out on the bottom bunk, dead tired from driving all night.

"No nappy time," Bill said, tossing my bag onto the bed next to me. "We're wasting daylight. Let's go skiing."

"Sure thing," I said and dumped my bag out on the floor, picking out the essentials and leaving everything else out on the carpet. My boots were cold and stiff from the back of the Jeep and from sitting unused since last winter, but I crammed my feet in.

Outside, I pulled down my goggles to shield my eyes from the fat flakes for our short walk to the lift, still in awe of the mountain before me.

"What were you doing inside on a day like this?" I asked.

"I had first tracks this morning," Bill answered. "Was out riding 'til noon and just went in for a quick lunch. Got caught up in a game of ping pong."

"Was that you I heard yelling in Spanish?"

"The Argentineans and I have a little wager going on table tennis. They win more games than me, I have to move down there at the end of the season."

"To Argentina?"

"To Argentina."

# SKI BUM

My skis felt heavy as I clicked into them for the first time of the season. I followed Bill pushing his board into the short lift line behind some ski school kids and their instructors.

"So what do you get if you win this bet?"

"I don't remember. I'm moving to Argentina anyway; an endless winter."

A class of tiny kids in color-coded vests stood in front of us with their teacher, a girl whose brown curls spilled from beneath a powder blue knit hat. Her boots matched the cap. Bill grabbed one of my ski poles and poked her with it.

She turned around and looked at me, confused. Then she saw Bill and nodded toward us, blue goggle lenses glinting in the snow-filtered white light.

"Boys," she said in greeting.

"My new roommate, Jimmy," Bill said. "Meet Kylie. She's part of our group."

"Pleasure to meet you, Jimmy," she said. "Welcome to Silver Mountain."

Compared to the lifts in Michigan this chair went on forever. Rather than skiing down we loaded another chair, Bill greeting the lifties by name as we got on. Once we reached the top the sky cleared and I had my first view of the jagged peaks in the distance spread out for miles.

Bill took off down a short bump run, the moguls and their troughs almost hidden in the fresh snow. I followed, skiing timid for the first few turns, afraid that I wouldn't remember how it felt. Each turn, though, brought the familiar feeling of freedom I hadn't experienced since last winter. With each turn I wanted more—this feeling was the only thing that mattered.

The bump run dumped onto a cat track where Bill slowed for a second, making sure I was with him before pushing off onto a cruiser. I hit the smooth snow and opened it up, my turns changing from tight weaves into long flowing carves. I made wide arcing turns on the gentle

slope then picked up speed as the trail steepened. I felt the edges of my skis digging into the hardpack underneath the fluff and I got low, my inside leg bent on each turn so that my hand and the handle of my pole skimmed the top of the snow. I passed Bill and then dumped speed as I remembered I didn't know where I was going.

Before long my thighs—and lungs—burned. I made a couple more giant slalom turns before stopping on the side of the run about halfway down the mountain. I gasped for air for a moment, not used to the altitude. Bill kept bombing the hill, so I pushed off, straightlining toward him with the ache in my legs never calming.

"You're pretty quick on that thing," I said, catching my breath aboard an old fixed-grip triple on some back corner of the mountain. "How long you been riding?"

"I skied as a kid," he said. "Started boarding when I moved out here six years ago." He took off his beanie. The sweat on the bald front of his head steamed in the cold air.

"And how long have you been bald, old man?"

"I wouldn't laugh if I were you," he said. "I had a big curly afro just like you until a couple years ago." He rubbed the back of his head. "It'll all be gone by the time I'm thirty."

The old lift moved slowly. We watched the only other people up there pick their way through the moguls under the lift line. When we got off the chair Bill had his binding strapped in seconds and was off into the trees. In the thick, steep glade, he was soon out of sight.

I blocked overhanging limbs with my fists until the trees got so thick I could barely squeeze through. Just when I thought about traversing out of there the trees opened into a small clearing where logs had been piled into an elaborate cabin style fort. Bill's board leaned against the entrance and he sat inside smoking a cigarette.

"All that hair must be slowing you down," he said as I unclicked my skis and went inside. "This old man is kicking your ass."

He was right. I sucked air while Bill sat there dragging on his cigarette. He offered me one. I shook my head.

"And it looks like you hit something," he said, pulling a small branch out of the hood of my coat.

"What's this place?" I asked.

"Smoke shack. We build them in the summertime when we're bored. Usually the Forest Service guys knock them down, but they'll never find this one."

I sat on a stump next to him, still catching my breath as he put his cigarette out in the dirt and pocketed the butt. Without another word, he put his board back on and dropped into a narrow chute off the backside of the fort.

We got off the next lift, and Bill started hiking the ridgeline. I followed him up the trail which steepened into stairs kicked into the ice. My throat dried, my lungs burned, and my skis felt heavy on my shoulder. I stopped to take off my jacket and tie it around my waist. Up ahead, Bill turned around. I thought he was going to say something, but instead he bent down and packed a loose snowball, lobbing it toward me and missing by several feet.

"This shit's kickin' my ass," I said.

"It'll do that," he said, grabbing another clump of snow and biting into it like an apple. "Bigger than the trash heaps you're used to back home, isn't it?"

I kept hiking toward him in methodical steps. He climbed slowly also, in a meandering way that told me he was forcing himself to slow down so as not to ditch me.

"You'll get used to it," he shouted down as if reading my mind.

Finally, when I looked up, he stood on a rounded summit not too far above me. Pretty soon I joined him.

I dropped my skis to the ground, picked up a snowball, and took a bite. The snowfall had stopped. I could see peaks in every direction jutting out into a cobalt sky. The skiers riding the backside of Silver were tiny dots as the afternoon sun lit the Ten-Mile Range in gold.

Bill strapped in and, without hesitation, got a running start along the lip of the bowl and hucked himself off a corniced section. He must

have flown 20 feet before touching snow. When he landed his body whipped back, shoulders hitting the powder. I thought he was eating shit, but he somehow managed to right himself and lean into a huge, heel-side powder carve.

My own turns were deliberate, tight weaves in a couple inches of fresh snow. My thighs burned, a pleasurable ache. At the bottom I looked over my shoulder to admire my tracks.

We rode one more lift to get back to the front side of Silver. On blue cruisers I made huge railroad track carves. This time Bill struggled to keep up with me, my skis faster than his board on the cruisers. He straightlined the last pitch toward the base area, passing me. I bent down into a racer's tuck and chased him, catching him just before we reached the bottom.

# 3

People milled around the base, done skiing for the day. Bill cruised around them like slalom gates, bobbing his head to music bumping from the patio. I followed him to an outdoor bar covered by a huge umbrella where people surrounded two empty chairs. They'd been saved for us.

Bill pushed his way through the crowd and grabbed the shoulders of a dude who still wore dark tinted goggles, goggle strap wrapped around a head of messy brown hair.

The dude looked up and nodded at Bill then continued his conversation with Kylie, sitting a few seats away. "But, man," he said, swigging from a pint of orange beer, "you honestly want me to just sit there and wait?"

"Of course," Kylie said. "It's crazy that you wouldn't date someone just because she can't keep up." She sipped her cocktail and looked up at us with a smile, goggles propped on top her head showing off her freckles and deep goggle tan.

"Who can't keep up?" Bill asked.

"This chick I met at Cuddy's last week," the kid, Ryan, said. "It's not going to work out."

"This girl is a skier, right?" Bill asked. "Is that the deal? You have it in your mind that you only want to date boarder chicks?"

"Not at all," Ryan said. "I show no prejudice."

Bill spun around to face the bartender, a girl with light brown skin and long black hair. "Double Jack and Coke for the bald one?" she asked in a strong Latin accent.

"You know it," Bill said.

"You the one living with this clown?" she asked me, reaching over the bar to shake my hand. "What's your drink?"

I ordered the same orange beer as Ryan.

"That accent," Bill said as she walked away, "I love that accent. I'm going to marry that girl."

"But she doesn't know it yet," Kylie said.

"Where's she from?" I asked.

"Argentina," Kylie said, sliding her drink down the bar next to us.

"Bill did say he was moving to Argentina."

"Think that's a coincidence?" Kylie said, rubbing the top of Bill's head. "This boy's in love."

The bartender, Aurelia, sat our drinks down. I pulled the few remaining bills from my wallet and handed them to her.

"Don't worry about it, Jimmy," she said, pushing them back toward me. "Glad to have you here."

Before I could thank her, she turned to help an obnoxiously loud middle-aged guy in a one-piece ski suit who called for tequila shots for everyone around him.

"She doesn't know it yet," Bill said, "but yes, she's going to fall in love with me very soon. We'll get married, and I'll become an Argentine cowboy." He took a long and determined swig of his cocktail, and then hummed the melody of an old-timey sounding country song.

Kylie laughed. She turned to me. "Where you from, Jimmy?"

"Michigan," I half yelled, trying to overcome the noise of the growing crowd. "You guys?" I leaned in to hear their answers.

"New Hampshire," Kylie said. "He's from Seattle." She nodded at Ryan, who had tilted back on his stool to watch a group of college girls take shots.

"Seattle," Ryan said, turning back to us. I couldn't tell if he was answering my question or just repeating what Kylie said. "You guys should have seen my lesson today. I had a bunch of little rippers from Frisco. We were in the park the whole time. They were learning 360s. I

spent the whole day showing off for them on the rails. Three boys and a girl. The girl was the best of all."

"You played in the terrain park all day and got paid for it?"

Ryan nodded. The lenses of his goggles flashed as the sun, now hovering just above the mountain tops to the west, caught them. "The girl's mom tipped me twenty bucks, too." He finished his pint with a large gulp and slammed the glass down on the bar.

I took a big gulp of my beer, too, finishing it. "You get a lot of lessons like that?"

He smirked.

"Don't be fooled," Kylie said. "You'll spend most days on the magic carpet picking four-year-olds up off the snow."

"I never knew how fat little kids could be," Ryan said in agreement. He flexed his biceps, muscleman style. "I spend all day curling them, and now I'm ripped."

"You ripped a fart," Bill said then struck a bodybuilder pose of his own. "Three-year-olds? Try picking up fatass fifty-year-old gapers all day. Half these rich assholes can't understand the concept of sitting down on a chair moving nine miles an hour."

The man in the one-piece got up to leave; the large group around him got up too. He dropped a twenty into the tip jar before staggering away. The bar quieted down as they left. It got a bit colder, too, as the sun dropped behind the mountains.

"What's a gaper?"

"*That* dude is a gaper," Kylie said, tipping her fresh bloody toward one-piece guy stumbling away.

Bill watched the guy go. "A gaper's a tourist who can't ski but pretends to be badass—taking photos in front of black diamond signs like his friends back home give a shit."

"A rich poser," Ryan said.

"You'll see them decked out in neon yellow and pink suits," Bill continued. "Look like sherbet."

"More concerned with counting their vertical than just enjoying their time in the mountains," Kylie added.

Aurelia finished cleaning up after the tourists and came back to us. "So did you pass the ski test?" she asked me.

"I haven't taken it yet." The question made me nervous. I'd spent the day skiing and hadn't thought about the test. What if I couldn't pass it, if I moved all this way just to end up bussing tables in the cafeteria?

"She doesn't mean that ski test," Ryan said. "She means *his* ski test." He raised his beer toward Bill like he was toasting him.

"Don't worry," Aurelia said. "I didn't pass it."

This scared me even more. These seemed to be my new instant friends, and I didn't want to be the gaper that couldn't keep up. I looked to Bill.

He waited a moment, taking a long drink, letting the anticipation grow before he said, "Flying colors. I even tried to lose him in the trees."

"If you can pass Bill's test," Kylie said, "then you can ski better than half the instructors you'll be working with. Welcome to ski school."

Aurelia set a shotski on the bar and emptied a Tuaca bottle into all five glasses, filling each one to the rim. She climbed over the bar and took her place beside us.

"To Jimmy," Kylie said, "and his first day living the life."

"To Jimmy!" they all repeated.

We hoisted the ski in unison and poured the shots down. I felt some of the booze splash down my beard but caught most of it in my mouth. The liqueur had a smooth caramel taste and made my throat warm. My cheeks went numb. I definitely felt a buzz. I shook my head to clear it.

"The best thing about this altitude," Kylie said, stacking the empty shot glasses and handing them to Aurelia, "you get drunk quicker."

The peaks to the west now completely blocked the sun. I put my coat back on. The tourists finished their drinks, paid their tabs, and left us alone on the patio.

# SKI BUM

Aurelia began closing the bar, loading liquor bottles into a box.

"Let's head to Cuddy's for another," Bill said. He chugged his beer then walked behind the bar and pulled the garbage bag from the can. He held the top of the bag in one hand and spun it with the other. He tied it off and threw it over his shoulder while I hurried to finish my drink before dropping my last fiver into Aurelia's glass tip jar.

Buzzed and with boots unbuckled, the flagstone sidewalk took some effort. Ryan followed Bill, weaving back and forth. Bill heaved the garbage bag into a big dumpster, taking three tries to get it up over the lip. Kylie seemed to be the only one really holding it together.

The sidewalk led to a round frozen pond, a lit Christmas tree anchored in the ice in the middle. A half-dozen skaters circled the tree and a group of boys in snow boots played broomball. We shuffled across the ice toward a two-story building on the other side. Ryan slipped and fell, sprawled on his back for a while before we helped him up. Kylie stumbled too, I grabbed her gloved hand, preventing her fall.

Guinness posters lined the walls and a soccer game played on a small TV in the dimly lit place called McGillycuddy's. The cook sat at the bar watching the game with the bartender, who started pouring beers before we even sat down.

"Who's playing?" Ryan asked.

"Who gives a shit," the bartender said, "it's soccer."

"The soccer lover is Muppet," Bill said to me.

He had a wide flat face with a nose that looked like it had been pushed in. A green Guinness baseball cap clashed with his bright red beard.

"Muppet?" I asked.

"Real name's Derek," he said, "but Muppet it is."

He set pints of PBR in front of us.

"I'll have a CC Manhattan," Kylie said.

"How about a sex on the beach? A red headed slut?" Muppet said.

"You know I don't drink that girlie stuff."

"You guys ride today?" he asked, pouring her drink. "Real nice snow in the Meadows."

"We were out all afternoon," I said, "and now I can hardly walk."

"He's from Michigan too," Bill said.

Muppet smiled, wide and toothy. "Me too. Came out here after college."

"You graduated?"

"Oh yeah. Got a business degree from U of M. I had a real job for a couple months. But it ate my soul. This is way better."

"See," Bill said to Kylie. "No sense in finishing college. It's a soul killer." He slammed his drink on the bar top like a gavel.

"College isn't the soul killer," she said. "His job was. I'm going back next year."

"Let's play some fricken foosball," Ryan said, putting his arm around me.

We followed him upstairs. He and Bill took one side of the table, with Kylie and me on the other. I controlled the forwards and Kylie the backs and goalie. We scored a quick goal, Ryan not paying close attention at first. Kylie high-fived me.

Ryan played with a big grin on his face. He leaned his weight on the handles and spun them so his players did endless backflips. He was having fun but wasn't any good, and we scored a few more points. Bill hit Ryan across the back of his head.

"What the hell?" Ryan said.

Kylie giggled at this, the first sign she gave of feeling anything other than sober. When we scored again Bill switched spots with Ryan, taking control of the goalie. Ryan concentrated now, his eyes squinted, almost closed. He scored one goal and then another then danced around in circles. "That's how you play foosball," he yelled. "Let me know if you want some lessons."

Kylie and I huddled up. She put her hands on my shoulders and leaned her head forward like she was a quarterback or something. "They're on a roll," I said. "Let's finish this thing."

She nodded, her tight curls bouncing with the movement, and I went back to my handles. We scored three quick goals and won.

"Suck that," Kylie said to Bill. She put her arm around me, and I side-hugged her back.

We played and drank, losers buying tequila shots. When we finally called it a night, I had to grab the railing while descending the stairs to keep from tumbling down them. The restaurant was more crowded now, half the tables full and people taking up every seat at the bar. Muppet flirted up a couple of girls standing there to order drinks.

"Later, Mupp," Kylie called out as we left, and he waved goodbye.

Outside the sky was dark and clear. Drunk, tired and happy, I clopped around in my ski boots, which felt nice, like an adventure or something. Bill and Ryan dashed off ahead, dicking around and tackling each other into snowbanks. Kylie and I walked slowly behind. I picked up my skis and threw them over my shoulder. She did the same with hers.

In her boots, she stumbled, reaching out and grabbing my arm for balance.

"Give them to me," I said.

"I'm fine."

"I know you're fine. Just let me carry them." I took her skis and carried a pair on each shoulder. She held all four poles, a pair in each hand. We walked the deserted flagstone back toward home, stopping once to tilt our heads back and stare up at the stars.

We reached the door, Bill and Ryan already inside, and I set the skis down in the snow. Kylie reached for hers and I took her hand. She looked at me, and I went in for a kiss. She kissed me back for the briefest moment before pushing me away, not real hard, but firm enough. "Easy, slugger," she said and then grabbed her skis. I opened the door for her.

"Aren't you coming in?" she asked.

"I think I'll stay out here for a minute. Get some fresh air."

She reached out and touched my shoulder, a sort of light pinch, and then went inside.

I sat down in the snow, letting it cradle me like a chair. "Jesus," I said to no one, feeling the booze swimming around in my head. I felt embarrassed but could always chalk it up to alcohol. At least I knew where I stood. I looked up at the stars again and took a deep breath of cold air. When I exhaled, I watched the cloud of my breath floating up into the darkness.

# 4

Blinding sun peeking over the mountains spilled in through the window. Bill fumbled around the room, getting ready for work. I sat up in my bunk, panicked I'd overslept.

"What time is it?"

"Don't worry," he said. "You've got time."

I sat up and stretched. It took my eyes a minute to adjust before I could focus on him behind the specks of dust floating in the air.

"I heard you tried to molest Kylie last night," he said.

*Goddamnit,* I thought. *Why the hell did I do that? My first night here and I tried to French everyone's friend.* "She told you that?"

"Aha," Bill said. "I knew it."

"She didn't tell you?"

"I saw that twinkle in your eye last night."

I walked to the window. The mountains didn't look real in the early morning sun. "And you knew she'd turn me down?"

"Kylie's a good girl. She wouldn't hook up with anybody she'd just met."

"I guess at least everyone has something to talk about now."

"Like how you're standing naked at the window?"

"Like how I put the moves on your friend."

"Don't give yourself so much credit," he said, throwing on his green liftie jacket and grabbing one of his several snowboards. "No one gives a shit. That's what people do. They get drunk. They screw."

"We didn't screw," I said.

"I know," he said, opening the door. "Toodles."

I didn't have to meet the ski school people until after their morning rush of assigning classes, so I took my time brushing my teeth, trying to get rid of any booze breath.

The kids' ski school building was on the other side of the base area, a ten-minute walk from the Block. It had been built to look like an old-fashioned schoolhouse. Outside, instructors lined their classes up on the tiny hill. Plastic playthings covered the gentle slope. A magic carpet conveyor belt built into the snow carried kids uphill.

Ryan walked out the school door as I walked in, four miniature snowboarders following him. "Beautiful day for a hangover," he said.

Kids packed the large room inside, yelling and screaming and climbing on plastic forts and slides while instructors rushed around trying to wrangle them into ski gear. I'd had a vision of what a Colorado ski school would look like; calm students eager to learn. This wasn't it.

I'd also pictured bigger kids, like slightly smaller versions of myself. A tall and hefty man, must have been six five, walking through the middle of the crowd made the children seem even tinier. A boy and a girl had wrapped themselves around the guy's legs, so he lifted them up with each step. He wore ski bibs that emphasized his beer gut, and he held a radio that made him look official. I walked toward him, careful not to step on any children.

"I start work today," I said to the guy.

"I've got to get out of here," he said. "Let's go for a run." He shook off the kids and stuck out his hand. "Paul. You ever taught before?"

"No," I said as we headed out to grab our skis.

"No worries," he said. "You'll pick it up real quick."

Paul didn't seem to have any misgivings that I might not qualify for ski school, which eased my mind a bit. We loaded the closest lift, an old double that moved so slow I knew it must be for beginners.

"It's not a bad job, being an instructor," he said. "A couple of years ago I was getting paid to ski with doctors and their 21-year-old daughters."

"Doesn't sound like a bad gig."

"Then they promoted me to head of kids' ski school, and now I spend my days listening to screaming four-year-olds and interrupting parents' vacations to tell them their kid just pooped his pants."

"That happen a lot?"

He looked at me and laughed, but I couldn't tell if that meant yes or no. He emanated nervous tension so I felt like I should do something to calm him down. But I also felt like I still had to convince him that I was qualified to teach kids to ski, or at least deal with ones who weren't yet fully toilet trained. "I guess a kid pooping their pants is better than losing one somewhere on the mountain," I said.

"Yeah, that pisses parents right off. You won't have to deal with that anytime soon," he said. "The ones we'll give you at first won't be anywhere near the chairlift."

"So it's more or less babysitting?"

He nodded slowly, gravely. "Babysitting. Pizza, French fries."

I knew that I'd be teaching kids, but for some reason I'd envisioned myself skiing powder in the back bowls with a bunch of little rippers following me like I was mother goose. And then their hot moms tipping me afterward and inviting me out for drinks.

"It's not so bad," he said as if reading my mind.

The lift kept stopping and starting, sometimes stationary for a minute or more while I knew one of the lifties was rushing around frantically trying to drag fallen children out of the way. Paul drummed on his thighs, erratic offbeat rhythms each time it jerked to a stop. It struck me that I was finally here, finally doing something I'd thought about for so long, finally in Colorado, in new surroundings with no stress about school or pressure to decide what to do with my life.

On the hill I surprised myself that I wasn't too nervous skiing with the ski school director, though Paul, despite his hulking size, didn't seem to be that intimidating a figure. He didn't even seem to be paying attention to my skiing anyway. Instead, he ripped down the mountain, carving big turns in a low, wide, powerful stance. He cruised past the herds of beginners who picked their way down the gentle, rolling slope.

I skied fast to keep up, straightlining sections while he kept up his huge and fast super G carves.

Near the bottom of the run an orange slow sign stuck out of the snow. Paul dropped into a low tuck, carving around the sign like it was a giant slalom gate before hockey stopping in front of the schoolhouse. A lady in a ski school vest hurried out of the building when she saw him. "I've been looking for you," she said. "There's a parent in there who'd like a word. She's been watching her son's lesson and says he isn't getting enough one-on-one attention."

"See what I mean?" he said over his shoulder to me. "Every day with this shit." He turned to the lady. "I'll handle it. Get Jimmy a uniform and then get him shadowing." He went inside.

I followed the lady in, past Paul who stood talking to a pissed off mom in furry boots and into a locker room that smelled like stale popcorn and feet. She issued me a locker and a uniform. The embroidered ski school logo gave me a sense of instant credibility.

I followed her out to the beginner hill where instructors herded their classes onto the conveyor belts and then escorted them back down on skis. Kylie stood at the bottom untangling a pile of kids, and I knew we were walking toward her.

*Shit,* I thought. I knew I'd be working with her, saying hi to her in the mornings, but I didn't think we'd actually be *working* working together.

"Jimmy, this is Kylie," the lady said, "one of our best youth instructors. Kylie, Jimmy will be shadowing you the rest of the day."

"We already know each other," she said, wrapping her arm around me in a half hug instead of a handshake.

I helped her sort out the mess of kids. Hers were the smallest on the hill, three-year-olds, she told me. She had six of them, color-coded in purple vinyl vests with handles on the back for picking them up off the snow. We set them, one by one, on the slow-moving conveyor bound for the top of the tiny slope.

"I'm sorry about last night," I said after we loaded the last kid onto the carpet. "I don't want things to be awkward."

"Don't be sorry," she said, climbing onto the carpet herself in boots but no skis. I got on behind her. "You gotta do what you gotta do," she said. "It might have been awkward if I'd fucked you. But probably not."

The word shocked me a bit coming out of her mouth, especially with all these kids around. But it also made me feel like making a dipshit of myself last night wasn't a big deal.

At the top, the kids getting off the carpet knotted themselves into another pile, not able or even willing to get out of each other's way. We picked them up again, lining them up at the top of the slope. Kylie took the first one down, following behind the tiny girl, keeping her from going too fast by holding onto a hula hoop wrapped around her waist. I did the same with a little boy.

Some of them did it without the hula hoop, and others were too damned jelly legged to even stand. Those we held upright as we ran down the slope with them.

"Is this how it is every day?" I asked. "Riding up and down the magic carpet?"

"We'll make it to the chairlift every once in a while," she said. "Not this week, though. Not with this bunch. They've been giving me the smallest of the small, the ones who can't even stand up. Yesterday I had one who was okay, so they moved him to another class."

"This is what three-year-olds look like, eh?"

"Supposed to be. Some two-year-olds with overzealous parents mixed in. Today's the kind of day we can be happy if the whole class can stand up on their own by the end of the day."

"So not a whole lot of powder skiing in the backbowls during class time?"

"Not so much, but if all the parents are on time to pick them up, we'll have enough time for a run or two of our own."

A free run with Kylie sounded nice. But hanging out with her on the bunny hill didn't seem terrible either, and I told her that.

"It's not bad," she said. "I enjoy it, and these ones are easier to deal with than the older kids. They pretty much do what you say. Any older and they start crying all the time or trying to escape."

"We could put them on leashes."

"You joke," she said, "but there are some parents who actually do that."

Inside the schoolhouse, lunchtime was chaos, a dozen instructors trying to get their classes ready for lunch while a hundred screaming kids ran and climbed all over the plastic play stuff. Across the room Paul looked to have barricaded himself inside a glassed-in office. He stood behind the window wearing great big headphones and seemed to be gazing not at the kids, but slightly above them.

I helped Kylie take off our kids' ski gear and stuff it into cubbies that surrounded the room. Without their gear on all the kids looked basically the same. I forgot all the names I just learned. We sat them down at a miniature cafeteria table and Kylie ran down the menu, having them choose between hot dogs, mac and cheese, or something called dino nuggets. She went to collect the food from the kitchen while I watched the kids. I sat in a tiny chair, legs outstretched and feeling like the plastic could burst under the weight of my fat ass at any moment. The kids' socks flopped around off the ends of their feet, and for some reason this grossed me out.

They all ate half their food and made a mess with the rest while Kylie and I took turns going to the real cafeteria next door to get our own lunches.

"We'll make this last as long as possible," she said joining me as the kids left the table to play.

"Tire them out?"

"With these kids we'll spend more time getting them into and out of their ski gear than we will actually on skis. They'll play until they get bored, and then we'll ski for a bit, take another good long break, and get them back on skis so their parents can see them on the hill for a run or two when they come to pick them up."

"And then it's our turn for a run?"

"That's the idea."

I watched all the kids play and tried to figure out which ones were in our class. It was impossible. "How do you keep track of them?" I asked.

She laughed. "Good question."

"I'm serious. All these kids look the same."

"I guess it's just something you get used to; count them a lot and hope you have the same number you started with."

"It doesn't matter which ones you have as long as the number adds up right?"

"That's right."

One of the boys outside the playhouse picked up a basketball and bounced it off a little girl's head. She started crying.

"Jeremy!" Kylie yelled. "Stop that!"

Paul stepped out of his office. "No more crying is allowed," he said, and the girl cried louder.

"Paul seems nice,"

"He was just joking," she said. "I think. He's actually a pretty nice guy; just not sure that youth ski school is where he's at his best."

Back in the glassed-in office, he pulled down a shade.

"He was an All-American or something when he raced in college. And was actually a really good instructor. That's probably why they put him in charge here. That's the cost of moving up, I guess."

"How long have you been teaching?"

"This is my third season. I go home during the summer and waitress out there. I wasn't planning on coming back this winter, but the mountains have a way of calling you back."

I looked up at the ski slope, the chairlift disappearing from view over a ridge and then reappearing, looking miniscule so far up there, beyond that rocky peaks jutting impossibly high. "I can imagine that," I said.

"Just you wait until next fall. Come September you'll be waxing your skis and itching to get out here.

"That sounds a whole lot better than studying for exams."

"I did a year of college," she said, "but I never figured out what I wanted to do."

"Welcome to the club. I think I've taken every gen ed there is."

"I'd like to do art or something."

"You're an artist?"

"I'd like to be one. I'll get a degree eventually."

"Bill said that too."

She laughed. "Bill's been saying that since I met him. I don't think he'd be able to stay put long enough to get a degree."

Our kids played a little longer before we started rounding them up and getting them dressed. By the time we had the gloves on the last kid, the first couple had taken theirs off.

The bunny hill felt pleasant, warm bright sun reflecting off the snow so that Kylie and I left our coats hanging over the railing. She took the kids up the hill and sent them down to me, one at a time. I caught each one, loaded them back on the carpet, and waited for the next. Between kids I watched Kylie standing at the top with the sun reflecting off her goggles, her sleeves rolled up exposing pale forearms.

The next kid to come down, a chubby little dude in a red jacket, made it halfway, crossed his skis, and crashed forward, his helmet bouncing off the snow. With his legs and skis a tangled mess, I had to take the skis off his feet to pull him up. The kid didn't cry but just stared at me with a dazed look on his face. I got down on one knee so I was face to face with him. "You alright, buddy?" I asked, holding onto his shoulder.

He didn't say anything, just looked at me for a moment longer, closed his eyes, and puked down the front of himself, not even trying to project the vomit out onto the snow. Some of it splashed onto my knee and down onto the toe of my boot, but most of it stuck to the front of his coat.

I'd always had this romantic notion of life as a Colorado ski instructor, but that all disappeared as Kylie took the kid inside and I scrubbed half-digested dino nuggets off my pants with snow.

We took a break while waiting for Kylie and then made it through the last hour of the day, minus one student, without incident. Kylie talked to the parents as they picked up their kids. One of them tipped her twenty bucks. She offered to split it with me, but I said no—it was her class.

By the time the kids and parents cleared out, the sun hung low over the peaks to the west, lighting up the east-facing slopes in a deep, golden glow.

"How about a run?" Kylie asked, and we stepped into our skis and skated toward the lift. Skis felt strange, having walked around in just ski boots all day, and the ride up the same slow-moving chairlift I'd ridden with Paul that morning felt good, like a reward after the day. On the way up, I caught a whiff of pot smoke. When we reached the top and saw Ryan up there, I knew that he'd lit one up on the chair ahead of us.

"How was the first day?" he asked through a big, goofy grin.

"Could've been worse," I said.

"Jimmy got puked on," Kylie said, smiling.

"That sucks, man," he said, "but yeah, puke over poop any day."

He took off down the slope, and we followed, cruising fast and plowing through the cruddy piles that a day's worth of riders had built up. Ryan veered off to play on the side hits. He dipped into the trees for a turn before bombing back onto the run. Kylie and I carved in each other's tracks, passing one another for a few turns and then falling back. We varied our turn sizes, a few big GS turns, picking up speed, and then some tight slalom carves.

By the time we reached the bottom the sun had dipped behind the mountains and a thin frozen layer had crusted over the snow. Through a bustle of gapers and employees ending their day on the mountain, we walked home, side by side, with the ice crunching beneath our boots.

# 5

On my first day teaching solo they gave me a small class, only four kids. Kylie took her older class up the chair, so I kept mine near Ryan and his tiny snowboarders. I copied his technique of hauling the kids around by the handles on the backs of their vests and followed his lead in giving them ample breaks and snacks and snowball fights. Even stuck on the bunny hill with a class of toddlers, spending a bluebird December day in the mountains made me so much happier than being stuck in some classroom.

I managed to keep track of everybody and avoided bodily fluids, shoveling the kids off to their parents in time to catch a couple of free runs in the golden late afternoon light. I carved wide arcs, bombing over the crud and tracks of a day's worth of riders, closing my eyes for a few seconds on an empty cruiser and just feeling the sun on my back, the cold breeze on my face, and my edges holding strong late in a turn.

Back at the Block I read an email that my fall grades were in. I didn't want to look, so Bill did it for me.

"Impressive," he said.

"I doubt that."

"You've about got the whole alphabet covered. An A, a B, a C, a D, and an E."

"Jesus Christ," I said. I knew it'd be bad, but hearing it all together like that was just embarrassing. If I were going back for the winter semester, I'd be on academic probation, one step away from getting kicked out—weekly appointments in some advisor's office to monitor my progress.

# SKI BUM

Kylie and Aurelia showed up to our room, excited to hear about my first day teaching. I was glad to delete the email and focus on the present. Bill opened the window and hauled in a laundry bag full of beers that had been chilling outside. He passed these around and then Muppet showed up with a box of wine, tearing open the cardboard to expose the plastic bladder inside. He held it up above Aurelia—her head up and mouth open like a baby bird—and opened the nozzle. After a good long first pull, she slapped the bag with vigor. We went around the room like this, Aurelia holding the bag for Kylie, Kylie for me, me for Bill, and Bill for Muppet, each of us slapping the bag with a firm thwack of the palm.

"Just like college," I laughed, "except no classes."

"College sucks," Bill said. "Let's play a game." He dragged a small end table to the middle of the room and tossed a deck of cards on top. Kylie sat down crosslegged and shuffled the deck like a pro. The rest of us crowded around the table, pulling up desk chairs and sitting on the bed with drinks in hand.

"Euchre?" I asked.

"We have five." Bill waggled his eyebrows. "Let's play poker." He dumped a bucketful of beer caps onto the table as chips.

"Texas Hold 'em," Kylie said and started dealing.

I knew I should fold my seven, ten of hearts, but I figured what the hell and called Muppet's bet of four bottlecaps. After a ten on the flop, I bet and Muppet called. By my third ten on the river all our caps were on the table. My three tens beat Muppet's queens, but raking in all the beer caps felt like I hadn't won anything, because, well, I hadn't.

"You know it's not really poker if there's nothing at stake, right?" Kylie must have picked up on my expression.

"Well let's put something at stake," Bill said.

"I'm not playing for money," Muppet said. "I'm straight up broke."

"It doesn't have to be money," Bill said. "We'll play for clothing." He took off his beanie and threw it at the wall as a gesture of goodwill.

"More dudes than girls," I said. "Not a great ratio." Though the thought of those girls, of Kylie, sitting across from me sans clothes would have had me playing no matter what.

Kylie and Aurelia looked at each other, gauging one another's reaction. Kylie cocked her head to the side, raising an eyebrow at Aurelia who wore a coy smile and nodded thoughtfully.

"What the hell," Aurelia said. "You have a game."

Bill shuffled and dealt as the rest of us passed around the wine bag again. No one really knew the rules of strip poker, but with something at stake the game took on a serious vibe. The first few hands ended with everyone removing hats and ski socks.

"Let's hurry this along," Muppet shouted. "We should all of us be naked by now."

"You boys will be long before we are," Aurelia replied.

"It's a game of skill, Mupp," Kylie said. "You have to be patient."

"Patient my ass." Muppet struggled to shuffle so he spread the cards out on the table and smooshed them around with his hands instead. "Counting cards in Vegas is a game of skill. This is a game of pure luck."

The next hand I went all in with my pair of jacks, not that the bottle cap chips meant anything at this point. Kylie crossed her arms and put her elbows on the table, lying her chin down on her forearms and gazing into my eyes as if deep in thought. I winked at her and she smiled, saying, "call," and pushing her chips into the middle. She flipped over two kings.

"Kings?" I asked. "You had to think that hard about kings?"

"Nope. Just thought I'd make you squirm a bit."

Aurelia dealt slowly as Muppet chanted for a, "jack, jack, jack," but he gave me no help and I ended up taking my shirt off.

"This isn't how I wanted this to go," Muppet said. "I'm here to see some titties."

Kylie scrunched her face up, grossed out by Muppet's comment. Aurelia, flirting with Bill across the table, didn't seem to have heard it. I

stood up and gave Muppet my best burlesque-style dance to show off my hairy chest.

"Not hairy titties," he said. "Not that you don't look good topless, you beast."

Kylie put her hand on my chest and scratched me like a dog. "How are you still wearing that sweater when you just took your shirt off?" Her fingernails feeling good against the skin beneath my chest hair.

The next several hands had us all shirtless, Kylie and Aurelia in sports bras and ski pants and us guys down to longjohns or boxers. The possibility of the girls soon being naked across the table had me reaching for the wine bag, which we'd half diminished.

Kylie shuffled and dealt like a pro, her fingers working the cards as if she'd done it a million times and her head up, smiling, not even looking down to concentrate on the deck.

"You sure look like you know what you're doing there," I said.

"You mean sitting half naked with a bunch of people?"

"Well you look good doing that, too, but I meant the cards."

"My dad and uncles used to play poker every weekend," she said, quickly dealing the cards as she talked. She threw them quickly, one at a time with a snap of the wrist so each card skimmed along the tabletop and slid into place in front of its player. "I started playing with them when I was tiny."

Bill stood up in just his undies and walked to the window to fetch another round of beers, which he tossed out to everyone. "So we've got a ringer on our hands," he said, cracking his beer, taking a long swig as he sauntered back to the table and pushing all his chips into the middle without even looking at his cards. "The only way to deal with a ringer is to go all in."

Aurelia called him with a laugh, flipping over two aces. When the board gave Bill no help, he was the first one naked. He kicked off his boxers and cupped his hands over his junk.

Aurelia laughed loudly. "Don't be so shy," she said, tossing Bill the wine bag so that he had to lift his hands off his crotch to catch it.

"Don't laugh at me, and I won't be shy," he said, taking a long pull.

"Too many dicks," Muppet said. "Way too many dicks."

Ryan busted into the room without knocking and sat down on the bed, pulling a glass pipe out of his coat and hitting it in a large drag. He looked up at naked Bill without questioning it. He joined the game, agreeing to the girls' condition that because he started late, he'd have to start in just his jeans. A few hands in he got into it with Aurelia. When she put him all in, he thought long and hard about it, almost in a trance that made us all think he'd zoned out completely.

"Can I pass?" he finally asked.

"You can fold," Aurelia said, "or you can go all in."

"Can I put in just the tip?" he said before throwing his few remaining caps into the pot with a *what the hell* shoulder shrug. He flipped over an eight of hearts and a ten of diamonds. "I like red," he said.

She just had a pair of fours but they held up, and he was naked. I quickly followed, chasing a straight against Kylie's two pair. Before stripping down to nothing, I grabbed the wine bag and took a nice long glug for a bit of liquid courage. I sat there a bit nervous, hands covering my bits. But soon it didn't matter; I was naked with friends, and the beer was flowing. Muppet went out next with Kylie still in a sports bra and long underwear and Aurelia down to bra and boyshorts.

"I wish I had a camera," Aurelia said.

"You sure you want a picture of this?" Kylie said.

"Not for me to look at, but it might be nice to have in case we ever need anything from any of these boys."

"Blackmailing us with our own dick pics," Bill said. "I see what you girls are up to."

Ryan shuffled, slowly, and began to deal when Aurelia asked, "Is there really much reason to play anymore, Ky? I think we won."

"Seriously?" Muppet asked, though neither girl paid him any attention.

"You know," Kylie said, standing up from the table, "you have a good point." She picked her shirt off the floor, holding it for a moment as she scratched an itch somewhere between her belly button and the bottom of her bra, teasing us intentionally or not. Aurelia shimmied into her ski pants.

"This just isn't fair," Ryan said.

"Come on," Bill pleaded. "Just a few more hands. Double or nothing?"

"Double or nothing?" Kylie asked. "You can't get any more naked than you already are." She tussled my hair, said, "Goodnight, boys." The two of them left, leaving us four dudes alone and naked. They'd played it perfectly.

"Pure luck," Muppet said, walking to the window, bare-assed. He cracked a beer and swigged, his wiener hanging free.

"Dude," Bill said, "put some clothes on."

Muppet grabbed a beanie from the desk, put it on his head, and held up his beer in a toast.

"I don't know about luck," I said. "They seemed to know what they were doing."

"Patience," Bill said. "It's all patience. They sat and waited for good hands. Knowing that us assholes would be all in all the time."

We all put pants on and finished our beers and then Ryan and Muppet left too, leaving us roommates alone.

"Those girls had a good time," Bill said. "They'll come around."

We made a silent toast and then finished off the wine bag, squeezing it into a crumpled mass of plastic in an attempt to drain out every last shitty bit of merlot.

# 6

The week before Christmas a cold front blew through the Front Range. One morning it was thirty below and the ski school snowmobiles wouldn't start. On my walk to the schoolhouse I felt the snot in my nose freeze and my pants harden like plastic.

Ski school was busy too; a lot of people on vacation who'd bought their flights and hotel rooms would be damned if they let a little frostbite ruin their holiday. I had six or seven kids in my class every day, but it was too freaking cold to do much but stay inside. We skied in half-hour clips interspersed with a lot of spilled hot chocolate and coloring with crayons. I found I really liked the kids when they were all coloring. I colored with them.

Kylie's class usually sat next to mine. She almost looked like one of them sitting there at the tiny lunch table, knees stuck up in the air, coloring intently with the tip of her tongue sticking out the corner of her mouth. She tore a page out of the notebook she'd been coloring in—a crayon mountainscape with intricate lines, a chairlift running up one side of the image and a pair of tiny skiers descending the other side. She'd written, "to Jimmy," across the top of the page. It was good; she was a real artist.

Ryan and his snowboard class played on the floor next to us. He kind of just lay there while his kids climbed all over him like a jungle gym. I was happy there in the warmth of the schoolhouse. I felt like a kid, playing with my friends during indoor recess because of a storm.

* * *

# SKI BUM

A couple of days before Christmas the snow gods dumped on Summit County. Everyone had the night off, a rare occasion, so we piled into the Jeep to go see a movie in Dillon like some big family trying to fit in the minivan. Muppet called shotgun before we even got to the parking lot, so the two girls and Bill sat in the backseat with Ryan on the floor in the far back playing with everything in the roadside emergency kit.

The traffic on I70 moved 25 miles per hour. We missed our show. The next one didn't start for three hours, so we went to a pizza parlor to eat and pass the time. We were the only people in the place.

"Snow like this gives me a hard on," Muppet said as he unwrapped the top of his straw and blew the wrapper across the table.

"Right?" Bill said. He gazed out the window in reverie.

"I'm tempted to call in sick tomorrow," I said, looking out the window at the thick white curtain of snow.

"Do it," Muppet said. "We'll drive up to Steamboat. They've got some sick trees up there, and I know where to find the stashes."

"I'm broke. Doubt I could even afford the gas to get there."

"You wouldn't get away with it anyway," Kylie said. "Calling in sick on the biggest powder day of the season? They'd call you on that lie." She leaned over the table, held her straw between her thumb and forefinger, and sipped her Pepsi. "The way to get out of work is to show up, punch in, then go to the bathroom or something when they do lineup. If it's a slow day, which Christmas Eve will probably be, you won't even get a lesson. You can ski all day and still get paid for that hour you were there."

"Sounds like you've done that a time or two."

"Hey, I love snow as much as the next girl."

"That, and you know as well as anyone how Paul works," Ryan said.

"That's true," she said.

The waitress brought our food, three large pizzas and a family order of breadsticks. We ate it all. She must have refilled our drinks five times while we sat there, and she kept asking if we needed anything else. After two hours she stopped bringing refills. When some guy

started mopping the floor and the waitress flipped every chair but ours onto the tables, we figured we were being kicked out and left.

The snow had eased up. The theater was just up the street, and we were the only car on the snow-covered road. It felt like we were the only people for miles until a big plow truck passed in the opposite direction, amber light flashing and the blade thundering against the pavement.

Six more inches fell during the movie. Big flakes still came down as we left the building, the empty parking lot a blanket of untracked perfection.

"Definitely calling in sick tomorrow," Muppet said just before diving into the snow. Ryan jumped on top of him and they wrestled until Muppet's face was buried. A snowball plinked me in the back. I turned to see Kylie pretending she didn't know where it had come from.

"That was a mistake," I said, running to her and lifting her up onto my shoulder. I tackled her in slow motion, laying her down in the snow on her back, careful to not bury her too deep.

In the Jeep I whipped some shitties in the fresh powder. I eased into each one and gave it gas at just the right moment. Most people jump on the gas too early, but my donuts were excellent.

"Why do American boys always have to do donuts every time it snows?" Aurelia asked.

"Because it's necessary," Bill said.

Every time the back of the Jeep started to whip, a cloud of nearly weightless snow exploded into the air. Bill kept yelling, "Yee Hoo!" from the back seat like my Cherokee was the General Lee. We tore up most of the lot. By the time we left, the tracks where we had started were almost filled in.

* * *

We all worked Christmas Eve, missing out on our powder day, though the snow kept up through the afternoon and Kylie and I managed a tree

run, making fresh tracks after our day of teaching. She brought a bottle of wine up to the room to share with Bill and me. We toasted to Christmas and to the still dumping snow that had all but blocked the view out the window.

"I went home for Christmas last year," Kylie said, gazing at the whiteout. "My grandma told me to get these adventures out of my system so I could settle down and become a good mother."

"And what does your grandma think of you coming out here for another season?"

"She passed away over the summer."

"I'm sorry," I said, trying to think of something better to say.

She smiled. "But I like to think that she knew that this makes me happy and would want me to be happy. There's more than one path in life."

I agreed completely. School, career, family was fine for some people and might be fine for me eventually, but travel and freedom and adventure were so much more romantic. "I'm sure she knew."

"I know," she said. "I eventually want to give my kids and grandkids the same kinds of lives, Christmas traditions, that I had growing up. Take them to see Santa."

"Fuckin' Santa Claus," Bill replied. "My uncles are deer hunters. One Christmas Eve Santa showed up. He told me and my cousins that his reindeer were up on the roof. So my uncles take this eight point out of the barn, just its head, and tapped its antlers on the window. I was mortified. I thought they'd killed Prancer."

"That's terrible!" Kylie laughed, covering her nose and mouth to keep the chardonnay from spilling out.

"No shit," he said.

"What a grump," I said. "How can you say fuck Santa Claus on Christmas Eve? Fuck your uncles but don't fuck Santa."

"Fuck them both. I don't understand worshipping some fat guy who breaks into your house."

"Cheer up," Kylie patted the top of his bald head.

"Yeah!" I passed him the wine bottle. "Cheer up!"

He put his arm around me and with the other hand took a long swig from the bottle then smiled wide. "I'm cheerful as a Christmas goose."

"That's what I like to hear." I took the bottle from his hand, drank, then passed it to Kylie. "How can you beat this? Christmas Eve in the mountains with good friends and dumping snow. What could be better?"

"It's better here than back home, eh?" Bill asked, and for the first time I heard a distinct Wisconsin accent.

"You betcha."

"You didn't like life in Michigan?" Kylie asked.

"It's not that. Not at all. I love Michigan, but I felt like I wasn't going anywhere. Treading water."

"College will do that to you," Bill said. "Life will do that to you."

"Just look at Derek," Kylie said.

"Muppet," Bill clarified.

"Yes, Muppet. He had a real job. He was about to get married and buy a house and all. But real life scared him off."

"What's real life?" Bill asked. "This isn't it?" He went to the window and hauled in his beer sack, grabbing the last three cans and passing them around. "Muppet just wanted an excuse to be a rebel."

"He's a bum just like the rest of us," I said. "Looking for some kind of adventure."

"Is it tough being a bum on a trust fund?"

"What makes you say that?" I asked.

"He's a total rich kid," Bill said. "Doesn't have to work for anything. The only reason he works at Cuddy's is for the free booze and tourist girls."

"Seems like a good guy to me."

"He's alright," Bill said then became silent as if deep in thought. "He's a good guy, especially when he pours them strong." He opened the window again and stuck his head out, leaning back and opening his

mouth wide, trying to catch the falling snow in his mouth. He shut the window and wiped the fat flakes off his head, leaving his scalp wet and shiny. "Just think; everyone else our age is laying in bed waiting for Santa Claus to put a new smartphone under the tree."

"Our age?" Kylie asked. "Aren't you way older than we are?"

"Hey. That hurts."

"Fuck their smartphones!" I held my beer up in a toast against our generation. We chugged the beers down and then Bill said goodnight, ruffling my hair and leaping up onto his bunk. He was snoring within a minute.

Kylie and I sat in the hallway, our backs against the cinder block wall, passing the wine bottle until it was gone.

"I'm glad you're here," she said.

"Me too."

We stood up and I wrapped her in a bear hug. "Merry Christmas," I said.

"Merry Christmas."

* * *

I woke to avalanche cannons blasting on Christmas morning and felt strangely out of place. Bill had headed off to work without waking me. I'd grown accustomed to his snoring, and without it the silence, broken every few minutes by booming explosions, seemed vast. The falling snow muted the light, dulling it into a far more soothing white than the sunlight that usually flooded in each morning.

A faint outline of the mountain disappeared into the curtain of snow. Infinite flakes, smaller than usual, floated to the ground as if in slow motion. I stood there in awe for a minute before getting dressed for work. I hoped that none of us would have to teach. This endless powder was my Christmas present.

Only six kids came for lessons. Kylie and Ryan both got classes, so I was alone with free time. The snow fell so thick that riding up the lift I

couldn't see the chair in front of me. The haul rope just vanished into nothing.

The snow offered a feeling of solitude. I couldn't see any other skiers and as far as I cared, they didn't exist. I hot lapped the trees under Sierra all morning without seeing another person besides the lifties. I made fresh tracks every lap. The champagne powder slowed me down and my skiing style became more fluid, almost graceful. Snow burst into my face with every turn. It stuck to me and froze in my beard.

Just after noon some kids found Sierra. They were half a lap behind, on the hill when I was on the lift. I could barely see them bobbing in and out of the coldsmoke. The intense snowfall muffled their screams and laughter like a mute in a trumpet bell. I caught up to them then took off to Silver Bowl to be alone again.

I didn't bother to go in for lunch; life was too good out there in the back bowls. This day didn't feel like Christmas. Christmas was in Michigan. This was a gorgeous December day, but it wasn't Christmas.

It was lonely back there but pleasant. There are no friends on a powder day anyway. Despite fogged goggles, burning thighs, and the dank smell of wet leather gloves I felt as happy and free as I could remember. I rode Mountain Chief until last chair and didn't want to be done.

Back in the village *Jingle Bell Rock* played over the speakers. A bonfire burned in the middle of the plaza and flames danced in the surrounding torches. I carried my skis to McGillycuddy's and dumped them in the snow outside.

The bar was empty except for Muppet who sat at a table watching *A Christmas Story* on the TV behind the bar. A small, Charlie Brown tree glowed in the corner.

"Merry Christmas!" he yelled, jumping up from his chair and running over to wrap me in a massive bear hug, lifting me off the ground.

# SKI BUM

"Doesn't much feel like Christmas. I need some boozy eggnog, or a beer at least."

"Sure doesn't," he said, heading back behind the bar. "You're first one away from home too?"

I nodded and then swigged from the pint of Guinness he put in front of me.

"My ma's called me three times today," he said, "crying that her baby isn't home for Christmas."

He poured a couple shots of peppermint schnapps. He raised his glass and said, "Here's to Santa Claus." We clanked them together. "And to Jesus and stuff." We knocked our glasses on the bar top then took the shots, which tasted like candy canes but so much better.

"Where is everyone?" he asked. "It's been me alone here since lunchtime."

"They all had to work. Who puts their kids in ski school on Christmas day?"

"Jews," Muppet said.

After a while Aurelia showed up, then Bill, then Ryan and Kylie, a few lifties. Pretty soon over a dozen people, mostly employees but a few tourists, drank hot chocolate and Baileys and sang Christmas carols. Someone brought sugar cookies. Now it felt like Christmas.

More people showed. Muppet tended bar, and he kept giving out shots and always pouring one for himself until he was by far the drunkest person there. Someone put a Santa hat on his head and he poured drinks while singing, *Grandma Got Run Over By A Reindeer* at the top of his lungs and telling girls to, "come sit on Santa's lap."

"This is what it's all about," Bill said.

"It's about having a grand old time."

"Damn straight. It's about having the greatest and grandest old fucking time we can have on this planet while we're here, you know." He put an arm around me. "And live it up now, brother, because it's on to the next adventure after this one—South America for me, and hopefully for you too."

It did sound good. Finishing one ski season just to fly south for another, but I didn't want to think about this one ending at all. Not yet. It had just started. "Why not just live in the moment, man? Why do we need to think about what's next when we're in the middle of something right now?"

"Amen," he said.

I'd been wearing my ski boots all day and after several drinks took them off, feeling good and free walking around the bar in ski socks. Kylie and I sat on bar stools looking out at the restaurant, at Ryan hitting on a middle-aged tourist woman whose husband didn't seem to mind and at Aurelia singing Christmas carols in Spanish with several of the other South Americans in the place. Bill joined them and sang as loudly as any of them though he didn’t particularly know the words.

Kylie ordered an old fashioned and I got one too.

"You know, I do miss home, miss my family."

"That's a good thing," she said. "I miss mine too, and being away will make it that much better when we go back."

"I just don't want you to think I'm some cold-hearted asshole who hated his life."

"I don't think you're cold hearted." She smiled and offered her glass up for a cheers.

Late in the night someone brought mistletoe and hung it above the bar. Kylie kissed me on the cheek, and before I could kiss her back Muppet grabbed me and planted one on me as well. We all partied well into the night. The snow had stopped by the time we left, but it had buried my skis first.

I carried them on my shoulder and Kylie walked with my poles as we all headed back to the Block together. The walk was awkward in unbuckled ski boots and full of drinks. A layer of fresh snow covered the lake and village. Everything felt calm and silent.

# 7

The week between Christmas and New Year's is a strange time at a ski resort, a depression after the buildup to the holidays, a trough in the wave. It's a busy time when the lift lines overflow their galvanized steel mazes and the ski school class sizes swell to nine, ten, eleven kids. It's a time when team teaching becomes the norm, because there's an illusion that it's easier for two people to keep track of twenty kids than one to keep track of ten.

I didn't mind working every day—I needed the cash—and the lift lines made free runs less pleasant even though I knew the backside wouldn't be as packed. With the new year looming, I couldn't help but contemplate the future. On one hand, everything about it seemed wildly unclear. On the other hand, that gaping hole, that lack of direction, left a kind of limitless freedom and potential. Most days after class assignments Kylie and I found each other. One of us stood at the top of the bunny hill sending them down while the other hung out at the bottom stopping the kids and loading them back on the conveyor. "You want to play pitcher or catcher?" she'd ask me in the mornings.

Even though the length of bunny slope separated us, I enjoyed working with Kylie. She helped keep me calm around the bratty kids and asshole parents. Those days were fun, not like work. I could tell she enjoyed it too. The day she got assigned a group of older, chairlift-ready kids was the worst day of my week—lots of crying kids and a couple of parents showing up a half hour late, clearly a few après ski cocktails deep.

I walked home from work alone and with the lifts already closed. Back in the room Bill and Aurelia had just started a movie, Bill in his bunk and Aurelia in mine. She climbed up with him when I got there. I was on the verge of sleep when someone pounded on the door. I ignored it, hoping whoever it was would go away.

"Let me in guys. Come on," Ryan yelled from the hallway.

I got up and started to open the door when he pushed his way through, a shit-eating grin plastered on his face and a plastic card in his outstretched hand. "Check it out, guys!"

"What the hell is it?" Bill asked.

"It's a key."

"No shit it's a key. A key to what?"

"A hotel key. Gets us into the hot tub."

"Where'd you get it?"

"I found it on the ground. Somebody must have dropped it. I tried it out and it worked. We're going to poach the hot tub." He left the room as quickly as he'd entered, yelling from the hallway, "Meet me in the lobby in five."

Aurelia went downstairs to get Kylie. Bill and I dressed in ski gear over board shorts. We followed Ryan as he power-walked across the village. He swiped the key at the side door of one of the many hotels in the village, and I wasn't surprised when the door remained locked.

"Damnit!" he yelled.

"Shit," Aurelia said, the word sounding fake in her accent and coming from her always sunshiny personality.

"We'll get in," Bill said, looking around intently, scoping out the situation.

We walked around the building, avoiding the grand front entry and trying to look nonchalant as we trudged through the snow toward the back, mountain-facing side. Steam rose up from the tub. An eight foot, wrought iron fence surrounded it. From where we stood at the corner of the fence a tool shed obstructed our view. Bill tossed his towel over the fence and climbed. I locked my fingers together, giving him a step and allowing him to clear the spikes atop the fence.

He dropped to the ground on the other side, landing with knees bent, low to the ground. He covered his mouth with a forefinger, a *shhh* gesture, then sprinted silently toward the rising steam like a ninja. He tiptoed to the edge of the shed and peered around the corner, coming back to us and whispering, "Just some old couple making out. We'll drive them out."

Ryan scampered over the fence so fast that he just about impaled himself on the spikes, falling onto the other side in a heap. He stood up and threw his hands in the air like a gymnast sticking a vault landing. I helped Aurelia and then Kylie over and then climbed over myself, lifting my crotch high above the spears to avoid a painful slip-up. As I lowered myself down one of the spikes sliced through my pant leg, leaving me hung up in the air. The other four helped lift me enough to untangle myself and get down to ground level.

The group of us walked out from behind the shed, trying to act naturally like we'd come out of the hotel. The make out couple didn't notice us at first, but as us dudes started stripping down to our board shorts, in Ryan's case, boxers, and the girls headed to the locker room to change, the woman whispered into the man's ear and they got out quickly and left.

"Don't leave on our account," I said, but they left anyway.

The water stung at first; then I felt my muscles relax. I leaned back into the jets and could have fallen asleep until Ryan cannonballed into the water.

Aurelia and Kylie came out of the locker room together, laughing. Kylie's white bikini looked like nothing against her soft skin. Aurelia got in quickly, but Kylie stood at the edge, dipping in just her toe. Her goggle-tanned face was so much darker than the rest of her body, and I tried hard not to stare at the freckles on her white shoulders and chest. She finally slipped into the water.

I reached outside the tub and grabbed a chunk of snow, rubbing it on my forehead and letting the cold water drip down my temples. Then I dropped the snow into the bubbling water and watched it melt. I

leaned my head back. The stars were bright, but I could only see a few through the steam.

"Undetected," Aurelia said. "Mission accomplished."

"Well the cops might still be coming for us," Ryan said, "So live it up while you've got the chance, *mamacita*."

She splashed him.

"Don't splash Ryan," Bill said, playfully dunking Aurelia's head under water. She got up and tackled him.

"Do you guys want the key?" Ryan asked. "Maybe it'll work if you can figure out which room it belongs to."

Kylie sat on the edge of the tub with just her legs in the water. She laughed at Bill, who swam under the churning surface trying to pull Ryan under. Then Ryan reversed, chasing Bill for a few circles before reemerging to splash Kylie. She kicked water back at him. He grabbed her by the ankle and pulled her in. She surfaced, giggled, splashed him again.

I dove toward Ryan. I grabbed him by the waist and pulled him under, trying to seem playful enough to disguise the not-too-little pang of jealousy I felt at seeing him play with Kylie. I held him down under the surface a second longer than what would have been comfortable. He came up, coughed, gave me a little grin, and then took off toward Bill and Aurelia again.

I went toward Kylie in the same motion as I had Ryan, but I wrapped her up gently, holding her legs, her body draped over my shoulder. She playfully hit me on the back. Instead of taking her down into the water, I picked her up and set her down gently on the edge of the pool.

"I missed you today," I said.

"I missed you too."

"Sure you did. Up there on the chairlift, skiing the big stuff, I'm sure you couldn't wait to get back on the magic carpet."

"I did!" she said, kicking her toes into the water and splashing me. "It was so busy up there that I was terrified all day of losing a kid. Days are better with you there. You're my partner."

"Likewise," I said. "How about a roll in the snow, pard?"

I pulled myself up onto the ledge, stood up, and reached out to grab Kylie's hand. She hesitated, looking down at the water. I'd thought of her as so outgoing and ready for anything, but I realized then that she was a little bit reserved, maybe even a little shy.

"You're leaving me hanging," I said, "and it's pretty damned cold out here."

She stood up and we ran over to the corner of the patio, jumping up and down in the snow like walking on hot coals. I tipped over into a pile of powder and she did the same. We both rolled in it and made a few rushed snow angels. It burned but felt good, exhilarating.

I started to get up, but she pushed me back down like a kid at recess, getting up herself and running back toward the tub and warmth.

I walked back, letting my body experience the extreme cold before the burn of the tub. I sat down next to Kylie, my back against the jets. Bill stood in the middle of the tub, looking down at his chest and spinning around to show everyone a white chest hair.

"I found a grey pube, too," he said, to which Aurelia squealed in laughter. "It's not funny," he said, though still grinning. "My body is starting to wither up and die."

"It may be time for you to retire," I said.

"No shit. *Siestas, cervezas,* and *montanas:* South America, here I come."

"You're really going to do it?" I asked.

"You betcha. The day this season ends. You should see the pictures of these mountains in Patagonia. They're so fucking big—they just explode up into the sky. Make these mountains look like bunny hills."

"He says this stuff about the mountains, but he's really following me," Aurelia said, scrunching up her face like the idea creeped her out.

"And you're coming with," he told me.

Bill's plan sounded like a grand adventure. Like something I should join without hesitation. Yeah, I had more money in the change jar next to my bed than in my bank account—quarters already removed on laundry day. But the season didn't end until April so there was plenty of time to save. I looked up at the mountains surrounding us. Their black silhouettes jutted up into a deep purple sky on all sides of us like some giant amphitheater. I couldn't imagine how the ones in South America could be any bigger.

"South America sounds nice and everything," Ryan said, "but we've all gotta get out of town sooner than that. Let's make a Steamboat trip soon."

"Let's go tomorrow," Aurelia said.

"Tomorrow it is," Kylie nudged my arm. "How 'bout it, pard?" She nudged my arm again.

"I, for one, have to work tomorrow," I said.

"We all do," Ryan replied. "But we'll call in sick."

"I hate the idea of calling in sick," I said. "It screws over everybody else."

"This is a ski resort. They expect you to call in sick."

It wasn't just the skipping work thing; I thought of that change jar again. Bigger mountains. Were there even enough dimes in there to pay for gas to Steamboat? Not to mention pizza and beer. "I'm broke," I said.

"Fuck," Ryan said. "Get a credit card. Charge the shit."

"Don't charge the shit," Kylie said. "Come along and you'll be alright. We'll take your car, so the rest of us will get the gas, cover your food."

I didn't want to be a mooch like the kids back home who showed up to our parties without the five bucks for a keg cup. I wanted to take Kylie out, not count on her or anyone else to keep me fed. And if I was going to head south with Bill, four months really wasn't much time to put together a grubstake. The thing that sucks about trying to live in the

moment is that you end up broke and hungover when you wake up tomorrow.

"We'll see," I said.

We sat there for over an hour. Snow began to fall again, most of the flakes melting in the steam with just a few survivors reaching the water. I kept getting out to sit on the snowy ledge until it got too cold then sitting back in the water until I started sweating again. When we got out I felt totally relaxed—clean and happy and tired.

While the rest of us dried off, Ryan stayed a little longer pulling a one hitter out of his coat pocket for a little alone time in the water. Bill and Aurelia hurried back to the Block, almost running to get out of the cold, so that left Kylie and me, walking slowly. We were still damp and the air was frigid. It felt good, though, after the heat of the water.

"As much as I want to go to Steamboat tomorrow," I said, "I can't do it. I can't call in sick and I don't want someone else to have to pay my way."

She looked disappointed but didn't argue it. "I think it's admirable," she said. "Nobody else takes anything seriously."

"Ryan's right, though," I said. "It's a ski resort job. There's no reason to take it too seriously."

"That's not true. You committed to working tomorrow and you're looking out for your coworkers. I can get behind that."

"But you're going tomorrow, right?"

"I promised Aurelia I'd go," she said. "I can't back out now."

"Well that's admirable too."

She didn't look convinced.

"It sucks that being admirable means just doing what someone else expects of you," I said.

"I know, right?" she said, reaching up and touching my hair. "Your curls are frozen. Do you want my hat?" She pulled one of the frozen ringlets and let it spring back into place.

I looked at her purple knit cap and the curly auburn hair that spilled out of it. "I think it looks better on you."

"Thanks, pard," she said. "We'll miss you tomorrow."

"I'll miss you too."

"It won't be anything too exciting, just another day of skiing and drinking beer."

"That sounds like a pretty perfect day to me. I'm there next time, for sure. I'll be working hard to save up some money."

"Money isn't so important," she said. "Time is the important thing."

"Time doesn't pay for gas."

She tilted back her head, looking up into the falling snow. A fat flake drifted slowly toward her face, and she stuck out her tongue just in time to catch it. She was a natural.

"It'd be nice if this was everyday life," she said, "hot tubbing, catching snowflakes."

"Why can't it be?"

"Do you feel like you're being pulled in two different directions?"

I told her I felt that exactly.

She thought for a minute as we walked slowly toward the Block in the exhilarating cold air. "You're right," she said. "This should be it. We should be doing this every day, doing new things, experiencing new places."

"You mean life isn't about making a lot of money and living in a giant house?"

"I think life is about seeing as much and doing as much and making as many friends as possible," she said.

I agreed with her, though I sensed in her a sort of melancholy, perhaps a post-Christmas funk, maybe the sense of the year coming to a close without much to show for it. I felt it too, kind of, but it also felt good, like this upcoming New Year simmered with possibilities. We strolled in silence for a while, taking the long way home, not an awkward silence, but a sort of comfortable quiet like we didn't have to talk to enjoy each other's company.

"If you want company while you're out experiencing the world, you can always count me in," I said as we neared the Block.

"How about heli-skiing?"

"I don't know that that fits the best things in life are free idea, but hell yes, someday."

"Well someday it is," she said, and we shook on it. "Teaching four-year-olds together will have to do for now." And that certainly didn't sound bad either.

When we finally got home we agreed to spend New Year's Eve together in a couple of days and hugged goodnight. Back at the room I passed out still wearing my ski pants, and I slept like I'd never wake up.

* * *

I woke up kicking myself for not making a move with Kylie; if there was a perfect opportunity, last night's walk home from the hot tub was it. As Bill got his gear together for the Steamboat trip, I almost said fuck it to work and to not having money and tag along anyway. I probably should have. Instead, I thought about them having fun as I taught. Then I headed back to the room for a ramen dinner and watched a movie from my bunk, passing out halfway through before Bill got home.

New Year's Eve morning I paired up with Kylie, as usual, at ski school, and our day of skiing together with munchkins flew by like we weren't getting paid for it. The parents were there on time and tipped us well; plus we managed to get a few runs together in the golden afternoon light.

As dusk neared, we met up with Ryan to head up the mountain for the ski school torchlight parade. Paul handed out beers at the base of the Eagle as we loaded the lift. He juggled a case of Coors in one hand while holding his own open can in the other. He seemed happy, just a giant jolly dude and not the bundle of manic stress that was his typical ski school demeanor. Once we all arrived at the top he gave out road flares while we waited for the sky to darken. From high on the mountain the village looked tiny. I'd never seen it from up there at night, and it looked how the North Pole always looks in kids' Christmas movies, all lit up in tiny warm lights.

The sky darkened to a greyish blue, the cloud cover holding in ambient light and preventing total darkness. It may have been the beer, but I felt warm up at the top. At Paul's command we lined up, myself between Ryan and Kylie, and lit our flares, the group of us sending up a plume of black smoke that smelled like the Fourth of July. Paul held his flare in one hand and his banquet beer in the other. "Try not to eat shit," he said, and as the leader of our parade, he took off in wide, snaking turns. Night had turned the day's snow to icy moguls and we chattered along in bone shaking, tail wash turns that reminded me of night skiing back home.

We approached the lit-up base. Torches aflame surrounded the plaza, and a large bonfire burned front and center. Around it a large crowd of cheering revelers gathered. At the bottom, we held our flares up, and at Paul's command bowed, extinguishing our torches in the snow. We retired to the back of the crowd where a couple of kegs sat in a snowbank on reserve for the ski school. Paul stood at the tap in a cardboard party hat, pumping it with vigor so that beer sloshed out of his party cup onto the beer belly poking through his ski school jacket. He held the legs of random kegstanders and then did a stand himself that lasted damn near a minute.

"You better be careful," Kylie said, joking with him, "you don't want ski school parents to see you drunk in your uniform."

"Screw 'em," he said. "I got kicked off my high school ski team for throwing a kegger. It can't happen twice."

"What's your resolution?" Kylie asked me as we sat around, waiting for midnight.

I didn't know what to say. I looked into my beer for a second and took a swig. "I guess save up some money out here, enough to pay for school so I can graduate before too long."

She nodded but didn't look convinced. Neither was I.

"What?" I asked.

"School is great and all, but I think you have more exciting things on your plate."

"Hey Ryan," I yelled to him, knowing he'd have an answer, "what's your resolution? What do you want to do this year?"

"This is it, brother," he said. "Exactly what I'm doing. Riding every day and having fun and loving life."

He was right. That's what I wanted too. Saving money and finishing school was what everyone else wanted of me, what was expected. I wanted all that stuff too, I guessed, kind of, but not yet. That was all in the future. This was now. This was why I'd come west.

"What's yours?" I asked Kylie as the buzz of the crowd grew in front of us, the New Year now minutes away.

"Same as you, pretty much," she said. "Go back to school, maybe. Maybe do some painting. Get a decent job this summer. Save up some money to travel. I want to start having adventures, start seeing the world this year. So far my life has consisted of New Hampshire and Colorado." She paused for a long moment like she was deep in thought, her silence emphasized by the building hum of the crowd around her. "The other night you said you'd come with me anywhere I'd like to go." She looked at me.

"I did. And I will. Where do you want to go?"

"Everywhere. And do everything. It's too tough making one choice. My resolution is to do and see as much as possible, to live a big life full of adventure and fun and love. You in?"

"You bet," I said, and I grabbed her by the hand and led her into the crowd. We weaved in between people, heading toward the front, toward the mountain, to the bonfire, for a front row view of the fireworks.

The fire's heat radiated off my back as the crowd finished its countdown to midnight. I heard Kylie's voice above all. The buzz of noisemakers erupted as the New Year began, and the plaza speakers blared *Auld Lange Syne.* We all sang along, and though nobody knew the words, it sounded immensely beautiful nonetheless.

# COLIN CLANCY

I wrapped Kylie in a tight hug as fireworks shot into the sky from somewhere high on the mountain. She watched the blasts; I watched her. Then she looked at me and I went for it. Her lips were soft and her nose cold against mine. I felt my forehead against hers. The explosions echoed around us. She looked me in the eyes—hers light blue with a navy ring around the outside.

"Finally," she said.

"Finally? I tried it once before."

"You were supposed to try again."

I kissed her again and then felt Aurelia, Bill, Muppet, and Ryan wrap us up in a group hug. Muppet pulled cans of PBR from his backpack and passed then around while Aurelia hugged me and kissed each of my cheeks. Then Bill planted a sloppy, wet one on my cheek. We toasted the New Year and everything to come as the explosions cracked the cold air.

I stood there with my friends, our futures wide open, my arm around Kylie. We watched the blue and red and green flashes illuminate trails of smoke. The light of each explosion reflected off the low clouds and the snow of the slopes and made those New Years' fireworks in the Rockies the brightest I'd ever seen.

# 8

The sunrise view from our seventh-floor room—smoke rising in tall, thin plumes from the chimneys of the buildings of the village backed by the surrounding peaks—was damn near too much to bear each morning. Most of the time, I'd see it after waking up next to Kylie in my tiny twin bed, which made it all that much better. Other times she'd stay in her own room with Aurelia, and on those mornings, I'd get dressed while looking out at the world then head down to her room to walk to work together.

Her free spirit, in contrast to the world around her, muted the world's imperfections like a fresh snowfall. The stress I'd felt before—about school, about a future, about the lack of money in my wallet—she made that stress disappear without even trying; those things didn't matter yet.

The girls had a coffee pot so Kylie always made a to-go cup for each of us. Our teaching together only lasted so long, though. Paul assigned me chairlift-ready classes for a week. For the first time I felt like a ski instructor, actually skiing and having my class follow in slow and winding turns rather than simply babysitting and picking up fallen children.

When I finally had a day off I skied all morning making big, relaxed turns on groomed cruisers. The sun shone in a brilliant blue cloudless sky, though it was still cold enough for breath to linger in the air on the chairlift—bluebird. The corduroy felt smooth under my skis. The beautiful day made me calm and happy.

I ran into Paul at the base, he beckoned me to follow him into the ski school lane to avoid waiting in the lift line, though we had no class with us.

"Had to get away from the schoolhouse for a while," he said. "Driving me fucking nuts. They think I'm in a meeting."

He pulled a pack of smokes from his jacket pocket and offered them to me. I didn't usually smoke, but I took one. I struggled to light it on the moving chair then blew out the smoke in long exhales, the high-speed quad pushing us ever ahead of the lingering cloud.

"This bureaucratic bullshit," he said. "It sucks balls."

"You miss just teaching?"

"Hell yes, brother. I'd rather be skiing with beginners any day than dealing with you all calling in sick with hangovers and dipshit parents complaining."

"Why do it then?" I asked. "Why not just go back to teaching?"

"Same reason as everything else in the world," he said. "Money." He flicked his cigarette butt from the lift in deliberate motion, watching it fall toward the ground.

"What do you do in the summertime?" I asked.

"Build houses for rich people. Fly fish. Drink beer."

"Seems pretty good to me."

He shrugged his shoulders and made a little grunting noise.

"It's something to aspire to, at least, spending your days outside, communing with nature."

"I didn't peg you for a hippie," he said.

He was a brand of asshole I didn't mind too much, maybe even a decent guy once you learned to ignore the *woe-is-me* attitude. We took a couple of runs together before going separate ways, fast, hard charging laps in big wide carves, launching off rollers, and hitting the ski school lanes each time.

* * *

# SKI BUM

I found Bill working at the top of Storm King. We sat in the shack together for an hour in the toasty propane heat. In that time only a handful of people made their way to the top. I envied him sitting up there every day at the top of the world looking out at the distant peaks where they met the sky. He got to sit up there relaxing in that little sauna on that perfect spot every day while I babysat down at the bottom of the mountain.

"You should be here on a storm day," he said. "I was up here once in a thunder blizzard. I thought this whole damned fucking shack was going to blow off the side of the mountain. They closed the lifts early and ski patrol called to see if I wanted them to escort me down the hill."

"That was sweet of them."

"But I've been up here on days so calm that I've gone into a trance, like back in Wisconsin when I used to go outside in the middle of the night when there was a lot of snow on the ground, and I would go sit in the snow on this ridge and just look down over the fields and forests. I'd just sit in the snow with my dog for an hour or two or who knows how long. I'd just sit there. It was so damned peaceful. Everything was dead. Dead quiet. Every now and then I'd hear an animal or something. There was something about how calm it was that I loved; I miss that."

"That's pretty and all, but *this* view." I gestured out the shack window to the peaks in the distance and then another range of peaks behind them, and then another and another out to the horizon. "This view reminds you of Wisconsin?"

"It's not about the view. It's about the feeling of it."

I knew what he meant about the feeling of it, of how the perfect place on Earth could be inside this top-of-the-world lift shack and could also be on a pontoon boat on Gull Lake back in Michigan, feeling the lake water evaporate off your skin, or of how peering off the edge of a cornice in howling winds at 12,000 feet gave you that same tickle down in your gut as the moment after jumping from a 20-foot cliff toward

Lake Superior, still icy on a scorching August vacation afternoon, that split second of limbo between earth and water.

After a couple more runs I went in early. I wasn't tired, just tranquil, and I laid down for a nap. I fell asleep thinking about what Bill said about Wisconsin, and it made me think about Michigan. It was my home and I loved it, despite feeling the need to leave. I hoped that I could show it to Kylie someday. I could see myself back there but not yet.

That night Paul pulled his old Winnebago up in front of the Block and a ton of us piled in to go ski the full moon up Loveland Pass. We threw our skis onto the queen bed in the back of the 20-foot rig. The couch and chairs were taken, so we found places to sit on the nasty shag carpet, Kylie nestled beside me. Metallica blared through wood paneled speakers bolted over the curtained windows.

"Dude, I've got to get me one of these," Bill said, admiring the motor home's old water-stained paneling. "I'd need nothing. Strong and content, I'd travel the open road."

"You've been reading Walt Whitman on the shitter," I said.

"Damn right."

Paul climbed in through the side door, slapping hands with everyone else in his overzealous style. He addressed the crowd. "First of all," he said, "this thing smells like patchouli because I bought it from some hippies. But it's still my baby, so treat it with respect and don't be a douche. Secondly, no shitting in the bathroom. It smells. Thirdly, I'm going to drink, so someone else needs to drive." He looked around for a volunteer.

"Fuck it," I said, volunteering for the first half of the trip so that I wouldn't be the one stuck driving home. "You don't need a CDL to drive one of these things?"

He shrugged his shoulders. "Don't think so."

Sitting up in the driver's seat scared the crap out of me, so far off the ground in this bus-sized thing, about to drive up a mountain pass in the nighttime. I gave it gas and felt the engine rumble as the beast

lurched forward. I took the turns wide, terrified I'd side-swipe somebody. By the time I merged onto the interstate I felt kind of confident, even a little badass.

I turned off onto the steep, narrow road curving up toward Loveland Pass. The engine bogged down as we climbed. I had the gas pedal pinned to just maintain 30 miles an hour—flashers on. Halfway up the pass I saw a bunch of people crowded around a roaring bonfire in a dirt parking area just off the road. They sat on pickup truck tailgates and camp chairs, most wearing ski gear but some in Carhartts and jeans. A tapped keg rested in the snowbank. I pulled the 'bago up near the fire, threw it in park, and cracked a beer making it obvious someone else would be driving home. Several pickup trucks ferried people the rest of the way to the top, and we piled our stuff into one of them, climbing up into the bed ourselves for a chilly ride to the summit.

The cold night had a bite to it, exhilarating, and the full moon hung big in the sky. It lit up everything and tinted the snow a spectral blue. I hefted my skis onto my shoulder and hiked up a short rocky trail to the top of a bowl, the four of us beginning the ascent in a pack.

Bill climbed quickly while the rest of us took our time, and he dropped into the bowl as soon as the rest of us got to the top. I put on my skis and dropped off a small cornice. A thin crust covered the snow so turning took some muscle, though once the steep face shallowed a bit the skiing became more fluid. I followed Ryan as he ducked into the trees. The moonlight didn't penetrate through the pine branches. Ryan continued into the darkness.

Kylie passed me just as I headed out of the pines. I followed her as she made quick turns in the crystalline snow. I crisscrossed her tracks, snow from her twin-tips kicking up at my face. I pulled my goggles down over my eyes, but the tinted lenses were too dark for the moonlight. I flipped them back up squinting away the cold air instead.

The trail became a glade for a while, then we followed the smell of woodsmoke which popped us back out onto the road near the bonfire. Ryan hadn't come out of the trees yet and Bill wasn't around. Kylie and

I hitched a ride back to the top. We climbed the same ridgeline as before, alone this time, the crunch of snow under our boots the only sound. Craning our necks at the top, we gazed at the full moon hanging there big and bright over the continental divide.

"Pretty," Kylie said.

"Very."

I kissed her under the moon and then we dropped in, making turns down into the woods again. I turned between trees, cross-blocking pine bows with my poles until my ski clipped a branch under the surface, sending me somersaulting. I sat there in the powder and watched Kylie plow her skis and sink in the fresh snow as she came to a stop. Then she toppled over and shimmied up to me, skis still on. I put my arm around her and pulled her close.

In the deep silence of the night, each movement we made sounded immense. The full moon cast shadows of the trees, and of us, onto the snow. I kissed her and then pulled her atop me, her weight pushing me deeper into the powder and her skis tangling up with mine.

She pulled her gloves off and ran her hands up under my shell, the cool air exhilarating and then her hands warm against my skin. I did the same to her, running my hand up under her sports bra, cupping her soft, perfect handful breasts. We struggled out of our ski clothes and tried to do it with her skis on. That didn't work, so she kicked them off before she straddled me. The nighttime was so cold that our skin felt hot, our body heat melted us into the snow. I squeezed her close for mutual warmth and pressed my face against her warm skin. Afterwards, we lay there in the woods, embracing the cold atop ice formed into our shape. I pulled her close, kissing her forehead as she closed her eyes.

"We'd better get going," she finally said. "They'll think we were in an avalanche."

We found our clothes with some difficulty and shook out the snow. She kissed me, and then we struggled getting back into our skis. We cruised back down, taking turns leading figure eights—best run of my life. Back at the parking lot two police Jeeps sat with lights flashing along

the side of the road. Someone had dumped snow onto the bonfire and the officers broke up the party.

"Where the hell were you?" Bill asked.

"We got stuck in the deep stuff."

"Deep stuff," he said, laughing. "You guys are sick."

We piled into the Winnebago, me on the floor with Kylie on my lap, and we headed back down the pass with the flashing lights of the police Jeeps reflecting in blue and red off the snow behind us.

# 9

I slept until noon and felt guilty having wasted a morning of Rocky Mountain skiing. Looking out the window at the tremendous Sunday morning lift lines, I felt a bit better even though the stuff higher up on the mountain would surely be empty.

I got dressed and walked through the vacant ski school locker room toward the schoolhouse. Having always walked this path in ski boots, it felt strange being on the snow in tennis shoes. I stood outside the orange snow fence next to a couple of parents as Kylie skied backwards down the tiny hill holding the hands of a little girl dressed all in pink. The girl had noodle legs and couldn't stand up without Kylie's help. Her head, in a giant pink helmet, bobbed like a doll's. I watched Kylie and her class for a few minutes until they took a break. Most of the class sat down in the snow, though a couple of boys ran wild. I walked up to Kylie and kissed her cheek—one of the boys made gagging noises. She hugged me and smiled, her oversized rose-colored goggles making her face look small.

"Hey class," she said. "Say hi to Jimmy."

A couple of them greeted me.

"I was hoping I could take you out to dinner tonight," I said.

"Are you asking me out on a date?"

"Yes, yes I am."

That night I showered and put on my nicest clothes: clean blue jeans and a shirt with a collar. Kylie was almost ready when I got to her room. She wore a cream-colored sweater under a jean jacket, tucked her brown curls behind her ear but they wouldn't stay.

# SKI BUM

At an Italian place in Frisco, the waiter pushed in our chairs for us. We ordered food and glasses of wine and I didn't care too much about cost. I'd built myself a little nest egg of tips.

The place was stuffy and I felt out of place, white tablecloths and the lingering waiter who filled our water glasses every time we took a sip. We ate quickly, ready to get out of there.

"Want to dine and dash?" I asked, joking.

"Sure!" she said and got up to leave. I didn't know if she was serious or not, and I panicked as she walked away.

"Relax," she said. "I'm only kidding. Just going to the bathroom."

The guy brought the check as Kylie came back to the table and she grabbed it trying to pay. I said no, so then she tried to split the check with me, finally she settled for paying the tip. We left the restaurant but didn't walk to the Jeep, following the sidewalk instead down Main Street toward Lake Dillon. We walked slowly past old shops and restaurants lit up with Christmas lights behind massive piles of snow lining the street. An older couple dressed in ski gear walked past, hand in hand, with a shaggy dog at their side. I felt Kylie's hand grasp mine.

"Tell me something," she said as we walked.

"What do you want to know?"

"Anything," she said. "Tell me something about you I don't know."

"My favorite food is baby back ribs. I love me some baby back ribs."

"I want something more interesting than that. If you could go anywhere in the world, where would you go?"

"The Alps," I said before even thinking about it. "I'd go ski the Alps."

We were at the end of Main Street now. Dirty Jeeps and beat-up pickup trucks turned onto Summit Boulevard toward Breckenridge. Behind that, the Lake Dillon Marina and the snow-covered expanse of the icy lake. On the other side of the water, lights like stars illuminated the runs of Keystone for night skiers. We turned around.

"That's not a very creative answer," she said, "you being a ski bum and all."

"Well, let's hear yours then."

"A burger with lots of jalapenos on it," she said, smiling.

"You know what I meant."

"Italy," she said. "Ever since I was a little girl I've wanted to go to Italy. It always looks so pretty in pictures."

"How's that different than my answer?"

"It's more specific," she said. "And it isn't about skiing."

"There's skiing in Italy."

"There's more than just skiing in Italy."

"Well let's go then."

"Right now?"

I should've said *hell yes, we'll leave tomorrow*, but I didn't. "Maybe not right now," I said, "but next year we'll go. After we have time to save up some money."

"Alright," she said, squeezing my hand. "It's a plan."

There was silence for a minute as we walked, broken by the loud growl of a mufflerless car on the street.

"We'll have to ski for a couple of days at least," I said. "And live out of backpacks and stay in hostels."

"And stay in fancy hotels sometimes too," she said.

"Yes. But we can't be tourists."

"No?"

"No," I said. "We'll be travelers but not tourists."

"And then what?" she asked. "Where will we go after Italy?"

I thought about it for a minute. "Africa," I said. "What do you think of Africa?"

"We'll go on a safari," she said. "And I'll paint pictures of elephants and giraffes and sell them at a gallery."

"Can we climb Kilimanjaro?"

"Yes! We can do that too."

# SKI BUM

I thought about all the places in the world and how little of it I'd seen. I wanted to see it all. I wanted to see it all with Kylie and not go home for a very long time.

We were back at the Jeep now. I opened the passenger door for her then drove back to Silver. When we got there we walked some more, not toward the Block. The black mountain silhouettes surrounded us on all sides like we were at the bottom of some immense bowl. It made us, me at least, feel small.

I took Kylie's bare hand and held it, stuffing both our hands into the pocket of my puffy coat. We walked slowly through the village and around the small lake twice.

"Now you tell me something," I said.

"About what?"

"You. What made you come here, to Colorado?"

"My parents started me skiing before I could walk," she said, almost dreamily. "My first day of lessons I ditched the instructor and rode up the chairlift by myself. In high school, I started racing. A girl on my team and I always said we'd move to Colorado to be ski bums. After a year of college, I was ready to come out here. She had a boyfriend by then and didn't want to come."

"Did your parents care?"

"Not for the first season, but that was three years ago. Now they want me to move back home and finish school."

"I'm glad you're still out here," I said.

"Me too."

We had almost reached the Block, walking very slowly now. I didn't want to go home and neither did she.

"Let's go sledding," I said, and we headed off toward the ski school, stars and moon illuminating the wooded path. A fox darted across the trail in front of us then disappeared into the trees. The trail was different at night.

We grabbed a couple of sleds stashed outside the schoolhouse and found a clearing of untouched snow. We stepped off the trail and sunk to our knees, then trudged uphill for a few minutes, feet post-holing with each step. It became thigh-deep, then waist-deep, then up to our stomachs. Halfway up the slope I gave up trying to move forward and fell back into the snow. Kylie did the same thing next to me and wrapped her arms around me.

"So much for sledding," she said.

I pulled her in tight as the snow enveloped our bodies and held us in place like a tucked in blanket. We didn't move or talk for some time, our breathing the only sound. Lying in the snow in the dark, I felt a strange warmth.

"What are you going to do with your life?" she asked.

"Do with my life?"

"Yeah."

"I don't know," I said. "I want to travel. I want to ski. I want to see everything and do everything and meet as many people as I can, just like you."

"That's a good answer, I guess," she said. "But I mean in the real world, like a career. Or are you going to be a ski bum your whole life?"

"I'm going to marry a rich girl, I think." She punched me in the arm at this, and I pretended it hurt more than it did.

"I'm not sure yet," I said, because I truly didn't know. And I didn't know that I even wanted to decide that yet. That kind of stuff felt less scary when kept at a distance. "Maybe go back to college at some point. Get a job, I guess. But living at a ski hill for a good long time could be fun too. What about you? What are your big plans?"

She took a good long time to answer. The cold night calm around us, we'd rested there long enough to feel that we were a natural part of the landscape. An immense quiet surrounded us.

"I don't know either," she finally said. "I'll go back to school soon. Really study art, or maybe graphic design. Someday I'll have a family but not for a long time." She breathed deep, her breath spilling out in a cloud as she exhaled. "And I want to travel, live places, experience

them," she said. "That's what's cool about people here. Everyone talks about doing things, but these people actually do it."

We seemed to be on the same boat, drifting not quite aimlessly but almost. "You'll figure it out," I said. "And so will I. But here, now, there's nothing wrong with living in the moment."

She made a small noise, like she agreed with me. I held her hand. We stayed there a long time and let the snow around us harden into the shape of our bodies, watching a lone black cloud float across the purple sky.

# 10

At its best, skiing distills life to one run at a time, a two-thousand-foot burn from top to bottom—the world becomes a single mountainside—your tracks behind you your past and the untracked snow ahead your future with the endless possibilities of trees, bumps, cliffs, and groomers. Each chairlift ride is resurrection. Of course, fresh, bottomless powder is the Holy Grail, but pow is elusive. True enlightenment can be found in things like soft corduroy on a 27-degree bluebird day. It's times like these when the perfect wax, sharp edges, and strong legs can make you feel part of the mountain, allow you to create carves as organic as the snowmelt streams that'll rush downhill in April.

Find a steep and let it take you—play on the slope's every undulation—don't just carve into the butter snow with your inside edge, but bury the outside edge of your inside ski so that even your pinky toe generates immense power. Get lost in the speed; embrace it. Let the carve take you so deep that your skis are completely on edge, perpendicular to the snow so that your boot buckles and knee skim the corduroy surface, followed by a thigh—maybe even your ribcage, forearm, hand, and pole. Fly along the top of the snow, inches off the surface without touching it. That's when it's time to come back the other way.

At speeds like these the best thing the mountain can give you is a roller, a launching point to send you airborne, not up but out so that you might fly a few hundred feet, falling with the shape of the slope. You'll never be more than a few feet off the ground, and when you finally land you'll hardly be able to feel the difference between earth and air.

Kylie, Muppet, and I skied like this any time I wasn't working, which was now becoming more and more frequent for me. Christmas had been a month ago, though white Christmas lights still glittered on all the buildings of the village giving it a perpetual winter wonderland feel. The winter break vacationers long gone, spring breakers still at least a month away, these weeks were slow and peaceful times. Fewer guests, though, meant reduced hours and wages—reduced from not all that much to begin with. I still taught three or four days a week, though, with classes of four kids being much easier to manage than the ten kid classes of Christmastime. We all got by on ramen and cheap beer.

For a week or so every day was perfect, cold but with the sun shining bright enough to take the bite out of the air and soften the slopes to an ideal consistency. Up high, snow dusted the mountain at night, not enough for powder skiing but enough to make the mountain as gorgeous as possible—the pines near the bottom green, fading to frosted white up top. I felt a connection to the place. It may not have been home, but it was mine nonetheless.

Kylie still worked a full load, having seniority and being well-liked by Paul, so Muppet and I skied together most mornings, ripping as fast as gravity could propel us. Muppet seemed to lack the ability to ever slow down, charging hard no matter what was ahead of him. Once we tore up all the corduroy we'd hit the glades and bowls.

One payday I dropped into Patrol Chute, made jump turns for a couple hundred feet, and then turned around to watch Muppet drop in. He hit the cornice with speed, launching off the lip, landing on the near vertical face, and straightlining the thing with hardly a speed check. He shot past me then made a couple of short turns before catching an edge and somersaulting. He lost a pole and then his hat and goggles as he rag-dolled all the way down to the bottom of the slope. I took off after him, grabbing his lost gear along the way, sure that if he wasn't dead he'd at least broken something major.

As I skied up to him he sat up. "Holy crap," he said. "Let's do that shit again."

We took another run before he left to go open the bar. I skied alone for a while, slower now, trying to find perfect lines through mogul fields. In the bumps I found my Zen.

I made my way down to the ski school where I had a paycheck waiting for me. I watched Kylie with her class for a bit; the ease in which she did everything stunned me. When she saw me she waved and then had her class attack me with snowballs. Then I rode back up to the top of Storm King and sat with Bill in the lift shack, watching the westward facing slopes of the Ten Mile Range shine in the afternoon sun, a deep golden hue of hayfields back in Michigan in July.

Done skiing for the day, I headed to the bank to cash my check. Rather than paying the three bucks to cash it, though, I opened an account, giving my room at the Block as my address. Being a Colorado resident now in some official capacity made me feel good and feel at home for whatever that was worth. Plus, it was payday and my legs were good and tired from skiing—all was good in the world.

That night all the boys and I took Muppet's truck to Aspen, Muppet driving at top speed through a whiteout blizzard so that I finally just closed my eyes and tried to sleep, sure that we'd all die. One of his college ski racer friends worked and lived at Snowmass. She shared the shitty top half of an old house with a bunch of guys who were all drunk when we got there. Someone threw us cans of beer before we could even put our backpacks down, a strong welcome after a harrowing drive through the dumping snowstorm.

It wasn't clear who actually lived in the house, who was visiting for the weekend like us, or who was couch squatting, but the place was packed. Muppet's friend, Danielle, introduced us around but hers was the only name I bothered to remember. The place reminded me of my college party house by the train tracks—full of people, messy, empty liquor bottle décor, and with piles of dirty dishes covering the kitchen

counters—the clear differences being the trail maps covering the walls and the dozens of skis and snowboards piled in every corner.

"Let's jumpstart the night," Danielle said as she grabbed an old Olin Mark IV from the kitchen and filled shot glasses superglued to the topsheet with Jägermeister.

"Here's to a powder day tomorrow," she said, and we tipped back the shotski, the syrupy black licorice taste oddly pleasant. Not twenty minutes in Aspen and I already felt buzzed; it was going to be a good weekend.

We sipped more beers and listened to Muppet and Danielle reminisce about their college ski team. Muppet tried to convince her to move to Silver, but she was trying to find a real job in Denver. They had an easy familiarity with each other, like they'd dated.

After we finished all the beer in the house, Danielle passed around the Jäger and we took bottle shots, cowboy style. Half-drunk I had the urge to call Kylie and tell her I loved her, but I at least had enough sense to suppress that thought. It seemed too soon to tell her that, and a drunk dial wouldn't be the right way to say it.

Our whole group walked as a herd through dumping snow the mile into town. Us Silver boys walked with Danielle while her roommates and their friends lingered a bit behind. Muppet bebopped around, play-fighting with me and Bill and talking about how he wanted to get weird and rowdy. Huge fat flakes fell in heaps, which gave the night a kind of giddy excitement.

We entered the Mountain Dragon, a red pleather night club with a weird bro brah vibe. Shitty screamo music blared at top volume. I sensed our night might turn south at some point. Muppet ordered a round for our whole massive group, bloody marys with beer backs for everyone except for Bill, who insisted on his typical Jack and Coke. Muppet slammed his credit card down on the bar with authority.

"Where's the money coming from, Mr. Bigshot?" Danielle asked.

"I have ten grand in savings," he said.

"Holy shit," I said before I thought better of it; I could travel for years on that kind of money.

"Don't be too excited," he said. "I also have nine grand in credit card debt."

"Why don't you use the savings to pay off the debt?" Danielle asked.

A fair question, to which Muppet responded with a look of disdain. "Then I wouldn't have ten grand in savings," he said.

The bartender served our bloodies, big fancy ones with shrimp and pickles and all kinds of shit. We took our drinks out onto the dance floor where I felt plenty drunk enough to enjoy stumbling around to the terrible music. The bloody mary sloshed around in my glass, some of it spilling onto the floor. Muppet dripped sweat as he danced, wild and energetic. He ground up on Danielle and kissed her neck. She laughed but didn't push him away.

The crowded line for drinks spread out onto our dance floor, but Muppet didn't seem to notice or care. He twirled Danielle, trying to dance fancy, flailing and bumping into people in the bar line. On their next spin Muppet slammed into some yuppy gaper on vacay, which knocked Muppet's drink, shrimp and all, down the front of Danielle's shirt. Muppet shoved the guy, who got all broey and pissed, puffing out his chest in a douchebag *come-at-me* gesture. Muppet laughed and slapped the guy's tallboy can out of his hand then pulled his shirt up over his head. The dude upper cut Muppet in the guts then managed to tackle him to the floor, rolling around in the bloody mary remnants. Muppet climbed on top and landed a couple of punches before Bill went in to pull Muppet off the guy. I went in to help, though I would have liked to see how it would have played out, and the guy's buddies did the same for him.

One of them pushed Bill in the back, to which Bill said, "Eat shit, dickweed."

I grabbed that guy by the arms and dropped him to the ground, pinning him down with my knee on his lower back. I saw olives, shrimp,

and god knows what else there on the beer-soaked floor so I grabbed the guy's hair and rubbed his face in it for good measure. He flopped under me like a fish. I waited until he stopped moving before letting him up.

Ryan stood there sipping his bloody while Danielle shook her head and yelled, "Derek!" a couple of times, but his given name worked to no avail. Muppet thrashed and yelled as we tried to help him to his feet. He swung his arms wildly and I took his elbow to my face. I slapped him hard, open-handed across the cheek. This seemed to gather his composure enough to get him to his feet, though he kept running his mouth. I felt my lip swelling up, could taste the raw iron of blood, though it didn't seem to be dripping.

"Geeze, dudes," Ryan said. "I'm glad I'm on your side."

Danielle bought the gaper a fresh beer to avoid any further confrontation. She knew the bartender, which was the sole thing keeping us from being kicked out. The guy's friends took him to the other side of the bar, but Muppet wouldn't stop running his goddamned mouth. He talked loud, almost yelling. "Fucking pussies," he said, looking at the group of bros. "Fucking bunch of motherfucking pussies!"

They pretended not to hear, probably thinking that to acknowledge the insults and not defend themselves would be dishonorable. I was glad. The initial moments of a scuffle are always the fun part, and we'd had that. Both sides had experienced the adrenaline rush and had a story to tell; anything more than that and you start thinking about getting arrested, or breaking some expensive shit, or landing a blow on the temple that could send someone to the hospital, or having that blow landed on you.

Danielle flirted with Muppet now, facing him on a barstool, not allowing his attention to wander from her immediate vicinity. It was clear she knew how to react, how to deal with him; she was used to this behavior. Things calmed down a bit, and we sat there at the bar regaining our composure, swaying drunkenly on our stools. We drank beer; three bloodies had been enough. Danielle finally trusted that Muppet had calmed down. She headed to the bathroom.

Muppet slid over onto the barstool next to me. "I just want to go over and kick that fucker's ass," he said in a slur, even though the guy and his group had already left. "Then when we get back to Silver you and I should kick Paul's ass."

"*Paul's* ass?" I asked. I didn't know Paul and Muppet even knew each other. "Why kick Paul's ass?"

"For you, man. You must want to. Must piss you off that he and Kylie hooked up. Fuck that guy."

I thought he misspoke at first. "What do you mean?"

"Kylie and Paul," he said. "They hooked up. They dated for like two years. You didn't know that?"

I got up and stumbled to the bathroom. I wanted to be angry, but more than that it just made me sad, made my stomach feel hollow, not just that they'd dated—whatever—but the fact that nobody had bothered to tell me. I pissed, drunkenly swaying, trying to keep it in the urinal. At the sink I looked in the mirror, closing one eye, leaning in so that my face was inches from the glass, and studying my prominent goggle tan; I looked like a real ski bum now. The whole thing pissed me off, but I smiled a shit eating grin at myself in the mirror anyway—the absurdity of everything. My swollen lip bulged. The skin felt raw and tight; it felt good to be hurt.

Bill walked into the bathroom. He'd been throwing darts with Ryan and hadn't heard what Muppet had told me.

"You're a fucking dick."

"Nice to see you too," he said, walking to the urinal. He started pissing. "What's your problem?" he asked over his shoulder, his nonchalance pissing me off.

"Why the fuck didn't you tell me about them?"

He pissed in silence and then zipped up, turning around and giving me a weird look. "Tell you about who?"

"Paul and Kylie."

"Oh, them."

"So you knew?"

"Of course I knew."

"Jesus Christ, you're a jackass," I said, tempted to hit him. Instead I grabbed the garbage can by the door and threw it to the ground, its lid toppling off and wads of paper towel spilling at his feet. It was childish but so what? He told me to fuck myself and I stormed out into the dumping snow in just my t-shirt, feeling the spinning world of my own drunkenness. I pulled out my cell phone and dialed Kylie without a second thought.

She didn't pick up, so I dialed again. After several rings she answered. She'd been sleeping. "What's up, babe?" she said.

I had half a second of clarity standing out there in the cold, the large snowflakes coming down thick.

"Hello?" she said.

The clarity faded. I knew I'd regret it but went through with it anyway. "Why the hell didn't you tell me you were fucking Paul?"

"Excuse me?" she said.

"You heard me."

"Fucking Paul? Are you kidding me?"

I said nothing.

"Well?" she said.

"So is it true?"

"Is what true?"

"You're fucking Paul?"

"I'm not fucking Paul."

"But you did?"

"Not that it's any of your business, but he and I dated."

"So you fucked him?"

"You're hammered."

"Fuck you, I'm hammered," I said, not caring that the statement made no sense. She said nothing. "Hello?" I said a few times before realizing she'd hung up. I pitched my phone into a snowbank then stood there freezing in the falling snow. I knew I should go dig it out, but that would've ruined the gesture.

My head spun as I walked back into the bar. Bill looked at me with either disgust or concern and Muppet ordered me a beer. Things got hazy from there.

* * *

I woke up sweating bullets in the dark, wishing the world didn't exist. I lay on the carpet of the condo next to the fireplace, the logs still smoldering, heat resonating off the brick. My head pounded in a fierce pulsating rhythm. An insatiable thirst raged inside me. I took stock for a second before remembering Kylie. The thought brought a rush of bile, but I swallowed it. I just wanted to sleep some more and wake up when the world was a better place.

I stood up instead, shaky, and stepped over bodies on the floor to the kitchen where I rinsed a dirty glass and filled it with tap water. I chugged that and filled it again and then laid back down on top of my sleeping bag. Head throbbing, I turned my back to the fireplace. I suppressed another urge to puke before falling back into a fitful sleep, a sleep disturbed far too soon when Muppet jumped on top of me.

"Wake up, man," he said. "It's a powder day."

I groaned and sat up. Everyone else was already awake, most of them half dressed in their ski gear.

"I called Kylie last night," I said.

"Probably not something you want to think about," he said. "Eat some eggs."

He dragged me off the ground and pushed me into the kitchen where Danielle stood at the stove, fully dressed, frying a huge pan of scrambled eggs. Bill stood there sipping coffee.

"You're a huge fucking dick," he said but he was smiling. He handed me a cup of coffee and then grabbed the trash can. "Watch out!" he yelled. "He gets off on dumping garbage cans."

"I know," I said. I was definitely a fucking dick; the fact that Bill wasn't pissed was a slight reprieve. I tried to think of the phone call with Kylie as only a dream. It certainly felt that way, and I was glad I didn't remember each and every detail.

Danielle placed a plate of eggs in front of me. "Dude," she said. "You look like shit."

I thanked her for the food.

"Hurry up and eat then get dressed," Bill said. "We're getting first tracks."

I tried to choke down the meal but only tasted bloody mary and thought the eggs would come back up. "Not gonna eat?" Muppet asked as he doused my plate in Cholula and Sriracha, scarfing down the whole thing. *How is he not hungover?*

My head pounded as I got dressed and coffee only seemed to make it worse. It intensified things, made them more real, or at least made me more aware of my misery.

I squinted in the bright sunlight and pulled my tinted goggles over my eyes, seeing stars from the glinting light off the fresh snow. I kept asking myself what the hell I'd been thinking last night. The cold walk eased my stomach a bit. Us boys and Danielle got on a chair together; her friends got on behind us. I hoped the group would split up, not wanting to deal with human interaction.

"You guys sure picked the right day to come out," Danielle said.

I looked down at the fresh glittering snow beneath us nodding in agreement. As shitty as I felt, both physically and mentally, I had to admit this day was perfect. I breathed in crisp mountain air and felt the burn of my cut lip. I'd forgotten that part of the night, a part which had been pretty exciting. Nobody had gotten hurt, and if the night had ended there, I'd have been all smiles today. We'd come into town with guns a blazin' and lived to ski the pow. At that point Muppet was the only one of us who'd been a total asshole.

We unloaded the chair and got onto a creaky old double with the bar in the middle. I sat next to Muppet.

"That fight last night," I said.

He nodded. "I can be a real dick," he said, his candor surprising me. "Get a few whiskeys in me and I'll pick a fight with the president. It's gonna get me in trouble someday. It was fun though, right?"

"Totally." And it had been fun to a point. Muppet was one of the nicest guys I knew, but also the biggest asshole and the meanest drunk, and this revelation made me think of my own psyche and what led me to call Kylie last night. I needed to call and apologize, but this might be beyond apology, which made me sick to my stomach. The Paul thing still pissed me the fuck off anyway. Maybe I wouldn't call, but I reached to check my phone to see if she'd called before remembering that'd I'd thrown it into the snow.

"Fuck," I said.

"Damn right."

At the top of the lift we looked down into a massive bowl of burnt up trees. So many peaks stuck up in the distance. While the view was no more spectacular than Silver, it was new, and that made it better somehow. Muppet dropped into the ten inches of fresh, eager for pow and not bothering to wait for the rest of the group. I followed. Face shots of weightless snow dissipated my sick and general bad feeling about the world, at least until we got to the bottom where the blinding sunshine got my head pounding all over again.

We took another run and followed Danielle and her friends through the glades and steeps. They could ski, and they knew every secret spot on the mountain. I struggled to keep up and forgot that I was hungover until we came to the end of a long bump run and I felt the reflux and tasted the Tabasco from last night's drinks.

I stood at the base of the lift and wretched a while before puking blood red liquid all over the pristine snow. The tomato and vodka smell of the steaming puddle of puke made me gag again, but my stomach was empty. I rinsed out my mouth with snow and rubbed a handful against my sweating forehead. I felt better and was surprised that they'd waited for me.

I got on another double chair with Bill. He'd joked around but we hadn't really addressed the shit that went down last night. "Still pissed?" he asked.

"Not at you. Just confused. I don't know why she didn't tell me about them?" He just nodded. "Why didn't you tell me?" I asked.

"I didn't think it was my place."

This made sense. "But he's so fucking old," I said.

"Old balls, man."

"Fucking gross. I can't believe she dated him for two years, my boss, and didn't even bother to mention it to me. I work with the fucker every day."

"Two years?" he said. "Where the hell did you hear that?"

"Muppet said they dated for like two years."

Bill laughed. "Muppet's a dumbass. They *maybe* dated for two months. Probably more like two weeks."

A mix of emotions bombarded me with this statement. I felt better about Kylie not having told me; it wasn't anything serious. But I may have fucked it all up anyway with my call last night. *Why'd I have to fuck with a good thing? Why do I shit in my own bed?*

I knew I'd have to be the one to make the call. I knew I was the one in the wrong. I'd borrow a phone and call later. I'd spend the powder day nursing this hangover and pretending that last night hadn't happened. I'd ski the rest of the morning trying not to worry, trying to just enjoy the good snow that was being tracked up way too fast, as always with everything.

# 11

We walked past the Mountain Dragon at lunch, and I got on my hands in knees to dig though the snowbanks in search of my phone. My memory of last night hazy, I couldn't remember where exactly I'd thrown it. I searched in vain for a few minutes, Bill helping me look, before saying fuck it.

Danielle and the guys stood outside a swanky looking boutique, browsing through a rack of furs next to a Sidewalk Sale sign. Her roommates had stayed out skiing.

"You thinking about buying?" I asked Ryan as he fingered the tag on a long brown coat. He flipped the tag my way so I could read the original price of $2,900, which had been crossed out and replaced with a hand-written $2,200.

"Hard to resist a deal like that," he said.

Muppet threw open the door of the shop, bells clanging, and went inside. The squat dude manning the counter in a three-piece suit shot us a look of disgust. Muppet pulled a white rabbit fur shawl off the shelf and put it on over his duct taped North Face shell while Ryan draped some dead animal scarf over his shoulders and just said, "Dahling."

The attendant ran out from behind his counter, moving faster than expected on his tiny legs. "Take that off," he yelled. "Take that off right now!"

He grabbed the jacket and pulled it off Muppet. While Muppet laughed at him, the dude herded us toward the exit like a bunch of feral dogs.

"How many hamsters do they have to kill to make a nice coat like that?" Muppet asked as the guy pushed him through the door.

We followed Muppet, Danielle giving the asshole a big, toothy smile. "Have a nice day!" she told him.

"I'd like to skin that dude and make a coat out of him," Bill said as we strolled down the sidewalk toward the village.

Muppet nodded. "I don't think he took my buying interest seriously," he said, picking at the duct tape on his sleeve. "I do need a new coat."

"Assholes," Ryan said. It was the first time I'd heard anything negative out of his mouth. "Lift tickets are damn near two hundred bucks now. Can you imagine paying that for a day of skiing? Who can afford that?" Ryan's typical mellow voice rose to politician level. "This should not be a sport just for the rich. It should be a sport for everyone."

"Amen," Muppet said.

"Look at them," Bill said, nodding toward a posh couple arguing near the base of the lift. "They're not even having fun. They do this because it's fashionable, just to tell their shitty friends that they spent the weekend at their vacation home in Aspen."

"Fuck!" Muppet yelled, gesturing toward a bathroom in the crowded base area, it's hardwood door and golden placard declaring it the Gentlemen's Lounge. "Gentlemen's lounge?" he yelled, gapers all over the veranda giving him looks. "It's a fucking shitter!"

Danielle seemed a bit embarrassed, possibly fearing that someone she worked with would see us, but she laughed anyway. We sat down and ordered eight-dollar beers. I thought about the absurdity of these people spending more than any of us made in a year for a week's vacation they didn't even seem to enjoy. I'd thought of Silver as a big, fancy resort, but spending the day in Aspen made Silver seem bucolic. The posh couple's quarrel had escalated and the platinum blonde wife now screamed at her asshole husband, her fur-lined hood bobbing with each emphasized syllable. We leaned in, trying to hear what was going on. The guy smiled a clench-toothed grin, clearly pissed though he said nothing. He'd lost control of the situation.

"I'll see you at the condo!" the wife finally yelled loud enough for us to make out before penguin-waddling off on her skis. She slid backwards several inches with each six-inch step forward, the motion diminishing the gravity of her statement. The dude saw us grinning and flipped us the bird, at which our table erupted in laughter.

"Is that what your fight with Kylie looked like last night?" Bill asked.

"Oh no," I said. "Ours was a whole lot worse."

I swigged my beer, feeling it cut through the acid in my throat and splash oddly into my hollow stomach—hair of the dog.

"You talked to her yet?" Muppet asked.

"No," I told him, "I threw my phone into the snow last night. It's gone."

"Jesus," he said. "When you do something, you do it whole hog."

Our waitress came and our whole table acted extra friendly toward her; she was one of us. Nothing on the menu looked appetizing but I ordered a bowl of soup anyway—15 fucking dollars; two hours of work after taxes.

"You've just got to call her, bud," Bill said after we'd ordered. "Sometimes you have to suck it up and apologize. Even if it's not your fault, it's best just to get it over with."

"Oh it's my fault," I said.

"Well, even more so then." He looked contemplative, staring into his beer. "Jesus, I've had some fights with Aurelia."

"You two are official now?"

"I don't know what that means," he said. "But yes, we've had some fricken fights—those Latin women are good at it."

"About what?" I asked.

"Jealousy," he said.

"She doesn't strike me as the jealous type."

"My jealousy," he said. "Know all those Argentinean dudes that work in the kitchen?" I nodded though I didn't. "She's like their queen," he said. "Seems like she's dated half of them. Every time they go out she ends up dancing all twirly and whatnot with them to salsa music.

There's all this cheek kissing. It pissed me off and I told her so; I guess that's just how things go and there's nothing to worry about, but it used to piss me off anyway."

He slid his cell phone across the table toward me as the waitress brought our food. "This shit never solves itself," he said. "You just have to say you're sorry, even if you're not."

I slurped down my soup before it cooled and then bit the bullet. I walked away from the table and dialed Kylie. I counted the rings as my nerves almost forced me to hang up. I had 100 percent expected her to answer, and when she didn't after five rings the letdown was also a relief. I left a short message asking her to call me back on Bill's phone.

The food had calmed my stomach a bit. Now I felt like a nap. I feared what I'd done to my relationship with Kylie, what I was capable of in a single brief dumb moment, how fleeting everything is.

We headed back out, finding a corner of the resort that we had mostly to ourselves—a creaky old double chair that, thankfully, made me feel we were somewhere other than Aspen. I rode up with Danielle.

"I've dated some assholes," she said. "You, you don't seem so bad."

"Thanks," I said, truthfully. It felt good to hear kind words from someone I didn't know well.

"It's just a blip. If you want to make up with your girlfriend, you should. If you want it to happen, make it happen. You guys will recover."

"And what about you and Muppet?" I asked.

She laughed out loud at this. "We had our time," she said. "Derek's a good guy, sort of. I still love hanging out with him, but I don't see anything long-term there."

I thought about the phrase long-term—I'd known Kylie for a month and shouldn't even be thinking beyond the immediate present. All I had to do was have fun and walk the not so thin line of not being a giant dick.

"Nothing wrong with living in the moment," I said, to which she pulled a flask from her coat pocket, unscrewed the lid, and gave a cheers to that. She passed it to me and I felt a gut gurgle before sipping—oh so delicately—at the cinnamon whiskey inside. It felt good, warm, even though I felt the possibility of coughing it back up as I handed back the flask.

Off the lift, we followed a long traverse then took off our skis and hiked. We followed Danielle to the top of a steep, narrow chute between thick pines. I watched from above as Danielle and Muppet skied the chute, one at a time in precise, athletic jump turns.

I'd never truly realized just how strong a skier Muppet was, and Danielle was even better. I dropped in next and fought against burning thighs as I made the tightest jump turns I could manage. The chute opened onto an untracked face just below treeline. I followed as Danielle bee-lined for a cliff and hucked herself off with barely a speed check. She disappeared for a second and then reemerged below, still on her feet.

I slowed as Muppet followed her off the edge. Bill stopped beside me as Ryan passed us with tons of speed and launched off the thing. He grabbed his board and tweaked it behind his back—huge—while letting out a wild madman scream. I couldn't see him touch down but the way his yell cut off abruptly told me that he hadn't stuck the landing.

Muppet waved at us from below, urging us on.

"Screw that," Bill said and went off to find a route around the cliff.

"Fuck it," I said to no one then aimed my skis at the cliff and hit it with speed. The drop felt good, long enough to contemplate life. I looked for the landing and couldn't help but roll up the windows the whole time. I hit the snow a good long moment after I'd expected to and was leaning way too far back when I finally touched down. I bounced up and overcompensated into a couple of forward somersaults. My skis stayed on and somehow I wound up on my feet, skiing away without ever coming to a stop.

"Almost like that's what you were trying to do," Danielle said as I skied up beside them.

"Who says I wasn't?" Then I burst out in relieved laughter.

On the way back to the condo after the lifts closed, Kylie called. Bill handed me the phone and gave a thumbs up when I walked away with it for some privacy.

"Hey," I said, trying to be nonchalant.

"Hi," she said—then a long silence.

"So," I finally said. "I'm sorry about last night."

"Why am I calling you on Bill's phone?"

"Did you try calling me on mine?"

"No."

"I threw it in a snowbank last night."

"I'm glad I'm dating someone so mature."

"You're still dating me then?" She was silent. "Well?" I asked.

"I don't know. I just don't know."

That answer pissed me off, the way she didn't seem to care either way. "What does that mean?"

"It means we have some shit to talk about," she said. "All you ever want to do is get drunk and fuck off. What are you going to do with your life?"

I said nothing but inside I raged, biting the inside of my cheek to keep from going off. *Who the hell is she to say that? She fucks off as much as I do.* "Well," I said, "we sure do have some shit to talk about. I'm looking forward to it." And then I hung up.

Even though I knew I was in the wrong I felt pissed off. But in some ways I didn't care, like this kind of shit is inevitable, and we might as well get it out of the way now and each get back to our freedom. I rejoined the group and handed Bill his phone. I must have had some glimmer in my eye because nobody asked how it went.

Back at the house, more of the same, the monotony wearing me down though I knew it was the fight with Kylie more than anything else. We took up a collection for beer and pizza while Danielle's roommates played video games in the filthy living room.

The drinking began again. I wondered what the hell was the point to it all. The games on the tiny TV went on for hours and got more

heated as the guys kept drinking. I'd always been suspicious of anyone really into video games, and these guys annoyed the hell out of me.

Muppet joined the game and played for a few minutes, but he clearly wasn't in the same league and didn't last long. We sat at the kitchen table, half-assed playing cards. The tone on the couch shifted from good-natured competition to actual anger. The younger of the two guys lost, I guess, because he threw his controller at the TV.

"What the fuck, man?" the other dude yelled.

"Fuck off," said the kid before he swept his hand across the coffee table, knocking a dozen empties to the carpet.

Two fights in two nights was too much. I slumped in my seat, not even interested in watching this thing. The dude grabbed the kid by the shirt and threw him up against the wall, knocking over several pairs of skis, including ours. At that, the kid kneed the dude in the nuts. Dude keeled over for a second, regained his breath, and then tripped the kid who fell onto the coffee table, shattering the glass. The kid seemed pretty un-phased. He stood up barefoot in the glass.

"You take no responsibility for your actions," the older dude yelled. "You need to grow up!"

The kid stood there and said nothing. At first he seemed stoic but that quickly faded until he looked on the verge of tears. "You think you're so tough," he said, slurring his words. "You think you're so smart." The fight clearly delved into something that went way beyond this weekend.

I looked at Bill, then at Ryan and Muppet, and it was clear that they were also ready to get the hell out of there. We scrambled around grabbing our stuff, tiptoeing around the broken glass. The assholes didn't even seem to notice us.

"I'm sorry, guys," Danielle said, following us out the door. "I'm so sick of this shit. I need to get a real job and get out of here. Something like this happens every weekend." She hugged each of us goodbye, and then we were gone.

"At least you only knocked over a garbage can instead of throwing me through a coffee table," Bill said as we pulled out of Aspen. "That shit looked painful." He reached over and tried to give me a weird tickle on my belly, trying to make me laugh. It sort of worked.

*What a strange fucked up weekend,* I thought, and as shitty and uncomfortable as it was watching those strangers fight over something so stupid, it heartened me a bit knowing I wasn't the only jackass in the world.

As Muppet hauled ass through the dark I sat in the backseat thinking about the fight with Kylie, the deteriorating hours at work, and what the hell I was doing with my life. I questioned my existence, yet in truth, I just wanted to go skiing.

# 12

My hangover was gone, but I woke up feeling like shit anyway. We'd gotten in late—I'd thought about knocking on Kylie's door but hadn't, and with my phone buried in snow back in Aspen, texting her hadn't been an option. I wasn't angry anymore, just sad. I felt sick to my stomach.

With Bill and Kylie both working, I skied a bit by myself, thinking about Kylie. I just wanted things to be okay with her if that was possible. I forced myself to think about my cell phone problem—whether or not I needed, could afford, or even wanted a new one—though my mind kept wandering back to her.

I skied hard, ripping the steeps off the backside and bombing tree and mogul runs on the verge of losing control. Skiing like this felt good. The pure rush of it pushed the thoughts and feelings about Kylie out of me, and if I did wreck into a tree at top speed, I probably deserved it.

On the lift rides I felt guilty about being able to erase it from my mind, if briefly, so I stopped skiing for the day to just wallow in the shitty feeling of it. I wandered around the village for a while before running into Ryan who was just sitting in a hotel lounge chair in the sunshine. I wondered if he did this often. I sat in the chair next to him. He didn't notice me, so I lounged back for a couple minutes before saying hi.

We took his Toyota into Frisco where we walked around a cell phone store picking up the chained display phones. The salesman was an ass and wouldn't leave us alone until some girl with a *live, laugh, love* tattoo came in and took his attention. *Screw it,* I thought. I didn't even want another phone.

# SKI BUM

Ryan didn't mention the Aspen fight or why we were looking at phones at all, which I appreciated. Then we stopped at Cuddy's because Ryan wanted a drink, and of course I couldn't say no. There was nobody behind the bar when we walked in. After a couple of minutes Muppet rushed out of the kitchen carrying plates of food. There were only a couple of occupied tables in the place, but he was frantic.

He set a pitcher under the PBR tap and flipped open the handle. The beer flowed while he scrambled around doing other stuff. He caught the pitcher just as it started to overflow and set it in front of us with a couple of pint glasses, though we hadn't ordered it—or said a word to him yet for that matter.

"Assholes called in sick," he said. "Both of them. Cook and waitress. I'm so damned sick of it." He sped off to the kitchen on some other task. "So what do you think?" Muppet asked me when he returned.

"About what?"

"Do you want a job? Can you grill a burger?"

"Sure," I said without even thinking it over—a job dropped in my lap like an answer to a prayer if I had those.

"Lunch rush is about over," Muppet said. "Be here for dinner and the chef will get you started."

So I had a new job, and now it was time to talk to Kylie. I walked down to the schoolhouse to catch her as she got out of work. I felt like I could puke, but I also felt oddly good, as if the Aspen shit hadn't happened—not that Kylie had any reason to feel the same way.

I watched from a distance as the instructors gave their kids back to the parents, then I intercepted Kylie as she headed back toward the Block. She didn't look altogether pissed off to see me—so far so good—but she didn't seem all that happy about it either. "Hi," I said, falling in step with her.

"Hey."

"I got a job."

"Where?" she asked, her tone not exactly friendly, but going along with the conversation regardless.

"McGillycuddy's."

"Bartending?"

"Cooking."

"Wow," she said. "All that ramen noodle experience adding up," a sort of joke that lightened the mood a bit, made me comfortable enough to get into the meat of the conversation.

"About the other night," I said.

"The other night *and* the phone call yesterday."

"Right. Both. I know you're probably through with me, but I just wanted to tell you how sorry I am."

"How sorry you are? Do you really think you can just say sorry after the way you treated me and everything just goes back to normal?"

I took the question as rhetorical and said nothing.

"You know the thing I had with Paul was tiny, right?" she asked, more a statement than a question. "So short, and so long before I met you."

"Like I said, I'm sorry for bringing it up."

"Maybe I should have told you about it. Probably I should have. But at first it didn't seem like it mattered, and then once it did, it seemed too late to mention it."

We walked on a bit.

"You know I have no feelings for him, right?" she said.

"I know," I said. "It's fine. I overreacted." An understatement for sure.

"I'm sorry for that, but I don't think that's an excuse."

"It's not," I said, biting the bullet. This was going well, the needle tipping from dumpster fire back to something manageable. "You said all I ever want to do is get drunk, that I'll never do anything with my life."

"I did not."

"You implied it," I said. "I'll go back to school at some point. I'll get a degree and a real job. But for now, why can't I just enjoy it?"

"You're right. I was mad when I said that shit, and I'm sorry."

"You're fine," I said. "The goddamned things I do when I'm mad. I dumped a garbage can on Bill's feet."

She laughed at this. "You didn't!"

"Bet your ass I did."

"Will you dump one on Muppet next?"

We walked a bit in silence, the first rays of sunlight after a storm. "So, can we be good?" I asked. "Can we put this shit behind us?"

"I don't know," she answered, and then after a long pause, "we can try."

This was all I could ask for, giving it a try, and it's all we're all doing anyway. I kissed her and headed off to my first day of work as a line cook.

* * *

Tickets filled the shelf of the pass-through kitchen window when I showed up to Cuddy's. A short, intense looking bald dude worked the grill, sweat soaking through the bandana on his forehead.

"Hey," I said, walking into the kitchen, stepping over empty French fry bags littering the floor and avoiding the spilled jug of barbecue sauce on the prep table. "I'm Jimmy, supposed to start working."

"Dex," the dude said without looking up from the grill. "Drop some fries, will you?"

I vaguely knew what this meant, but it took a second for me to realize that there'd be no small talk. I was being tossed into the fire here.

"Well don't just fucking stand there!" Dex yelled.

Unsure of where things were in the kitchen, I reached into a chest freezer and grabbed a bag of frozen waffle fries. I ripped it open and dumped them into a deep fryer. Not knowing what to do next, I bent over and picked up the empty fry bags off the floor. Dex ran behind me, carrying two plates of food to the window, bumping me out of the way with his ass. This guy was a total fucking dick.

"I feel like I'm the only one working here, man," he yelled.

"You know this is my first day, right?" I said. "And I have no goddamned clue what I'm supposed to be doing."

"Oh, right," he said, his tone slightly gentler. He continued working the grill.

"So what the hell do you want me to do then?"

"Look at the tickets." He pointed at the window full of them. "Read the tickets. Get the plates prepped. And drop anything that's deep fried: chicken fingers, fries, that kind of shit. Got it?"

"Got it," I said, though I didn't. The waitress' scribbles on the tickets didn't make sense half the time and I had to guess where anything was. It took me a while to get into a rhythm, what with not having a minute of training and showing up to my first day in the middle of the goddamned dinner rush. Dex's constant yelling and throwing stuff didn't help.

He manned the grill, myself at the fryer. There seemed to be more and more tickets in the window. All I wanted was to catch up so that we could calm down and regroup. Each time we got down to one or two tickets, the waitress filled the window back up. I was sweating freakin' bullets when Dex smashed a basket of fish and chips on the floor because it wasn't plated right. I almost punched him but just bit my lip instead.

When a pan of potato skins started to fall out of the oven I reached out without thinking and caught it barehanded. I winced as it seared into my skin, and then I ran to the sink to rinse it in cold water.

"Suck it up, man," Dex said. "You're a cook. It happens."

"Just shut the fuck up for a minute, man," I yelled.

At this he grinned and yelled a loud, "woohoo!" slapping me on the back. "Now we're getting somewhere!" he said.

*Who the fuck is this guy?* I took a breath and walked back to the fryer. I tuned everything out: the noise, the mess, the pain in my hand,

Dex. I just concentrated on one thing at a time, working quickly but deliberately, not rushing.

Pretty soon the window was empty and it was 10 o'clock, kitchen closing time.

"I'm going out for a smoke," Dex said.

I didn't answer, just went to the sink and rinsed off my hand. I put a bandage on it and got to cleaning the kitchen.

Dex came back after his cigarette with two bottles of Budweiser and a couple of shots. He handed me one of each and took his shot without a cheers. "Well I think we've got you broken in," he said. "How's the hand?"

"It's alright," I said, still pissed at the guy.

"This is why I like working with dudes," he said. "You can work a whole shift wanting to kill each other then have a drink and be over it. Women hold grudges."

God, this guy was a dick. I wasn't sure that being an old cook made someone a chef. But, as I sipped Budweiser while he cleaned up the kitchen, he didn't seem all that bad.

Kylie stopped by and sat at the bar sipping an old fashioned while I mopped up the kitchen. Dex gave me a bro hug as I left and said he'd see me tomorrow. I walked home with Kylie. Hand in bandaged hand, under the stars. Things were looking up.

# 13

Grey dishwater filled the stainless-steel sink. I stuck my arm in up to my elbow and pulled the rubber stopper. It made a sucking noise as the water drained. I dried my wrinkled hands with the towel that hung from the grease-stained apron tied around my waist. A bottle of Budweiser sat on the counter next to the pile of drying dishes. I wiped the cool condensation on my forehead and took a long drink.

I'd been working at McGillycuddy's for a week now and was starting to get the hang of this cooking thing—I'd also warmed to Dex a bit. He wasn't as bad as my first day made him seem. For him, any cook who wasn't an asshole to the guy next to him didn't deserve to be working in a kitchen. I'd worked a couple of days at the ski school, but that was more of an afterthought now, any remaining romantic ski instructor notions gone. Most importantly, though, things with Kylie seemed as good as ever, both of us being overly nice to each other—a wild course correction from the shitstorm of last week. It felt fragile, but that beat the alternative.

"Hey there, chief," Bill said as he appeared in the kitchen window wearing snowboard gear, holding his beanie in a gloved hand. "When do you get off?"

"Just have to mop up and I'll be done,"

"Great. Come sledding with us."

"Sure thing," I said, wheeling the mop bucket out of the closet. I mopped the floor in sloppy quick strokes and drained my beer. I slapped Dex on the back as I walked out.

"Take it easy, man," Muppet yelled from the bar. "You coming in tomorrow?"

"Nope," I said, a feeling of absolute freedom. "Got the day off."

The stunning cold air bit through my sweat-soaked t-shirt as I opened the door to leave, and it felt great after a shift behind the grill. The crew leaned against a massive January snow pile outside the door, wearing snow gear and watching ice skaters on the frozen pond. Ryan wore ski goggles and held a plastic sled while Bill stood with arms wrapped around Aurelia for warmth. Kylie had a stack of cafeteria trays under her arm. We walked off toward the mountain.

"How was work?" she asked, a cloud of steam spilling from her mouth.

"No burns. No fights. A good shift."

I walked in my t-shirt for a minute before putting on my sweatshirt and puffy, taking in the cold as long as I could stand it. I was glad I had a hat and gloves in my pocket.

"Here you go, bud," Bill said as he handed me three Blue Moons from his backpack

I put two of them in my coat pockets and opened the third, feeling the cold bottle through my deer hide gloves. We walked in silence toward the base of the mountain. Walls of snow taller than us lined the sidewalks that were mostly empty except for a few tourists on their way to the bars from their hotels. Strings of white lights ran from building to building above our heads.

Speakers played classic rock and flames danced in the torches surrounding the plaza. We stepped from flagstone onto snow. A closed chairlift sat in the middle of the plaza, its haul rope and chairs climbing high up the mountain.

Kylie handed me one of the trays, I looked up the slope to the top of the halfpipe a few hundred vertical feet above us. The moon illuminated the mountain and cast shadows from the trees and the walls of the pipe. High up on the mountain the lights of groomers shone through the darkness, and above that, stars in a cloudless sky.

Snow crunched beneath my tennis shoes as I hiked along the side of the halfpipe. Ryan went ahead, scurrying uphill on all fours. Bill and I

climbed together, the girls below us. In the slippery snow I struggled to find traction. The slope steepened so I couldn't go any farther with just two feet. I stopped for a moment to finish my beer and then stashed the empty bottle in my pack. With both hands free, I scrambled on.

Halfway up, we stopped to catch our breath. Sitting down in the snow, the cold radiated through my blue jeans. I got up and sat back down on my tray, digging my feet into the hill to keep from sliding down. I tilted my head back to look up at the sky—no clouds and a million stars.

"Doesn't look like snow tonight," I said.

"Nah," Bill replied as he packed a snowball in his gloved hands. "There was still some untracked in the Enchanted Forest this afternoon. Get out there early and you'll get some." He leaned back and threw the snowball down the hill. The girls were getting close now and the snowball landed between them.

"Quit it, you jerk!" Aurelia yelled.

"Hurry up then!" he said.

They climbed up next to us and flopped on the ground, breathing heavily.

"We're almost there," I said.

We waited a minute and then headed up. We climbed quickly now and when we got to the top Ryan was lying on his back in a spread eagle, his plastic sled upside down next to him.

"Four-year-olds," Ryan said, sitting up.

"Huh?" I asked.

"Four-year-olds," he repeated. "My lesson today. I had a pooper and three criers. Don't know how much longer I can deal."

I laughed at this and pulled out the last of my Blue Moons. Ryan took a beer from his pocket, took his glove off, and popped the cap with the ring he wore around his middle finger.

We sat at the top of the halfpipe on the edge of the deck with our feet dangling against the vertical wall. White lights glistened below, crisscrossing above the sidewalks of the village which still looked festive

a month after the holidays. Music from the bars and the plaza speakers echoed, barely perceptible. A few small dots walked between the bars and glided on the pond. Beyond the village, lights of semi-trucks moved quickly along the black ribbon of I70. They came out of the east, curving around the purple silhouette of the Ten Mile Range. They straightened, gradually gaining elevation, then disappearing around more mountains to the west toward Vail Pass.

Aurelia and Kylie arrived at the top, dropped their sleds, and flopped down on their backs in the snow.

"Did Ry tell you about his new girlfriend?" Kylie asked, snuggling up next to me. I shook my head.

"It was that blonde from ski school," he said, "That Kiwi that tele skis. She wouldn't stop trying to dance with me."

"You're complaining about that?" Aurelia said.

"Nope. Nope." He stared up into the sky.

Kylie laughed and patted him on the back. I smiled, enjoying this moment, then drank the rest of my beer in long gulps.

Lights from a groomer approached—time to head down lest we get caught. Ryan sat on his sled and shimmied so the front of it hung off the edge of the halfpipe deck. He pulled his goggles down over his eyes and dropped in. In freefall the sled sped down the wall, climbed halfway up the opposing side, and then nosed straight down the fall line. I watched him for a while and then followed. My tray wasn't big enough for much more than my butt, so I lifted my feet up as I dropped in. The tray spun around backwards and I dug my foot into the snow to turn it back around.

It was impossible to steer and all I could do to control my speed was dig my feet in. Every time I did this, snow sprayed up into my face, so I just straightlined it. It took only seconds to slide down the length of the giant halfpipe. By the time I reached the bottom my tray was going so fast that I had to bail off it to keep from hitting the empty ski racks that lined the base.

Ryan helped me up and we watched Bill spin out of control and fall off his tray. Aurelia did the same. Kylie followed them, in and out of moon-cast shadows, her feet kicking up a cloud of snow that rose into the cold, still air. She rolled off her tray, but the tray kept sliding. It got close and Ryan stomped on it, arresting its motion.

# 14

A warm-up the first week of February melted off a good chunk of the snowpack and gave the feeling of an imminent spring. The temperature was in the forties every day exposing rocks and bare spots in Resolution Bowl. We needed a storm. Everyone on the mountain seemed happy though, basking in sunshine. The skiing wasn't bad either, carving through slushy snow like a slalom water skier—hoodie and sunglass weather—idyllic.

Work at ski school picked back up a bit, busier and with a few of the other instructors having quit or moved on. A busy ski school was great for me, but Paul seemed stressed as ever, locking himself in his office for hours at a time and sometimes shoveling heavy snow around the schoolhouse from one spot to another quickly and angrily for no apparent reason. He seemed to be cracking up, though I didn't particularly care.

He had me teaching older kids. These five and six, sometimes seven and eight-year-olds were able to turn and stop on their own and were mostly housebroken. I took my class up the chairlift every day, which never happened with the threes and fours I was used to teaching.

A few times that week Kylie had older kids too. We ventured together mostly on the gentle green runs above the schoolhouse. Our two classes took up four triple chairs and loading the lift with all those kids was always precarious. On the hill Kylie made slow, wide turns while our ten kids followed in her tracks. I skied cleanup, picking anyone who'd fallen up off the snow.

I enjoyed this slow skiing together—almost as much as I enjoyed skiing fast with her. Teaching, Kylie seemed totally in her element. The kids loved her too. At the bottom of every lift they'd clamor to sit next to her on the chair.

The kids never seemed to like me that much, which may have been fitting because I didn't particularly like them either. There were exceptions, of course. Like the ones that were happy and inquisitive rather than whiney little brats. Or the times when we took them out to the stables behind the schoolhouse and fed carrots to the horses.

On Superbowl Sunday our group class skied really well. We made it onto some real lifts and blue runs high on the mountain, not just the greens and the slow beginner chair we were used to. Kylie led us to parts of the mountain I'd seldom been before, meandering trails that cut easy curving paths through the pines. She'd stop and let our snake of children catch up. A few times we all took our skis off and found a log to sit on for a break. Ky kept a pocket full of Swedish Fish and handed them out to the kids like dog treats, which kept them happy and attentive like a herd of wagging Labradors. I liked all of them then. The slushy snow made for perfect snowballs and the kids, under Kylie's direction, would usually gang up on me. They all cheered when I picked a lift tower 20 yards away and pelted it dead center, channeling my old little league fastball so the wet snow exploded against the tower on impact.

It was by far my best teaching day of the season, so much so that it made me want to come back next season—not to work at Cuddy's as I'd been thinking about, but just to teach. I'd have a bit of seniority and could probably get enough classes to make it a full-time gig, maybe even get certified and get a raise. Maybe Kylie and I'd get an apartment together in Frisco or Leadville, skip the Block altogether.

This daydream continued as we snaked our way down the last run of the day. I skied as the tail to our long snake in wide and slow arcs that traced the route of Kylie and the rest of our class.

As we neared the bottom, though, angry voices from the vicinity of the schoolhouse tore open my reverie. At first it was vague, too distant to hear exactly what was being said, but definitely shouting and definitely coming from the schoolhouse. Then as we got within earshot, Paul's voice rang out clearly in the midst of a rager with one of the parents.

"This is how we do things around here, lady," he yelled, his voice quavering. "If you don't like how your brat son's being treated, you might want to pony up for a private lesson, or better yet a birthday clown babysitter to keep your son entertained!"

The woman, in a fur-trimmed coat and vacuum tight jeans, struggled to stand in the slush snow in high-heeled boots and seemed not to notice or care how nonsensical Paul's birthday clown comment was. Our class skied into the base, where I left our kids with Kylie and jumped in, trying in vain to stop Paul from taking it any farther. He was half-cocked, about to go off on any other uptight parent who got in his way. The mother was fired up too and seemed fixed on furthering the screaming match.

"I paid two hundred dollars for my kid to learn to ski!" the mom yelled. "And you have him inside all day doing what? Eating snacks? Taking naps?"

"I guess now I know where your kid got it from," Paul said, about to lose it if he hadn't yet. "Sounds like his mama's a whiney little bitch too."

The lady slapped him across the face as a crowd of parents gathered around. Paul grinned, licked his lip.

I clicked out of my skies and threw my arm around Paul, forcing him out of there as a couple of other ski school people came running to deal with the mother.

"You got my class?" I asked Kylie over my shoulder.

She nodded, mortified. Paul thrashed his arms for a moment. I struggled to keep him restrained and pushed my weight into him to keep him walking. He lost heart pretty quickly, the force behind his thrown elbows diminishing.

"I'm fired," he said to me as I led him away, my arm still around him. "I'm fired." Now he seemed dejected rather than angry, the passion that burned in him moments ago totally extinguished. "I can't live on unemployment again. The wife will divorce me."

I didn't know what to say to him. I knew for a fact that he wasn't married, that his bartender girlfriend lived with him at his place in Frisco. Maybe she'd leave him and that's what he meant. Maybe he was just at the end of his rope.

I let go of my grasp—he was no longer a threat, benign. He followed me, slump shouldered, toward the village. I'd buy him a beer, probably his last as youth ski school director. He sat with his head in his hands as I went up to the bar and ordered a couple of pints.

"What the hell happened back there?" I asked him as we sat down at the cafeteria bar, our uniform coats turned inside out on the backs of our chairs.

He just shook his head at first then downed half his pint in one long gulp before speaking. "She probably wasn't even out of line," he said. "At first at least. These rich parents complain every damned day. You usually just have to sit there and take it. Today I didn't want to take it, so I went off on her. She sure as shit didn't see that coming!" He laughed at this last line, which was good, I guess. "She got a little feisty in return," he continued. "It was kind of fun. She was actually sort of sexy."

He finished his beer and slammed the glass down on the table, mine still three quarters full. I patted him on the back, this strange ass man who conjured in me such mixed feelings. I had a soft spot for him despite his tense as a piano wire attitude and his history with Kylie.

"You really think you'll get the can?" I asked, knowing full well that he would but not really sure what to say to the guy. He'd called a paying guest a bitch to her face.

"Fuck it," he said and walked to the bar. He ordered a pitcher, set it on the table in front of me, and walked away.

"Where are you going?" I called out to him.

"Home," he yelled back, a smile on his face now. "Don't worry about me. They can't fire me if I'm not here."

The logic didn't make sense, but whatever—it wasn't my problem anyway. I had a pitcher to work on, and pretty soon Kylie joined me. I grabbed her a fresh glass and filled it up.

"Where is he?" she asked.

"Went home. He calmed down quite a bit. Said he thought that lady was sexy."

"What in the holy fuck," she said. "He's gone insane. Fucking insane."

I nodded in agreement, thinking that he'd been on the edge of crazy the whole time I'd known him. It was just at the forefront now. "What the hell happened out there?" I asked. "Did the lady calm down?"

"Hell no. She was still irate when I left. Parents gathered around checking out the commotion. Needless to say, we didn't receive any tips today."

"What are they doing to calm her down?" I asked, picturing the woman still out there screaming her fucking head off.

"Free shit," Kylie answered. "They offered her kid free lessons for the rest of their trip, but she said hell no she didn't want her kid back in this ski school. Last I heard they were trying to give her a week's worth of free lift tickets and a hotel room for next season. All expenses paid."

I raised my glass. "Here's to Paul," I said. "May he not get arrested. Or have an aneurysm."

Kylie cheersed and drank, but there seemed to be a concern in her eyes, like my comment hit a nerve. As we finished the pitcher she seemed to relax a bit.

We got last chair for a single free run together, an all-out burn, super-G turns and launching rollers, no one else on the mountain but the ski patrollers beginning their sweeps. Outside the Block people were already tailgating for the game. A bunch of foreign employees played pick-up rugby in the snow and the Aussie from the housing office had bratwursts sizzling on a grill. He called them snags and offered them to anyone within earshot. Bill stood next to a barrel of Pabst resting in the snow, pumping the tap and handing out red party cups. He wore a Packers cheesehead, though we both knew they weren't in the game.

"Nice hat," Kylie said.

"Wisconsin pride, baby."

"Packers playing today?" I asked.

"Ha. Ha," Bill said. "They may not be in the Superbowl, but they beat your Lions this season. Twice."

"The Packers and everyone else," I said.

"Tell him about Paul," Kylie said, which was odd. Why not tell him herself?

"What about him?" Bill asked.

"He's getting fired.

"Is that a surprise?" Bill asked, unphased by the news, not even asking me to go into detail. He chugged what was left in his Solo cup and crushed it against his cheesehead. "Let's go play some rugby, eh?"

We ran into the game, replacing a couple of guys coming out for a break, one of them bloody and both of them drunk. I had no idea what I was doing and Bill didn't seem to either. I made some tackles that made me miss my high school football days. After a few minutes someone passed me the ball and I ran it into a herd of tacklers, plowing a couple of them over before being laid flat by a giant Australian liftie who had me seeing stars. That was about enough of that for me.

Inside the Block they'd set up a projector TV with a huge screen. Everyone crowded together, sitting on couches and the floor. We managed to snag a couch where Kylie sat on my lap and Aurelia on Bill's. Pretty much everybody talked through the actual game, paying attention only to the commercials.

"I don't understand this game," Aurelia said halfway through the first quarter. "Why does it keep stopping and starting?"

Bill explained first downs but Aurelia cut him off before he went any farther. "You're going to put me to sleep," she said. "It just looks like a bunch of fat American men beating each other up like savages." She turned to Kylie. "You like this game?"

"Yup," Kylie said. "I like their tight pants." Aurelia agreed with this at least.

At halftime Ryan stumbled in drunk and with a bunch of beads around his neck, purple and gold and white. He flopped down onto the floor in front of us, sprawling out and leaning on his elbow like a centerfold.

"Where the hell'd you come from?" I asked.

"Frisco," he said, his voice slurred and dreamy. "I was out at the bar with a girl I met on the chairlift."

"Where's the girl now?" Kylie asked.

"Don't know," he said. "I left. I wanted to hang out with you guys."

"That's sweet of you," Bill said.

"His chairlift girl might think otherwise," Aurelia said.

"What's with the beads?" Bill asked

Ryan looked around and then down at the necklaces hanging around his neck as if surprised to see them there. "These? The bar was handing them out. Mardi Gras is Tuesday."

"Mardi Gras," Bill said. "You guys want to go?"

"Definitely," Ryan said. "It's half-priced rum drinks and free beads."

"Not to the bar," Bill said. "To Mardi Gras. New Orleans."

"New Orleans?" I chewed on the word like steak fat. "How far is that?"

"I don't know. Not far. Maybe twenty-something hours. We can leave in the morning and get there just in time for Fat Tuesday."

"You're serious?" Kylie asked before answering her own question. "Of course he's serious."

"I'll go!" Aurelia said. "Someone needs to keep you guys out of trouble."

"I've got the next couple of days off anyway," Bill said. "And the rest of you can call in sick."

Ryan nodded, not even having a second thought. Bill turned toward Kylie and me. "You guys?"

"I'm in," Kylie said, and I agreed. Why the hell not?

And that was that. A plan to check off a line on the bucket list, and the second half hadn't even started yet. The idea was crazy, of course—an entire day of driving for less than a day of partying, and that accounts zero time for sleep, and then another day of driving just to get back in time for work on Thursday morning. Lots could go wrong. It would be the most spontaneous thing I'd ever done. My friends back home would never do something like this, which probably made them smarter, but I was glad for friends here who were game for it.

I had a tough time sleeping that night, my body and mind jittery with an excited, nervous sort of tension. I called the schoolhouse knowing that nobody'd be there—certainly not Paul—and feigned illness, saying it felt like food poisoning or something. I hoped my message wouldn't be time stamped. Then Kylie called. She didn't pretend anything, just said she was taking a few personal days.

We were all in the lobby, mostly on time, with the exception of Muppet who'd been working last night. Kylie and I went up and knocked on his door. He didn't answer so we pounded harder and nonstop. He finally opened it, groggy, in boxers, his morning wood popping through without shame.

"Jesus Christ," Kylie said. "Cover yourself."

"Oh," he said, holding his hand over his junk. "Sorry."

"What the hell's wrong with you?" I asked. "You want to come with us to Mardi Gras?"

"Let me put on some shoes," he said.

We loaded up the cars, my Cherokee and Ryan's Toyota, and then stopped in at McGillycuddy's. Muppet opened the door with his key and scribbled a note in all caps on a napkin.

*DOG ATE HOMEWORK. GRANDMA DIED. FUNERAL IN NEW ORLEANS. JIMMY COMING WITH. LOVE, DEREK*

He left the napkin on the bar top, grabbed a bottle of Jägermeister for the road and let out a *whoop*. By nine we were headed east on I70, happy to be on the road. The sun shone down on the highway like a summertime road trip. Life was good, pushing it as fast as Ryan's beater four-banger Toyota could go.

# 15

The first light of morning hit us somewhere near Baton Rouge. I rolled down the window to breathe in some thick, warm Louisiana air. Out the window the bayou passed at eighty miles an hour. In the rearview I could see Kylie and Aurelia asleep in the backseat. I shook Bill awake in the passenger seat next to me.

"Wake up, sleepy head," I said. "It's time to party."

He woke with a smile on his face and grabbed a Nalgene bottle from under his seat into which Muppet had dumped half the fifth of Jäger he'd pilfered. Bill took a big swig, contorting his face at the first-thing-in-the-morning liquor drink then handed me the bottle. I steered with one hand and took a slug with the other, coughing and feeling that shitty licorice burn that made today feel like an adventure already. Some of the syrupy liquor dribbled down into my beard and disappeared there.

"It's a little strong," Bill said.

"It's not mixed with anything."

"Exactly." He smiled like a giddy little kid at his own birthday party. He couldn't sit still as we approached the city and kept giggling and chanting "we're going to Mardi Gras," in a strange falsetto.

I watched Ryan's car in the rearview as he swerved into the passing lane and inched ahead until he was side by side with us. I gave a thumbs up as Muppet cranked the window down. He shifted around in his seat, dropped his pants, and stuffed his ass out the window. I knew exactly what he was doing as it happened but I couldn't look away. Bill screamed and Ryan and Muppet both giggled like a couple of kindergartners as they fell back in line behind us. The girls woke up at the commotion.

"What'd we just miss?" Aurelia asked.

"Just a whole lot of man ass," Bill said.

"Damn."

"It was Muppet."

"Gross!" she yelled.

Kylie and Aurelia both swigged their Jägermeister like champs as the sky lightened into an overcast grey. We followed signs to the French Quarter where we turned onto a wide boulevard. Curtains of hanging moss hung from the tall trees. Vines and flowers grew in the median like some sort of jungle. With the windows down, we heard the distant sound of drum beats.

In Elysian Fields, we paid a lady twenty bucks to park on her lawn then jumped out of the cars like dogs from a cage. My knees ached from a day crammed in the Jeep. It felt good to be sweating and breathing the heavy, humid air.

We weren't the only ones pulling into the French Quarter ready to party; the lawn on which we'd parked quickly filled with people. We all changed into shorts and flip flops as we passed around the Jäger again and headed off toward the distant sound of a brass band. Others around us pulled coolers from their trunks and cracked open beers there on the grass, like a football tailgate, though it wasn't even eight in the morning yet.

We followed the crowd toward Bourbon Street where we stopped at a vendor's cart and bought hurricanes in giant plastic cups. The guy asked how strong we wanted them. I said strong, and he dumped what was left of a bottle of rum into my cup.

We stood on the curb of Bourbon Street and drank as a Dixieland band paraded by. Its leader, a short dude in a three-piece suit, danced ahead of the rest of the band holding an umbrella, sweat rolling off his face.

People, tons of them, gathered on the street corner to watch the band pass. It became clear that our group was out of place in t-shirts and khakis, our intense goggle tans the only distinctive thing about us. Bill talked to some guys dressed as Dr. Seuss characters while Muppet gaped at a topless middle-aged woman in a feathered mask whose enormous breasts had been airbrushed with green and yellow fireworks. A pot-bellied man wearing just a purple thong and pink feather boa crossed the street hand-in-hand with a woman dressed as a giant penis.

"Good God," Bill said, at which Aurelia giggled in excitement.

"Did you bring your penis costume?" Kylie asked me.

"Damn," I said. "I forgot it at home."

Bourbon Street buzzed as we walked through hordes of people, everyone jovial, laughing and dancing and yelling though it was still early—the crowd ready for a party. We bought two-dollar beers from a cart; the cold condensation on the cup felt good against the growing heat. The weather itself seemed exotic after months of winter in Colorado. Despite the buzz of the crowd, I sensed a foreboding calm, like one that lingers in the air before an immense summer storm. I knew that today was going to get wild. This excited me.

Some stranded beads lay in the street. Bill rushed to pick them up and handed them out to our group, trying to help us fit in. People sat on elaborate wrought iron balconies overlooking the street, drinking and throwing beads to an occasional flasher who was eager for the party to start in earnest. Muppet gaped at the breasts of every woman who exposed them, and so did the rest of us, really.

"Tits, man," he kept saying over and over.

As we wandered the street, sounds of jazz music coming from inside a club faded into the sound of the next like turning a radio dial. The occasional spicy hint of Cajun food wafting out of one of the many restaurants made my stomach tense with hunger. Bill and Muppet crossed the street to buy beers from another cart while the rest of us went into the beaded entrance of a voodoo shop that turned out to be

just a touristy gift shop selling beads and tiny alligator heads. We bought feathered masks. Bill and Muppet didn't recognize us as they walked back from the beer cart until Aurelia lunged at Bill and kissed him. They handed out overflowing 32-ounce plastic cups that said *Big Ass Beer.*

Another jazz band came by, this one smaller, just a few guys. A dude on a clarinet played a high obbligato part while the trumpet player soloed over it, bending the pitch with a plunger. They didn't quite march by, but rather danced, bobbing their heads to their own music.

Further up the street, the party grew more raucous. A huge group of drag queens gathered under a balcony where more queens in floral print sundresses stood, tossing beads into the mass of people from above. They threw down cans of beer, blew kisses, and poured tequila into a two-story beer bong for the crowd below. I got pushed underneath the bong and took a tequila shot, the velocity of it hitting my mouth with the force of its freefall. Its sweet, sweet liquor burn hit me hard and felt like a jolt of lightning in my gut. I let out a *whoop!* and gave a thumbs up to the busty bearded queen who'd poured the liquor.

As we walked on, a big bald queen in a leotard waved to us with his fingertips and said, "Hey boys." Ryan waved back and she blew him a kiss.

"Please don't let me kiss a man today," Muppet said.

We finished our beers and went into a bar to use the bathrooms. The place was small and the line for the toilet was a dozen deep, so we sat down at the bar and ordered shots from a bartender dressed in a full body skeleton suit and face paint. My buzz felt good and mellow, and if I could keep it at this level all day things would be good—stay in the pocket. Muppet and Bill had both hit the Jäger a little harder in the car and were feeling rowdier than I was.

"Every day should be Mardi Gras!" Bill yelled even though we were sitting right next to him. Aurelia put her arm around him and kissed him on the cheek, a big wet one.

Muppet yelled back, "Cheers to that, buddy!" and ordered up another round of shots.

Kylie came out of the bathroom and slumped on the barstool, her eyes a bit squinty and a big grin on her face. Muppet slid her a shot of rum. She shook her head no, so I took it instead.

I put my arm around her. "You doing alright?" I asked.

"Doing fucking great!" she said. "Just pacing myself a bit."

"Pacing yourself?" said Muppet. "What does that mean?" Then he took two shots in a row.

We bought each other drinks, even bought ones for strangers and they for us. So much different than our ramen noodle stinginess back at Silver, it was a party and money didn't matter.

Outside, the celebration had erupted, people everywhere, the crowd so thick we could barely move. We randomly ran into some other Silver employees we recognized. We cheersed and drank together before they disappeared into the mob.

Kylie held my hand as we navigated the sea of people. Pretty soon Aurelia and Bill grabbed on, then Ryan, trying to stay together. We lost Muppet for a few minutes and then found him next to a zydeco band playing on a street corner. A bunch of people danced in the street, though Muppet just stood there on the outskirts head banging to the music.

Bill jumped in and danced like a madman, flailing his limbs around so that the crowd gave him space. Ryan walked into a group of college girls on the sidewalk and, without saying a word, grabbed one of them by the hand and led her into the mix. He held her by the waist and she wrapped her arms around his neck, like two kids slow dancing at prom. Their slow swaying looked awkward against the up-tempo zydeco beat, but they both seemed to enjoy it.

Kylie and I joined in. So did Aurelia, who grabbed Bill by the shoulders. He dipped her low to the ground, about to drop her I thought, but he didn't. I held my drink in one hand with the other around Kylie's waist. The booze sloshed around as I did my best fancy dancing with her, drunk enough that I felt like I was dancing well.

"Twirl me!" she yelled.

I handed Muppet my cocktail. He kept head banging with a drink in each hand. I grabbed Kylie and spun her to the music like I imagined salsa dancers would do. Then she spun me. I dipped her low to the ground as Bill had done with Aurelia, and I kissed her. Nobody cared that our dance moves were absurd. The crazier we were, the more we fit in.

I felt the sweat dripping down my back and by the end of the song I was soaked. The band took a break. Ryan's girlfriend Frenched him right there in the street before returning to her friends and disappearing into the crowd.

We pushed through people again, past a group of zealots holding signs about sinners burning in hell. They huddled in a group in the middle of the road where nobody paid them any attention. Next to them stood a bearded guy dressed as Jesus Christ who held a beer in one hand and a sign in the other that read **Though Shall Drinketh and Make Thyself Naked.**

I felt a drop on my arm and thought it was beer spilled from the balcony above. I looked up just as a clap of thunder echoed through the French Quarter. One more drop splashed on my face and then the sky opened up and the rain came in heavy, thick, long streaking drops. Thunder rolled so loud I felt it in my bones. Warm rain splashed off the pavement with enough force it soaked my legs from the knees down.

We made a mad dash for the closest restaurant, which was perfect because I felt starved. The hostess sat us in the back corner of the place at a plastic patio table that had obviously been crammed in as extra seating for the celebration. The waitress squeezed between chairs to take our drink order. When Aurelia ordered just a water the waitress told her she had to get a drink or lose her seat. So she ordered a beer and a pitcher of water for the table. The waitress seemed annoyed at the request.

"Can I get an old fashioned?" Kylie asked.

"We've got beers, margs, and shots," the waitress said.

Kylie ordered a beer. The waitress walked away without any acknowledgement.

*"Anda a cagar, hija de puta,"* Aurelia said toward the waitress as she walked away. I didn't know what the Spanish meant, but I knew it was bad and it held extra weight coming from Aurelia.

The waitress brought out a tray of microbrews, forgetting the water. We nursed our beers while waiting for our food, maintaining that perfect, happy, life-is-good kind of buzz.

Looking at the restaurant's entryway packed with people waiting for a table made me glad we'd managed to snag one. It felt good to sit down for a minute. I shivered as my damp clothes began to dry in the air conditioning. The waitress brought our food, mine a massive steaming bowl of gumbo that smelled so good I could hardly wait for it to cool down before stuffing it in my face. It burned my mouth on the first bite but I couldn't stop myself. The Cajun spices sopped up the booze in me even as I swilled beer to combat the heat. Fucking delicious.

"Think we can learn to cook like this in our room?" Bill asked me.

"On the hot plate sitting in the bathroom next to the toilet? I don't see why not."

I ate my entire bowl and then finished Kylie's jambalaya, which she'd ordered extra, extra spicy. It set my whole mouth on fire and brought tears to my eyes. I sniffled with the heat and poured beer on top of it to try to drown out the burn.

"Goddamn that's good!" I yelled, feeling the snot starting to bubble in my nose.

"I don't know what's better," Bill said, "the food or the booze!"

"Or the tits!" Muppet added.

"You're a pig," Aurelia said, joking, at which Muppet snorfled like a pig and giggled at his own joke.

"You going to whip out your boobs out there?" Kylie asked Aurelia. "I will if you will!" The comment surprised me a bit. It excited me.

Aurelia pointed to Bill with her thumb. "Nobody's going to see these babies but him."

Bill smiled at that and held his beer up in a cheers. We all raised our bottles and drank what was left of them.

"*I* will if you will," Ryan said to Kylie after he'd drained his beer.

"Deal!"

I leaned back in my chair and rubbed the top of Kylie's back. It would be fun to see her go a bit wild.

Lunch sobered us up a bit. I felt fat and tired and knew if I didn't get moving and drinking I'd be wanting a nap.

The waitress brought our check. Muppet put the whole thing on his credit card, not a care in the world. "Time for round two!" he shouted as he bolted from the restaurant for the nearest street vendor cocktail cart. And we were off again, running through the sodden street, hell bent on going crazy.

# 16

The rain muddied the sidewalks and my damp flip-flops squeaked as I walked, kicking specks of mud onto the backs of my calves. With the rain, it seemed everyone else had taken a lunch break as well. Soon the celebration was back in full force and crazier than ever, the crowd so thick we had to turn sideways to meander our way through it like a college basement house party that went on for blocks and blocks. Beer splashed from cups and spilled from the balconies above so that soon we were soaked in it. The rain had done nothing to diminish people's spirits.

Bill stopped to catch some beads that an elderly white-haired woman threw from a balcony willy-nilly into the crowd. She must have been 90 and struggled with each toss but seemed to be loving it. Bill took his shirt off and danced. The lady cackled with laughter at this and threw down beads by the fistful.

From the next balcony over, middle-aged men threw bigger, fancier beads, multicolored ones with blinking lights. Without hesitation, Kylie ran underneath them and pulled up her shirt and bra so her gorgeous breasts flopped out. She shook them around and squeezed them together like a burlesque dancer and let out a squeal of laughter. I looked at her beautiful pink nipples and felt a jolt of electric desire. The beads rained down on Kylie and she ate that shit up—as happy it seemed as I'd ever seen her.

Then I looked at Muppet who gaped at Kylie with his mouth open, and at the middle-aged ex-frat guys up on the balcony hooting and hollering and ogling her as well. I felt a sick punch of jealousy that I knew was undeserved. We were at fucking Mardi Gras after all.

I took a healthy swig of daiquiri to drown out the feeling. It worked for a while and I let myself enjoy looking at all the other breasts around me of all shapes and sizes and colors. And I enjoyed seeing Kylie's the most, watching her wild and free, seeing her tits bouncing merrily and knowing that I was the only guy in Louisiana who could get away with pressing my face between them and flapping my lips like a motorboat. So that's what I did, and she giggled with pleasure.

Muppet bought rounds of drinks faster than anyone could finish them, so we were all double fisting. He pulled me up to a bar cart and ordered six shots—two each of tequila, rum, and whiskey—which we took all in a row without even pausing to breathe in between. I let out a holler after the burn of all that liquor.

"Jesus!" he yelled. "Jesus Christ!" He slapped me on the back and howled at the sky. I howled with him. "God damn, I'm going to go crazy today," he said.

I was good to romp now, the jumpstart of the shots pushing me instantly from a happy buzz into a good ol' boot-stomping drunk.

I grabbed Kylie by the hand and ran out into the street again, dancing in crazed spins, flailing into people who couldn't care less about it. The rest of the crew joined in, Muppet dancing even wilder than the rest like a psychopath, purposefully obnoxious so that the people around him didn't take it so good naturedly when he flailed into them. He backed into some meathead in a Tap Out t-shirt, knocking the guy's beer out of his hand. The dude shoved Muppet, and I ran in ready to fight.

Aurelia got there first, though, and shoved her fresh drink into the guy's hand. "It was an accident," she said. "He's drunk. He didn't mean it." Her explanation appeased him enough to get us the hell out of there. Crisis averted.

I turned around to make sure our whole group was together, counting heads like I did at ski school. Everyone was there, except for Muppet. He was gone, running off down the street. I watched him stop beneath a balcony a block away and dance for beads. He took off his shirt and twirled it over his head, then ran it between his legs like he was riding it. He caught the beads that rained down and then took off again, out of sight. I thought about chasing him down but turned back to the rest of the gang instead.

"We've lost him," I said. "He's running wild."

"He'll be alright," said Bill. "He's a bigboy," *bigboy* coming out in a slurred single word. He sipped his hurricane as he swayed back and forth trying to appear sober. Kylie nodded at Bill, comprehending just how intoxicated he was. Then she looked over in the direction in which Muppet had just disappeared, and finally into the chaos of the euphoric crowd around us.

"This thing could get wild," she said in a serious tone like a nature show narrator.

"God damn," I said, "I sure hope so."

She grabbed my hand at this as the crowd around us became a conga line and we were enveloped by it. There was no controlling the thing and no avoiding it—people dancing, singing, screaming, stomping. We were either part of the mob or fighting against it, which was undoubtedly a bad idea. By luck, we'd latched on together, keeping our group intact with the obvious exception of Muppet.

Up ahead, a retiree in a straw hat let go from the line and tried to step out—a bad idea. As he tripped and fell out of view, I watched the spot where he'd disappeared and didn't see him pop back up as person after person danced over it. I saw his straw hat laying there in the mud, people stomping the shit out of it without notice as they danced by. It appeared that he'd been trampled. I hoped he'd managed to army crawl his way the hell out of there between the legs of the revelers, through the mud, beer, piss, and beads that covered the street.

As randomly as it had started, the conga line broke apart. We were now several blocks from where we'd joined it. Then I saw what had broken up the dance: four Louisiana State Troopers were chasing a shirtless guy through the street. The suspect was young and athletic in a

Yankees cap, in contrast to the overweight troopers struggling to keep up in their navy blue uniforms and Stetsons.

The guy put some distance between himself and his pursuers. He seemed about to escape down a side street. I was almost cheering him on when another dude, just standing on the sidewalk beer in hand, stuck an arm out and clotheslined the guy. The runner dropped in his tracks and the troopers swarmed him. One of the cops dropped onto the suspect with all of his 300 pounds of girth, his knee in the middle of the suspect's back while the cuffs went on. We all watched in rubbernecked, mouth agape excitement, like seeing a car on fire on the side of the freeway, until the troopers dragged the guy off.

"I sure hope I don't do what that guy did," Ryan said as he pulled his bowl from his pocket and lit up. As the cops marched the guy past us in handcuffs, they stared at Ryan, who seemed clueless that he too could be cuffed for smoking weed in public. I was sure they'd say something, but they must have had their fill of excitement for the moment and ignored him.

The crowd yelled and jeered at the running man as the cops dragged him off, though if anyone had any idea of what his original crime had been, they'd seen something I hadn't. This was the first time that this jubilant crowd showed the twinge of angry mob. I didn't like this new vibe.

I grabbed Kylie's hand and continued walking, Aurelia and Bill tagging behind, until we were once again amidst a group of jovial people whose happy dancing and laughing lacked any tone of menace. When I turned around, though, Ryan wasn't with us. I told the crew to stay put and walked back try to find him. No sign of him.

We were down another, though Ryan's disappearance worried me less than Muppet's. Ryan was less likely to piss anyone off or get himself into trouble. Just a stoner wild and free. My biggest worry with him was the fact that he might not be able to find his way back to the cars, though that was a problem for later.

Now down to four, we followed Aurelia as she wandered toward a club thumping music with heavy bass. Ready to dance, she led the way into a line that funneled us down a narrow set of concrete steps where a bouncer at the door collected $10 cover charges. The growing line behind us now blocked us in.

*Fuck it*, I thought, and I forked over all my cash in the world to get us all in the door. Money was money and I was too drunk to care anyway. Aurelia was the one to order up shots this time. She passed them around and then got to booty dancing up on Bill, rowdier than I'd ever seen her before.

"Come on," she yelled as she grabbed Kylie by the hand. "Let's dance!" She dragged Kylie up onto a little elevated stage where they danced up on each other in a way so out of character for Aurelia that I found it amusing and Bill seemed to as well. Then a bunch of men came up to the stage, front row, ogling the two of them and cheering them on. Bill and I forced our way through the dudes to get front row to the girls. I half expected these guys to retaliate as we pushed through their group, half ready to fight and too drunk to care if we'd get kicked out of the club. The guys were good natured about it though, happy drunks there for a good time.

Aurelia tried to coax Bill up onto the stage, but he was content watching. Without warning, she raised her shirt and bra, exposing her large brown breasts with a giant drunken grin on her face. The men behind us hooted and tossed beads up onto the stage, which Aurelia snatched up with relish. Bill didn't look amused.

Kylie walked toward me and danced as if she were a stripper and I was the guy with the stack of bills. She raised her shirt and flashed, getting a couple of wolf whistles from the crowd in response. She leaned down playfully and pressed her boobs in my face so that I could smell the sweet and faint lingering apple scent of her two-day old soap. Then she kissed me and wrapped her arms around me. I lifted her off the stage and set her down beside me.

That left Aurelia up there, still dancing by herself for a minute. Then she leapt off the stage onto Bill with a drunken laughing squeal. He caught her because there was no other option but immediately set her down rather than reciprocate her gushing affection.

"What's the matter, sweets?" she said loudly. "I thought you'd love to see my breasts."

"*I* do love to see your breasts."

She raised her shirt and bra again, pointing her tits at Bill though us and the rest of the world saw them as well. Bill just shook his head at this.

"Well, there you go," she said, stuffing her big boobs back into her bra. "Now quit being such a sourpuss, and let's get us another drink!"

She ran off toward the bar for another round. It would have taken me or Bill twenty minutes of standing there, three-deep at the bar, to get drinks. But the guys standing in line let her right up to the front. She got us a round within a minute and even had one of the dudes help her carry the drinks out to where we stood beside the dance floor. She seemed oblivious to the special treatment. Bill stewed, not saying much. He was short with Aurelia but acted overly friendly with the rest of us like he was trying to stay chipper.

"It's Mardi Gras, bud!" I said, putting my arm around him. He smiled, not at all enthused. "Just think," I continued, "you get to put your face between those tits and nobody else does."

Surprisingly, this line of thinking seemed to cheer him a bit, as it had done with myself, and he raised his hurricane in a toast. "Let's get fucked up," he said. And that's what we did.

We drank what Aurelia bought, the girls still dancing and giggling, and then Bill pushed his way up to the bar for another round of shots. *Jesus*, I thought, *it's still early*.

We cheersed and drank; that's when things began to turn sour. Aurelia reached up and put her arms around Bill's shoulders. She swayed drunkenly as she went to kiss him. Despite his anger, he kissed her back before pulling away.

"You okay?" he asked. She didn't respond but looked like she was about to speak. Instead, she puked, without warning. It splashed down the front of her shirt. Some on Bill, some on me and Kylie, some on the random people around us who scattered as the liquid vomit splashed to the floor. The bouncers were on us before the last bits of puke were even out of Aurelia's mouth. They shoved our whole group out the doors without a word and without a modicum of gentility.

"Watch it, dickheads," Bill yelled as a bouncer's shove caused Aurelia to stumble and nearly fall.

Bouncers tossed us into the thick of a large jostling crowd. The street looked like a cross between a funhouse and a war zone—beads and broken glass covering the muddy pavement. The noise of the ongoing party no longer particularly pleasant, it simmered with a sort of subdued rage that was just waiting for the chance to come to a boil. But this may just have been me, the first pang of a hangover before I was even done being drunk. A slight headache pulsed in my skull like the errant drumbeats echoing down Bourbon Street. It may have been the lingering acidic smell of Aurelia's vomit that made me feel that way—maybe not.

Aurelia had puked and rallied and Kylie was full-throttle as well. I tried to hang. I could with the drinking part—Bill and I both—but the rest of it was just too much. We chugged giant beers, me hoping to avoid the oncoming headache. As we pushed through the crowd somebody spilled their beer down the front of my shirt. Bill spilled his own on himself when someone ran into him. There was no avoiding it.

The girls took off down Bourbon Street toward more dancing, toward another bass-thumping night club. I looked to Bill seeing a dour expression on his face. He huffed but followed the girls, neither of us wanting any part of another nightclub scene.

"Can't we just find a bar where we can sit down for a minute?" I shouted to the girls up ahead of us.

"Can't we just find a quiet bar where we can sit down and be boring," Kylie called back in a mocking, snarky kind of voice that took me by absolute surprise. "What's the deal, grandpa? Can't hang?"

She was joking, I think, but I wasn't in the mood for it. I thought back to our last fight, though, and bit my tongue. Rather than saying anything, I thought of the image of Kylie's supple breasts out there for all to see, and of the gawking eyes of Muppet and all the other men standing around her. I stewed on this.

Bill and I followed the girls, about 20 yards behind. We somehow ended up inside a building walking up the back stairs. And then we were out on a balcony overlooking Bourbon Street with coolers full of beer that seemed to be up for grabs, a table laden with food and boxes and boxes of beads. On the balcony were several older businessmen types in golf polos and khakis. It seemed that they'd invited Kylie and Aurelia up to their perch, and the girls had gone up without a second thought. It hadn't been apparent to the men that Bill and I were with the girls. These guys wanted some young girls to hang out with, not their tagalong boyfriends.

They were nice, though, and drunk. Passing out beers and burgers and urging us to drink and eat all we could. They talked about their stock portfolios and speedboats and strippers they knew in Miami. Bill didn't talk much, but I bullshitted with the guys, talking about my nonexistent house in Vail and my equally nonexistent Porsche. Getting more food in my stomach seemed like a good idea, and this was all free. The douchier I acted, the more they seemed to like me. Nothing had any consequences.

The biggest of the men, with a paunch gut and legs as hairless as his bald head, also seemed to be the drunkest. He kept eyeing our girls without shame, whereas his buddies tried to be discreet about it.

"My, my," he said to Bill and me. "What I wouldn't do to be young again. Find me a pretty little thing like you guys got."

"Why do you have to be young?" I asked. "Bald men with dad bod are the hot new thing."

He belly laughed, which sent him into a coughing fit. His buddies clapped him on the back and then handed out beads by the fistful for us to toss down to the revelers below. Kylie threw out beads with vigor, indiscriminately, and so did Aurelia. Bill had no interest in it. I took a handful and looked down at all the women below. It amazed me how the prospect of cheap plastic beads changed them, and they all pointed their knockers up at me. I rained the beads down like goddamned Santa Claus tossing presents from his sleigh.

That's when I spotted Muppet on the other side of the street, shitty drunk and barking like a dog at a fat woman who tossed beads from the balcony across the way as her bare boobs flopped wildly atop her protruding belly. She laughed in grotesque guttural heaves, throwing down beads from a seemingly limitless supply. Muppet tried to catch them around his neck so that most of the strands hit him on the head and shoulders before falling down, wasted, into the mud.

He laughed crazily at this like it was the funniest thing in the world. No one around them gave two shits, but Muppet and the woman seemed to be having the time of their lives in this private moment.

"He's terrible when he's drunk," Kylie said, looking out at Muppet's antics before showering more beads onto the crowd below. I nodded and kept watching Muppet. He made me nervous. He barked again, then howled and panted like a cartoon wolf. The woman produced her most prized strand of beads. Like a queen from her throne, she held up a huge necklace, obnoxiously big, with bulbs that blinked like Christmastime. Muppet clapped, trying to coax her to throw it down. He'd have to give her a show first.

The people standing around Muppet began to notice him as he undid his belt and dropped his pants all the way to the ground around his ankles like a four-year-old at a urinal, his bare ass out for all to see. With a big, sloppy grin on his face, he grabbed his penis and started twirling it around, laughing at his own joke. I couldn't hear it, but I knew he was making a "chicka, chicka, chicka" noise like the blades of a helicopter.

The woman shook with laughter, which egged Muppet on so that he kept going more vigorously. The guys around him had had enough. One guy, looking disgusted, said something to Muppet, though we were too far away to hear. Whatever he said pissed Muppet enough that Mup let go of himself and took a wild swing at the guy. The momentum of his drunken roundhouse caused him to lose his balance, and he stepped forward so that his foot tangled in his pulled-down pants and tripped him. He fell face-first in the street, his ass pointing at the obese lady he'd been trying to impress. The guy's friends converged on Muppet like dogs on meat.

I rushed down the stairs to street level and then pushed my way through the oppressive crowd over toward Muppet. I looked up at the woman as I ran, knowing that I'd find my friend directly underneath her balcony. She hooted in delight at the chaos and, finally satisfied, tossed the blinking beads to the ground. When I got to the street I saw the dogpile and Muppet at the bottom of it. From what I could see, his face looked swollen and covered in blood, though I hoped it was more mud than anything else. I saw several cops, too, running toward Muppet, and also the fancy blinking beads lying in the street.

Another drunken topless girl, this one skinny with perky airbrushed breasts, came upon the beads and bent down to pick them up, oblivious to the scene playing out around her: the cops running into the pile, some of the guys scattering as the police approached, and my drunken bare-assed asshole friend lying there beaten on the muddy pavement. She put the beads around her neck, screamed with pleasure at her good luck, and ran off down the street, the blinking lights disappearing into the crowd.

# 17

As I closed in on Muppet I heard him shouting nonsensical gibberish. "I'll pummel you, you fucking cunts," he yelled. "I'll eat you for fucking dinner." Blood sprayed from his mouth so his words spilled out in a bubbling, gurgly lisp.

The last of the thugs landed one more haymaker on him, this one on his eye, knocking him senseless for a moment. I thought he'd been knocked cold and that would have been for the better. Instead, he came up swinging. I pounced into the melee, leaping at the dude and dragging him to the ground by his ankles like a cornerback making a touchdown-saving tackle. The guy kicked once like a mule landing a boot heel on my eyebrow. It hurt like hell and left me dazed for a moment. I lost my grip and the dude jumped to his feet and sprinted off into the crowd. I felt my forehead start to swell as a trickle of blood dripped down.

As one of the cops grabbed me in a bear hug from behind, I at least had the sense to quit fighting. Muppet, in some kind of delirious haze threw elbows and fists and knees in a crazed tantrum like a mental patient. He seemed to have no sense that the bodies around him were no longer his attackers but, rather, officers of the law.

The cops holding me realized I was no longer a problem and let go to help subdue Muppet. Time seemed to slow, my senses heightened to the details of the scene around me. I heard Aurelia screaming and Kylie yelling, "Muppet! You fucking asshole! Knock it the fuck off!"

Bill yelled in vain at the cops. "He didn't do anything! It was self-defense. Let him go, you fucking pigs!"

I heard the cackling of the woman who'd started the whole thing from her balcony above. Then I looked around us; the crowd had given us some space, but also encircled us as it looked on. The people gaped, their partying suspended because this spectacle was more amusing for the moment. Many in the crowd held their cell phones above their heads, filming the situation. This enraged me, us being gawked at like zoo monkeys. I raised both middle fingers in the air, pointing them straight at each cell phone cam.

"What the fuck are you looking at?" I yelled. "Don't you got some drinking to get back to?"

At this I felt Kylie grab me from behind and pull my arms down to my sides.

"What the hell are you thinking?" she asked me. "Calm the fuck down."

I turned back to Muppet and to the three officers scuffling with him. It took all three to get him to the ground but not before Muppet landed a blow on a cop's forehead, knocking off his Stetson and causing him to blink hard and sway in a moment of stupor. With Muppet face-down on the ground but still bucking wildly, one of the troopers pulled his Taser and shocked the shit out of Muppet before cuffing him.

At this, the world paused for a second as the cops, and the rest of us, caught our collective breath. In this impossibly brief moment of respite I realized just what kind of trouble Muppet had gotten himself into.

The cop who'd cuffed him stood up and jerked Muppet to his feet then hiked his pants up to cover his dick and ass. The electric jolt calmed Muppet a bit. He no longer flailed though he kept running his mouth somewhat incoherently, his words sounding mush-mouthed with his whole face swollen and bloodied. "What the fuck did I do?" he asked though the officers ignored his talk. "Since when is self-defense a crime? This is police abuse. An abuse of power!"

His tears flowed and his nose dripped a disgusting mixture of snot and blood. He blew it like a snot rocket but with his hands cuffed behind his back, the bloody snot just oozed down his moustache and bright red beard. Mud and blood and snot covered his bare chest.

Another of the officers ripped the beads from Muppet's neck and tossed them in the gutter with his shirt, his University of Michigan ball cap falling onto the muddy street as well. They marched him out of there and the crowd went back to their partying. We followed behind with Kylie doing the talking, though the police totally ignored her.

"Where are you taking him?" she asked. "Is he getting arrested?"

She slurred her words so that no matter what she said I knew the cops wouldn't take her seriously. She sounded about as drunk as I felt, which was the sort that left both my mind and body teetering.

"Let him go, you fucking fascists!" Bill yelled. Aurelia elbowed him in the ribs, knowing that was the kind of talk that would only do harm.

The cops escorted Muppet to a waiting cruiser and loaded him in the back.

"Where the hell are you taking him?" Kylie yelled.

My blood boiled at their lack of response. "Yeah," I said. "What the fuck?! You can't just take him like that. He didn't do anything wrong."

"Drunk and disorder isn't worthy of getting cuffed," Bill added.

One cop finally turned to us and spoke, calm as could be. "Your dumbass friend here showed his genitals. Maybe that's a sex offense, but even that would be the least of his worries. He also assaulted a peace officer."

"Assaulted an officer?" I yelled, drunk and angry, walking toward the cop. "What the fuck are you talking about? Were you watching the same shit I was? He was defending himself and didn't know where the hell he was swinging."

I was now standing face to face with the officer, a foot or so between us. I felt Kylie pulling on the back of my shirt.

The cop smiled at this and gazed into my eyes for a long moment, neither of us looking away. "Keep running your mouth, big shot," he said. "You'll be sitting in my car with your buddy."

At this he got into the passenger seat of the cruiser. It pulled off with Muppet inside, the crowd parting like the sea to let the car

through. I raised my middle finger at the cop car as it left. Kylie threw her elbow to get me to stop.

Aurelia grabbed me by the chin and gazed above my eyes. She took her forefinger and pressed it into the swollen part of my forehead. "You look like shit. But I don't think it's that bad. You might have a black eye tomorrow but nothing's broken."

The mass of people went back to partying without hesitation. Muppet's fight and arrest had just been a bit of afternoon entertainment. This pissed me off. That left us there wondering what the fuck to do. I thought we'd better drink a beer and think things through. Bill and I went to a beer cart where we ordered a round for the group then sat down on a curb to think and drink.

"What the fuck do you think you're doing?" Kylie asked me, her tone taking me by surprise.

"I don't think I'm doing anything," I said. "I'm sitting on a curb drinking this beer."

"In case you didn't notice, your friend just got cuffed and taken away by a cop car."

"Yeah. I was there," I said.

I sipped my beer then turned to Bill and Aurelia. "Bail money? What do you think we'll have to pay to get him out?"

Bill shrugged his shoulders.

"Maybe we won't need bail," Aurelia said. "Maybe they'll let him off with a warning?"

"They wouldn't have taken him away for a warning," Bill said. "It's going to cost money."

"I don't have shit for money," I said. "I spent the last of my cash at that shitty club and have probably fifty bucks on my debit card for gas to get us home."

Kylie rolled her eyes at this. Suddenly I was sick of her shit. Apparently we were fighting now and I was unsure how it had started but also too drunk to care. "What about you, princess?" I said to her. "You got money to pay his bail? I'm sure this crowd will throw some cash at you if you keep whipping your boobs out for any idiot who wants to see them."

Kylie just rolled her eyes again. Bill and Aurelia seemed to tiptoe around the volatility, not wanting to be the ones to send me or Kylie off the edge into an all-out rager.

"I've got a credit card," Bill said. "But I think it's maxed out."

"I have my savings for going back to Argentina," Aurelia said. "I can't spend it on Muppet, though. I can't afford to have him not pay me back."

"He'd pay you back, I bet." Bill said.

"You bet?" Aurelia's voice had some hostility in it. "How much would you bet? Your friend is an asshole and we all know it. If it's not an absolute certainty he pays me back, he isn't getting my money."

This surprised me. Yes, Muppet was surely an asshole, but I thought that everyone in our group considered him a friend. We sat in silence for a minute. Bill glanced at Aurelia from the corner of his eye, trying to gauge her precarious mood. I did the same to Kylie.

"What about McGillycuddy's?" Kylie asked, directing it more at the group than at me. "Could we call them and see if they'll advance us his paycheck?"

"Doubt it," I said. "They can barely afford to pays us as it is." I sipped my beer, the party around us intense so that us sitting on the curb seemed wildly out of place. I felt lightheaded and numb, incapable of the critical thought necessary to figure out this situation. "We don't even know what's happening to him," I continued, "don't even know if there is bail to be paid. Let's get that figured out. First things first."

"First things first," Kylie said, mocking me. When I just stared at her, she continued, "We find out where the hell Muppet is."

"How are we going to do that?" Bill asked.

Aurelia started walking around looking for cops to ask while I went to seek a moment of solitude. Kylie naturally followed Aurelia. I knew that Bill would come with me, but I needed a minute alone so I snuck

off. A block away I found a little café so tucked back in an alley that it went unnoticed to most of the revelers.

"I hope the other guy looks worse off than you," the waiter said as he approached my table.

"Doubt it," I said.

I sipped my beer and thought about what the hell was going on. I knew there was no stopping the oncoming freight train of a major blowout fight with Kylie. I had no idea what we were going to do about Muppet—or where we'd find Ryan—and I was running out of damned money. I felt fucked, like the world was crushing down on me and no one else. Sitting down thinking about it all calmed me a bit, slowed the drunken dizzying thoughts. I felt like I'd escaped something big and bad if only for a moment.

I closed my eyes as I sipped. I wanted to end this dumb fight with Kylie, for us to have a blast together at Mardi Gras and for this crazy impromptu road trip to be a fond memory for us. I wanted to make up with her, but I doubted my ability to do so. It seemed already too late to shove these beginnings of an altercation back into the box. I dreaded going back out onto the street but could only nurse my beer so long. I walked back out to where I'd last seen the group.

Kylie saw me before I saw her. "Where the hell were you?"

I ignored her and directed my question at Aurelia. "Any news on Muppet?"

"We found out where they have him," she said. "We think we found out at least."

"They have a makeshift cop shop set up in an apartment about a mile from here," Bill said. "Complete with a jail cell. Kylie called down there, and I guess it's so busy that they don't even know if they've processed him yet. But that's where he's gotta be."

We walked a few blocks down and a few blocks away from Bourbon Street, away from the party. It seemed to me a wild goose chase, but Bill was intent with the directions he'd been given. He and I walked together with the girls way ahead. He shouted out directions to them or else they'd have walked off into the bowels of the city. Just as I thought it was a lost cause, we saw it. The nondescript brick building didn't stand out, but the group of vagrant types and drunks hanging around the door did. They differed from the fun-loving crowd on Bourbon Street and had a bedraggled look about them.

The place was packed when we walked in. I shimmied sideways into what looked to be a small apartment turned makeshift booking station. An officer at a desk by the front door took fingerprints. Next to him, a camera sat on a tripod for mug shots. In the tiny kitchen, more officers crowded around a coffee urn.

Other officers escorted drunken partygoers while their drunken partygoer friends, like us, yelled at the cops. We crowded around the doorframe and slowly moved into the hallway of the apartment. The place had a pungent reek of vomit that damn near made me gag. In the back, a bunch of prisoners packed a holding cell and more of them sat outside the bars with their hands zip tied. Nobody looked up as we shimmied our way inside. It took us a minute to get anyone's attention.

I let the girls handle the talking while I scanned the place in a frantic search for Muppet. Once she got their attention, Aurelia seemed to have a way with the officers. I could tell that she was hammered, but her heavy accent and exotic charm seemed to mask that fact to the cops. She spoke to them firmly but thoughtfully, showing them a hell of a lot more respect than the rest of us had. She asked that we be allowed to see Muppet, though she of course called him Derek.

The cops relented and one of them took us back down a hallway and unlocked a cell in the back room of the apartment. They brought out a shirtless Muppet still cuffed with zip ties. He kept running his mouth but with much less vigor than he'd had before when out on the street, like a Christmas toy with dying batteries. They sat him down in front of us, blood crusted all over his swollen and bruised face.

"How's it going, buddy?" I asked.

"Bad," he said, like a kid whose sister had taken away his favorite toy. He sniffled and started to cry.

Aurelia grabbed his chin and inspected his injured face. She squinted in disgust at the bruises and swollen eye, shaking her head when her intent gaze reached a gash that ran under his right eye. She approached the cop who'd led us to Muppet tapping him on the shoulder.

"Excuse me," she said. "Has he been seen by a doctor? He needs stitches." The cop shook his head and turned back to his paperwork. She tapped him again and spoke more forcefully this time. "Have you even looked at his face? That gash is horrible and he needs to go to the hospital."

I didn't know about that. Yeah, he definitely looked beat to shit, but taking him to the hospital for it would have seemed overzealous to me. Had he cut himself like that, say, skiing, there's no way we would have taken him in. Still, it seemed like as solid a strategy for getting him out of here as any.

"You see how busy it is in here? If we took everybody in here who's been bruised up in a fight to the hospital, they wouldn't have any beds left. There's guys in here worse off than your buddy. Now say whatever it is you got to say to him, because your time is up." The cop turned back to his paperwork

"We're going to figure this thing out, man," Bill said to Muppet. "Aurelia's got a fire under her ass about getting you out, and you know how she is."

Muppet nodded, the tears still streaming down his face. "At least I'm not the only one in here."

"What do you mean?" I asked.

"Ryan's in here too."

Muppet looked over in the direction of another holding cell in the living room at the far side of the apartment. He nodded toward the group of people sitting next to the bars.

I looked over and saw Ryan sitting there outside the cell with his hands restrained. My heart sank. I don't know how I'd missed him before. Where Muppet was the deserving asshole, Ryan was just a good-natured stoner with no motives other than for everyone to have a fun time.

He looked up and saw us as we walked toward him. "Hey guys!" he said, cheerily like we'd just bumped into him on the street rather than a jail. "How'd you know I was in here?"

"We didn't," Bill said. "We came to find Muppet."

"Oh yeah," Ryan said. "He was in here earlier. He wasn't a happy camper. It looked like he'd been hit by a dump truck. I think he's back in one of the cells now." He looked at me intently, gazing just above my right eye. "Man," he said, "you got beat up too!"

"Yeah," I said. "Same fight that put Muppet in here. What the hell did you do, man? Why are you here?"

"Weed," he said, nonchalant about it. "So much for the biggest party in the world. Can't even light up a joint."

I looked over to Aurelia at the police desk pleading frantically with an officer. I turned back to Ryan, unsure what to do or say.

"They got me for dealing," he said. "Which I wasn't. I smoked a guy down and he bought me a beer. That ain't dealing. That's just sharing like they taught us in kindergarten." His carefree demeanor surprised me though it shouldn't have. Then his tone turned serious. "Listen, I need you to call my dad. He's a lawyer. He'll fly down and they'll let me go as soon as he walks in the door. He'll take care of Muppet too."

He gave us a number that Aurelia typed into her phone. I felt both elated and sick at this, pumped we had a lifeline in Ryan's dad but a sinking feeling at knowing how deep we were in it. The officers ushered us away from Ryan. Our time was up.

"Call my dad!" he yelled again as if we hadn't gotten the point the first time.

I felt like a child knowing that Ryan's dad would be the one to fix our problems, but it felt good to have this one weight off my shoulders. We went to tell Muppet the new plan but they'd already taken him away.

# SKI BUM

We left the station and Aurelia made the call. I didn't want to hear her end of the conversation, so I wandered off a ways and sat down on a curb. Bill followed and lit a cigarette. I asked for one too, and he gave it to me with eyebrows raised. I lit it and inhaled deep, nearly choking. It tasted like shit but was oddly satisfying. "You think his dad can really clean this mess up?"

"I reckon we're going to find out," he answered.

"I feel in over my head."

"What do you mean?"

"This whole mess," I said, unsure exactly what I was getting at. "What the hell are we even doing here?"

"We're having fun," he said. "Can't you tell?"

"Did you know he was a lawyer, Ryan's dad?"

"No idea," Bill said.

I smoked the cigarette down to my fingertips and felt like I could have another. Aurelia found us several minutes later having just gotten off the phone.

"Well?" Bill asked.

"His dad is on his way, getting the first flight down tomorrow morning. He didn't even seem surprised by it. Told us not to worry. He was intense."

"Intense?" I asked.

"No nonsense," she said. "Not like Ryan at all."

"Damn," I said. "I guess we keep on partying and wait for the cavalry to show up."

"Keep on partying?" Kylie said. "Are you retarded? Your friends are in jail. And aren't you the one who wanted to find a quiet bar to rest at, anyway?"

"There's nothing we can do for them now, is there?" I said. "So in the meantime I'm going to go get myself a cocktail and enjoy the party. You all can come with me if you want, or you can stay here and mope."

I thought turning Kylie's own argument against her might score me a point in this meaningless game. I knew they'd follow me wherever I went, and that's what they did. I walked back to Bourbon Street and straight into a bar with a live jazz band. There was either no cover or the doorman was too preoccupied to collect it.

Kylie pouted and Aurelia seemed in a daze. Bill, like me, was just trying to keep his shit together. The girls took the last two seats at the bar while Bill and I stood behind them. The bartender poured us tall cocktails from a slushy machine. I felt oddly sober after the whole Muppet incident, though I couldn't have been. The morose vibe of our whole group bugged me. I wanted us to be over it.

I grabbed Kylie by the hand and pulled her over by the band and tried to spin around in some shitty impersonation of swing dancing. This was my olive branch. She played along for a bit, but it was short lived. Then she pulled away from me and went back to her seat. That's when I grabbed another girl by the dance floor and spun her around. This new girl loved it and laughed as we danced with wild fury. As she twirled, her long brown hair cascaded around her. Beautiful and carefree, she laughed as we danced. When she looked at me I could sense her gaze moving up to the wound above my eye. She seemed to admire it, like it gave me some kind of rugged mysterious quality.

I let go of this girl and grabbed her redheaded friend, who was just as drunk and had just as much fun. She danced slower, leaning against me and swaying closely, though the zydeco music kept its fast pace. I knew I was being a dick to Kylie, but I didn't care. I'd given her the opportunity to put our fight behind us. She hadn't been interested.

Bill danced with Aurelia next to us and he shot me a *what the hell are you doing?* look as he swayed with Aurelia. That's when Kylie joined in on the dance floor, twirling and flirting with another dude who was real into it. At first they danced with their bodies well apart from each other, not touching at all. Then he grasped her hands in his. She laughed and smiled at him, and they inched closer to one another. I watched this as I kept swaying with the redhead. Then he pulled her close and ran his hand over her butt.

This pissed me off but I just kept dancing. I twirled my girl and led her close to Kylie and the guy she was dancing with. Kylie noticed this but pretended not to. It was a dumb game of chicken. I let go of my girl and went to try and cut in with Kylie. She pushed me away and so did the guy she was with. For a moment I thought I'd fight him, but I walked out the door instead. It was now dark out. I walked straight to the nearest liquor cart with Bill following behind.

"What the hell are you doing?" he asked.

"What do you mean?"

"Don't give me your bullshit," he said. "You want to fuck things up with Kylie, that's your business. But give me enough respect to admit to me what you're doing." I didn't say anything to Bill but I ordered him a shot, wondering when my debit card would finally max out. He took it and continued talking. "You don't have to take my advice. But I don't think there's any point in screwing things up with Kylie on purpose. Maybe you guys will last beyond the end of the season. Maybe you won't. But there sure as shit is no point in you spending the rest of the season pissed off at each other."

He was right. There was no arguing with it. I decided then to try my best to make amends, to try to right this sinking ship, but Kylie had already decided otherwise.

She left the bar and marched right past us, not even breaking stride as she walked by. I grabbed her by the arm as she passed and knew it was a bad move the second I did it.

"Get your fucking hands off me!" she yelled.

The crowd around us turned their heads. I thought someone might hit me.

"Kylie," I said, trying to think of something to say to reason with her. All I came up with was a pathetic, "Come on."

"Get away from me," she said, simple and concise.

I stood there trying to think of something to say but nothing came to mind. I'd felt my relationship with Kylie slipping away all day but now I seemed to have lost it completely.

"Come on, Kylie," Bill said. "Just let bygones be bygones."

"Don't defend him," Aurelia said to Bill. "He's the one in the wrong here."

I looked at Aurelia, disappointed. I always thought that she liked me.

"Oh Jesus Christ, babe," Bill said to Aurelia. "This is nothing. Just let it all blow over."

"Is that an order?"

"What do you mean?"

"I mean you boss me around because you're a man and I'm a woman? Is that right? Is that how it works here?"

"No. That's not right at all."

"And Jimmy can do whatever he wants to Kylie with no consequences because he's the man and she's the woman. Is that right?"

"No," Bill said, dumbfounded. "That's not what I was saying at all."

"It sure seems like that's what you're saying," Aurelia said.

Bill waved her off with a motion of his hand, and that sent her into a rage.

"Don't wave me away, you arrogant prick!"

He seemed genuinely hurt by this and didn't respond. And at that the girls marched off together into the crowd. I knew I'd lost control of the situation but I didn't want to leave it without saying or doing something. I wanted the last word at least. "Fuck you, Kylie, you fucking bitch!" I yelled after her—childish, petty, mean.

She turned around only long enough to flip me off and then was gone. Bill and I stood there stunned and drunk. I thought he might follow them; he seemed to contemplate that option before staying there with me. Closing one eye to see straight, I felt dizzy. I felt the swollen tightness of the skin above my eye but it no longer throbbed. I knew that I'd care in the morning, that tomorrow would be horrible, but tonight I didn't. Bill didn't seem to either. He was in the same stupor as I was.

Together, we staggered in a drunken daze around the French Quarter as the party escalated toward midnight. We walked through the same group of drag queens we'd seen earlier, now rowdier than before. The huge crowd was dizzying. Beer spilled from cups and soaked our clothes as we pushed through the crowd.

I remember holding onto each other to keep one another upright as we swerved across the street. And I remember motor-boating a middle-aged woman, giving her all my beads and shaking hands with her husband.

The memories from there are spotty. Vague recollections of yelling obscenities into the night and being thrown out of a bar. Closing one eye and laughing at the image of myself in a bathroom mirror. I know that we both smoked the rest of Bill's cigarettes, both puked in the street. There's an image of vomit spraying onto a gutter piled with beads and plastic cups.

By the time we got back to the Jeep in the early morning hours, we were bloodied and I was missing a flip flop. The sounds of the party had faded. The silence felt immense.

The girls had made it back as well and were cuddled together in the back of the Jeep. Bill and I each grabbed our sleeping bags and laid down in the gravel yard beside my car's tires and our own puddles of vomit, the world above us spinning and spinning out of control.

# 18

My dreamless sleep ended far too soon. Emerging from the darkness confused, it took me I don't know how long to realize the feet stepping over me were Kylie's. Then Aurelia's. Then Bill's. The sound of flip flops crunching on gravel mixed with a ringing in my ears.

I heard Bill's voice pleading but it took me a minute to comprehend the meaning of the words. "Auri, this is insane," he said. "Just stop a minute and think."

I raised my head, suppressing an urge to vomit. I felt like death, squinting, trying to get my left eye to focus with my right swollen shut. My forehead pulsed, as if the front of my brain were trying to press itself through the wound above my eye.

I was still drunk, a horrific kind of dizzy. My dry mouth tasted like rancid cigarettes. I could have chugged a gallon of water but didn't have the energy to stand up to find some. Then it hit me, the vague recollections of last night and the huge blowout fight with Kylie. I just wanted to shut my eyes and turn it all off.

"If you want your shit you better get it out of the car," Kylie said.

"What?" I asked, not comprehending as I wiped a bit of gravel from my bloody eyebrow.

"You heard me," she said. "We're taking the Jeep back to Colorado, so if you want your stuff you better grab it."

"It's my Jeep," I said.

"It's your parents' Jeep."

"Yeah, it's *my* parents' Jeep."

"Tough," she said. "You can wait here for Ryan and Muppet and go back with them. Aurelia and I have jobs to get back to."

"We need to get back to work too, Kylie," Bill said.

"Tough titties."

"We're going back now," Aurelia said. "If you really want to join us, fine."

"We can't just leave Muppet and Ryan here," I said.

Aurelia shrugged.

"So stay and deal with it," Kylie said. "You're the one who wanted to keep partying. You all can take Ryan's car home."

I finally stood up and tugged on the door handle of Ryan's Toyota.

"Locked," I said.

"You'll figure it out," Kylie said.

She got into the Jeep's driver's seat and started it up with my keys. She was serious. I thrust my body into the open driver door so that she couldn't close it. Over on the passenger side, Bill implored Aurelia to stay. The inside of the Jeep smelled terrible, like stale beer, vomit, and wet, muddy clothes. Kylie's beads still blinked in the backseat, their lights dim, slow and sporadic, nearly exhausted.

"You can't take it," I said without conviction. She didn't respond, refused to look me in the eyes. I reached in and grabbed my keys, trying to pull them from the ignition.

"You take those keys and I'll scream bloody murder," she said. "I'll scream, and people will come running. Get your crap out of the back. You can have this piece of crap car back when you get to Colorado."

I knew I was defeated. I opened the tailgate and grabbed my backpack. Aurelia gave Bill a forced hug before climbing into the passenger seat, but a hug nonetheless. They pulled out of the parking lot, leaving Bill and me stunned with just our backpacks, standing there like the bums we were.

I laid down in the gravel beside Ryan's car and pulled my pack over my head. I wasn't yet ready to deal with life. I regretted basically everything about yesterday though I couldn't remember significant swaths of it.

Bill pulled my backpack out of my hands. "No more sleeping," he said. "It's time to face the music."

He sat on the hood of Ryan's car where the uncapped, third-full Jäger bottle still sat like a totem. He took a pull then scrunched up his face in agony. He proffered the bottle my way. I about gagged at just the thought of it, but he insisted. I took a swig that immediately came back up. I stood there heaving onto the gravel, not much left in my system to purge. What did come out splashed in a puddle onto my toes. I felt oddly better after puking. I took one more quick swig for good measure, holding it down this time.

Bill laughed wholeheartedly at this until it sent him into a coughing fit. "Fuck," he said once he regained some composure.

I filled my mouth from a water bottle and spit it all onto the ground, trying in vain to get rid of the combined taste of puke, Jägermeister, and cigarette.

"What the fuck happened to us?" I asked. "What the fuck are we going to do about it?"

"Things tend to work themselves out," he said. "It will all end up being okay."

"Between you and Aurelia, yeah," I said. "But not for me and Kylie."

He shrugged. "Maybe. Maybe not. I'm more talking grand scheme of things. Things'll be fine in the long run."

"And what about my car, man? What the hell? They took it."

"They sure did," he said, laughing.

"I can't believe they did, but they did."

"You could always call the cops on them. Aurelia would have a fun time with that. Grand theft auto." He laughed at the thought. He took another pull from the bottle and offered it to me again, but I couldn't.

"That cop really didn't want to see Muppet's penis," he said.

I laughed at this, genuinely. The laughter bringing a wave of acid from my guts up into my chest.

"I guess we call back to Silver and see about our jobs," he said.

"Then head to the airport to meet up with Ryan's dad."

Bill pulled out his phone and looked at the screen. "Dead."

We wandered around looking for a bus stop or a cab, carrying our packs with us.

"You know I've got no money, right?" I said as we walked back toward the French Quarter.

He waved this off. "I'll float you."

The town looked like a technicolor bomb went off. An inches-deep layer of muddy plastic beads and beer cups coated the street. A crew of workers in coveralls scooped the beads up with snow shovels and tossed them into rolling dumpsters, the throwaway nature of it sickening. "Such a goddamned waste," I said.

"No doubt. These things all end up in whale's bellies."

We boarded a crowded bus to the airport, watching the town outside the window piece itself back together. I stood, holding a steel pole for balance, sweating and dizzy. Even the damned bus reeked like spilled booze and fryer grease. I about lost it by the time we got to the terminal.

At baggage claim Bill found an outlet for his phone and called his boss at Silver. "All's good," he said when he hung up.

He handed me his phone for my own call, which didn't go nearly as well. I was nervous as hell to dial up the ski school, especially with the whole show in turmoil after Paul's departure. One of the assistant managers answered, this lady named Sheri who never seemed to like me much, or Paul for that matter. I told her I was stuck in Louisiana and wouldn't be at work tomorrow or the next day.

"Aren't you with Kylie?" she asked.

"She's already on her way back."

"Shouldn't you be with her?"

I told her bits and pieces of the story, my brain struggling to make words. That I had to stay down here to help out Ryan who was in trouble. But I left out so much, most everything in fact, that she didn't buy it.

"Look, Jimmy," she said, condescending. "You haven't been working here long enough to no call, no show like this and keep your job."

"But I'm calling right now."

"I mean calling with a valid excuse. If Kylie can make it back in time for work, so can you. Sounds to me like you've been partying too hard and got carried away with yourself. I think that responsibility falls on you."

For a moment I thought about pleading, but I couldn't bring myself to care enough, so I hung up without another word. I owed it to Muppet and Ryan to stick around anyway. I knew trying to explain that to her was just a waste of time.

Other hung-over Mardi Gras revelers on their way back home occupied every part of the terminal. Everyone had a depressed and downtrodden look about them now that the party was over. We fit right in. I wondered if anyone else here had fucked their lives up as deeply as we had.

We sat down by baggage claim with an hour to kill before the Seattle flight was due. I laid down on the carpet and tried to sleep, head pounding. When it was time for Ryan's dad's arrival, we stood outside security waiting for him. I didn't know what to expect, a grownup version of Ryan I guessed. Maybe an old hippie who happened to also be a lawyer. I didn't give a second thought to the slick businessman in the navy blue suit until he walked right toward us asking, "Ryan's friends?"

"How'd you know?"

"Look at you. You're beat to shit and look like bums. Same melee as Ryan's other friend, I'd guess," he said. "No offense."

"None taken," Bill said.

He shook our hands with a power grip and said to call him Charles. He walked toward the rental car booth without another word and we followed. "You're lucky all you got was the black eye," he said. "Getting three guys out is tougher than two."

"You really think you can get Ryan and Muppet off?"

"Muppet?" he asked.

"Well, Derek," I said. "The friend in the fight."

"Absolutely, though you need to knock it off with the nickname. That sounds like the nickname of a guy who belongs in jail."

I felt like a helpless little kid as Charles drove us toward the police station in his rental car, Bill up front with him and myself in the backseat. He was down here to save our asses and we were along for the ride. He and Bill talked a little, Charles all business, but I mostly sat in the back suppressing the urge to vomit.

"Do you ski?" Bill asked him.

"Been skiing my whole life," he said.

"Ever been to Silver?"

"Can't say that I have. I get to Tahoe a couple of times a season." He parked the rental in the police station lot. "This is going to take me a bit," he said. "Best not to have you two milling about. Why don't I call you when we're through here? Should be an hour or two."

As we wandered New Orleans it began to rain, not the deluge of yesterday but a dreary misty drizzle. At first we tried to stay dry under the awnings of businesses but quickly gave up on that. We sat down on a bench to take stock. I reached up and touched my eyebrow, my fingers squishing into the swollen mass so that it sent a sickening jolt into my head. My mouth dry and parched, I could have heaved but lacked the energy to make myself vomit. My whole self throbbed, stiff and sore. Sitting in the rain helped.

I regretted a lot of yesterday, of what I'd said to Kylie, and I had the foolish thought that I wished I could rewind life back just 24 hours and try it over again. I couldn't remember what really had led to our fight or what it was about, but looking back it seemed inevitable.

We wandered without aim, got ourselves lost in a business district. Suits walked to work as if nothing abnormal had happened yesterday, which for them was probably true. I puked in a muddy alley next to a dumpster while Bill peed. I felt like I'd survived a long a perilous binge, if just barely. I just wanted to get back to Colorado though at this point I wasn't quite sure why—no ski school job or girlfriend to get back to. But skiing did sound nice.

After wandering in circles for a while we found a street corner we recognized and made our way back to the police station, no sign of Charles or the boys yet.

"Let's get a beer, man," Bill said.

"Jesus Christ, I can't."

"Hair of the dog," he said, walking into the nearest dive bar.

I knew I had to follow, that anything would be better than sitting here alone, wallowing in my own misery. We were the only ones in the place save the weary bartender. We sat down at the end of the bar and Bill ordered a couple tall boys despite my protest.

"Just drink the damn thing," he said. He took a long swig from his frosty can like he was drawing a deep breath then made a dumb, loud, *ahh* sound like some satisfied schmuck in a Pepsi commercial.

"How is it?" I asked.

"Tastes like shit," he said.

I drank too, and while the first sip hurt, it quickly became easier and tasted better.

"God," Bill said. "I hope I didn't screw things up permanently with Aurelia."

"You guys will be fine," I said. "She gets it. Kylie may never speak to me again."

He had no answer to this. He seemed to contemplate his response. "Lots of fish in the sea," he finally said. "Plus, you're young and dumb so it's okay."

I held my aching head in my hands. I thought he'd at least say something comforting about how I still had a chance with Kylie.

"Cheer up, sport," he said, clapping me on the back. "Finish your drink. Let's see if old Charles managed to get our boys out."

Outside the police station Ryan and Muppet stood with Charles, all three of them smoking cigarettes and the two younger men looking all the more disheveled when compared with Ryan's swank father.

"You're out!" I yelled to them as we approached, Muppet ecstatic but Ryan oddly subdued.

"Charles here is a total badass. Even better than O.J.'s lawyer," Muppet said, at which Charles gave the slightest grin.

"How'd you get them out?" Bill asked.

"I'll tell you all about it over a steak dinner, my treat," Charles said. "And then Ryan and I have a flight to catch back to Seattle."

"Wait. What?" I asked, turning to Ryan. "You're flying to Seattle?"

"It's dinner conversation," Charles said, clapping me on the back. "I'm famished and we'll need some drinks to celebrate these boys' freedom."

We piled into Charles' rental, Ryan sitting bitch in the backseat with me and Bill. Charles seemed to know where he was going. I felt weird around Charles, something like embarrassment, but I didn't know what about. I hadn't been the one arrested. So I directed my question at Ryan as Charles and Muppet gabbed up front. "Your dad said you had a flight to catch back to Seattle. He meant *he* has a flight to catch, right?"

Ryan looked grave. "He's making me come back with him to intern at his firm. Says I have to work off the debt from having him come down here."

This was a gut punch, the prospect of Ryan not returning to Colorado to finish the season. "But what? Why?" I asked, the obvious question being what would happen to Ryan's car and how we'd get back to Silver. But that part didn't matter so much to me. I realized I'd really grown to like him.

He shrugged. "You guys can take my car," he said. "I don't have a choice. It's a bummer, man. I know. A big bummer."

We pulled into the lot of a fancy steakhouse, the kind of place with a burger-free menu and waitresses wearing ties. Charles fit right in, but with us in our filthy clothes and backpacks, I was half surprised they even let us in the place. Charles ordered us big rounds of drinks, his attitude celebratory with the rest of us still tired and hungover. The exception to this was Muppet, who acted happy as ever and ready to party. He kept slapping Charles on the back and putting his arm around him.

"This guy," Muppet said and grinned at all of us. "This guy is the world's biggest badass. You should've seen him in there. Looked like a lawyer on TV or something."

"Yeah," Bill said. "How the hell did you both get out anyway?"

"You tell the story," Muppet told Charles.

Charles talked slowly and calmly, but I couldn't shake a hint of smugness. He liked having an audience. "Derek was easy," he said. "Look at that gash on his face. He should have been taken directly to the hospital for an evaluation and treatment. Simple. I threatened a lawsuit for negligence and they let him go without another thought."

"That's exactly what Aurelia said."

"So if he needs to go to the hospital, what are we doing here ordering steak?" I asked.

Charles laughed at this. "Relax. He doesn't actually need to go to the hospital."

"So it was a bluff?"

"Bingo," he said, draining his scotch and waving the waitress over for another. "Come to think of it, Ryan was pretty easy too. I asked for the evidence on his case and they had none. Probably confiscated his pot and piled it up with everybody else's. Or smoked it their damn selves." He paused to thank the waitress as she brought his next drink. "They make so many goddamned arrests during a festival like this and have too much paperwork to deal with already without having to worry about a lawsuit," he continued. "It's a numbers game for them. They make X number of arrests and ninety-five percent of them won't dispute anything about it. You come in with a suit and tie and threaten to make a stink and they fold."

We ate huge steaks with massive baked potatoes. It would have been in the top five meals of the winter if I wasn't too hungover to enjoy it. Charles ordered us several rounds of cocktails and by my third gin and tonic I felt a bit better and a bit buzzed, with my swollen brow

being the only part of me still palpitating with pain. I went into the bathroom and stared at myself in the mirror. I leaned in, my face inches from the glass. My eyebrow and forehead looked gnarly, puffed and purple, a bit of puss seeping from the gash. I pressed the wound with my finger and felt the heat of pain.

Charles got the check, obviously. "Time to hightail it, boys," he said.

In the parking lot we thanked him profusely and he offered a ride back to the parking lot with Ryan's car

"We'll take a cab," Bill said. "What do you want us to do with the car?"

"Oh, the car," Charles said. "I almost forgot." He pulled a crisp document from his briefcase and signed it before handing it to Bill. "Here's the title. The car's a hunk of shit worth maybe a couple hundred bucks. Keep it. Or sell it. Use the money to ship any of Ryan's stuff up to Seattle."

Ryan made no reaction to this as he handed over his keys. He acted meek and soft spoken in front of his father.

Muppet hugged Charles. "Thanks again. You're a boss."

I hugged Ryan goodbye with a sick feeling in my gut, knowing I'd likely never see him again. He seemed neutered, like his gusto had disappeared.

Then Bill hugged him as well. "We better be seeing you next season, bud. If not later this season. This is no way to end our party."

Ryan nodded at this. "I hope so, guys. I hope so."

And they were off.

When the cab dropped us off, parking tickets covered Ryan's windshield.

"At least they didn't boot it," I said as Bill swiped the tickets to the ground with a forearm like he was clearing off a dusting of snow. Then we put New Orleans behind us, westbound for Colorado in this crappy little rear-wheel-drive Toyota that reeked of weed and dirty socks. I was done partying for a while.

# 19

Ryan's car barely made it back to Silver, howling wind and torrents of crystalline snow pushing us all over the road for the last few hours of white-knuckle driving, ever ahead of the plows. When the mountain finally appeared in the windshield, it looked clean and pure, blanketed in a fresh layer of white.

"You're going to want to ski this," Bill said.

Though I'd barely slept, and my forehead throbbed, he was right.

I dreaded the walk to the ski school locker room, but that's where my boots were, and I figured if I was actually getting fired I deserved at least to have them do it to my face.

The place buzzed with the early morning chaos of people getting dressed and ready. A few people asked what the hell happened to me, but I assumed most everyone had heard the story. Some just stared at the gash above my eye. I walked straight into Sheri's office.

"Ah, good," she said. "You're here to clean out your locker."

"Actually, I'm here to ask you to reconsider."

"Reconsider what? Your losing your job here?" she asked, laughing. "No, no. Your actions might've flown with Paul in charge, but luckily he's no longer here."

She dug through a pile of papers on her desk and handed me an envelope. "Your official notice of termination," she said. "No hard feelings?"

I turned to leave but had to say something first. "Good thing you found this office job," I said, "because you can't ski for shit."

It was dumb but was the only reasonable insult I could think of. I could tell it got under her skin by the way she huffed at me, likely because it was true. She skied stiff and upright with her chest and butt stuck out, arms extended in front of her like she was steering a very large ship. Her easy turns were so slow that any dipshit in a snowplow could pass her.

Her smile turned sour but she nevertheless extended her hand for a shake.

"Fuck off," I said walking out. I cleaned out my locker and Ryan's. As I piled Ryan's shit into a cardboard box, Kylie walked in and pretended not to see me though she must've.

Back up in the room, I opened the envelope that Sheri had given me. It included a notice of termination that said they'd mail me my last paycheck. It also mentioned my spot in employee housing. I felt sick at this one. I hadn't even considered that I'd lose my room if I lost my job. My part time gig at McGillycuddy's wasn't enough to justify my spot. I had three days to figure things out or I was out on the street.

I considered laying down, but I put on my gear instead. The snow dumped as I walked down to the lift. The New Orleans trip had killed my financial situation among other things. I had a few crumpled dollar bills on the desk and a cup of change. I had to get my shit together, and fast.

As the snow cascaded down, my thoughts drifted to a bunny hill back in Michigan. I'd been maybe eight years old, two pairs of Hanes socks stuffed into rental boots, grocery store snow pants, a Detroit Lions Starter jacket, the hill around me packed with people in Carhartts and jeans who'd come up that morning from Indiana in the yellow school and church buses that filled the parking lot. I'd spent the whole morning riding the rope tow before my dad finally convinced me to go up the chairlift. I was terrified—the top looked so high up there, looked like you'd ski right off the side of the mountain if you didn't know how to turn—which I didn't. We got up there and he helped me get off the lift. Trees and farms and water towers spread out below as far as I could see. If I squinted I could almost see the glint of sunlight on Lake Michigan. We waited for a few people to go ahead of us so that we had the whole slope to ourselves and then we started skiing down, me going faster than I dared. That's when the fears faded, when I felt that feeling of flying. That feeling right on the edge of losing control, riding the lip of destruction. Nothing else mattered. I'd come to Colorado, I realized, searching for that feeling. I knew then that I wasn't going to find it. It wasn't here. It wasn't anywhere, because it didn't exist. It wasn't just a feeling or a place but was also a time, a moment, one instant of a Sunday afternoon in the February of a dozen years ago on a 200-foot ice-covered Michigan trash dump with my dad. Nothing would ever match that feeling. I'd keep on chasing it, but I doubted I'd ever find it again.

I got in the singles line of the Flyer and was about to load when I heard Muppet yelling my name from behind. He ducked a rope to get on the chair with me. I didn't want to see him today but here he was.

"Man, it's cold as balls out here," he said.

I nodded without saying a word.

"Pow day, man!" he said. "What're you bummed about?"

Him asking pissed me off, as if he hadn't been there for the whole damned Louisiana debacle—must have forgotten about it as he snored in the backseat with his dirty wadded up blue jeans as a pillow while Bill and I powered through the all-night drive.

I looked over at him; despite goggles and a facemask I could still tell that he'd been beat to shit, his face purple and puffy. My own injury was much smaller, but it still pulsed with a dull ache, the foam of my goggle frame pressing ceaselessly against it.

"I'm bummed that Ryan's not here," I said.

"Oh, yes. There's that. That's a bummer, for sure. But at least we're not both still sitting in jail cells. Good thing Charles showed up when he did."

"Why the hell do you think Charles showed up when he did?"

He shrugged. "Somebody called him is my guess."

Echoes of avalanche cannons rumbled as we got off the lift. He followed as I traversed over to Sierra then took off into the Enchanted

Forest at a frantic pace, not necessarily trying to ditch him but knowing he'd have to ski hard to keep up. We ducked a rope into a secret spot we knew, some thick trees that opened into a small bowl.

I skied straight for a ten-foot cliff in the middle of the bowl with barely a speed check and launched myself off the thing. I'd hit the damn cliff with so much speed that I startled myself, overshooting my expected landing point by a whole lot. When I finally hit the snow, leaning way too far forward, my right binding released with the pressure and my ski popped straight up into the air. This shot me forward into one somersault, then another. I just let myself tumble for a moment before digging my heels into the powder and coming to a stop as my one ski fell straight down and stuck into the snow like a javelin.

I let out a breath I realized I'd been holding the whole time as I felt my arms start to shake with adrenaline. I felt alive. I stood up and let out a howl without thought or pretense, then hiked up to fetch my ski and goggles which had also come off in the fall.

Then I watched Muppet huck the cliff carrying even more speed than I had. He hit the lip and tucked into a front flip. He over-rotated and landed on his back in the powder, somersaulting the same way I had. He crawled out of it, red beard caked in snow.

"Nice," he said to himself. He'd gotten so snow-covered that he took his coat off, draped it over his poles, and pulled his pants down to dump out the champagne snow.

I huffed and puffed with the pain in the ass of digging out my gear and clicking back into my skis in this knee-deep stuff. My right leg churned and churned and post-holed while my left leg stayed up there above the snow attached to my ski. It was a mess, and when I finally got both skis back on I flopped over for a moment just to catch my breath.

We charged like that all morning, Muppet right on my tails. Up at the top of Sierra, the wind picked up so hard that we had trouble standing. Sharp snow crystals pounded our faces.

"Want to head in a grab a cocktail?" Muppet asked.

"Fuck no," I said and skied away. I ducked into the trees and bombed the tightest line I could find, trying now to ditch him. When I popped back out, he was no longer behind me.

I sped off to hit the backside alone. The wind back there wasn't as bad, hiking the ridge off Mountain Chief and making first tracks all over Silver Bowl, where I found pockets of waist-deep. It was that perfect light fluff that you burrow into with each turn before popping back out. Face shots galore.

The bitter cold had a skin-prickling quality, a sharp intensity each time I inhaled. The snow fell harder and harder until I could hardly see and every track filled up within minutes so that every run was in total fresh. For a run or two I even quit thinking about Kylie, or Ryan, or the potential of losing my room.

I found Bill working at the top of Storm King. He sat in the top shack in a t-shirt with the door open. It was about 90 degrees inside. "The heater's stuck on high," he said as I shook snow from my coat. "But it's colder than shit outside so I can't turn it off."

"They're going to kick me out of the Block," I said.

"No way."

"Three days," I said. "If I can't figure out a job, I have to be out in three days."

"Not going to happen," he said. "Even if they do kick you out, it's still my room. There's no waiting list this late in the season. You lose your housing on paper but keep on staying there with me."

Though he said it with confidence, I knew they'd never allow it to happen. Plus, it didn't help my money situation—my couple shifts a week at McGillycuddy's wasn't enough to live on even on the cheap.

"We booked our Argentina tickets," Bill said.

"You and Aurelia?"

"Yup. Deals too good to pass up right now. Better get it while the getting's good because prices are only going up."

It sounded as tempting as it ever had, running south and starting fresh. But I knew Bill's reason for wanting me to go was to broaden my

life experience rather than fleeing from this one, and I couldn't afford a flight even if I wanted to.

"So you and Aurelia made up?"

"I told her I'd buy our tickets to Argentina and told her in Spanish that I love her and want nothing more than to live a life of adventure with her in Argentina."

"You said that all in Spanish?"

"Been learning it all winter. Reading a Spanish dictionary in bed. Got to get ready for South America. You can borrow it when I'm done. I was going to wait and bust out some Spanish once we got down there together, but I had to take out the big guns after our fight."

Hearing this from Bill made me question myself and my inability of drive or forethought to take on anything on that kind of level, and Bill knew it. He changed the subject but didn't turn the dial too terribly far.

"You talked to Ryan at all?"

"No phone," I answered. "You?"

"Not yet. Figured I'd give him a few days then text him. What a goddamned shitty way to go."

I said nothing, didn't need to. It was the truth.

"Get your keys back from Kylie yet?" he asked.

"Nope," I said. "I have nowhere to go at the moment."

The snow came down heavier. Bill went outside, still in his t-shirt, and began shoveling off the ramp. I grabbed an extra shovel and went out to help him.

When we were done I gathered some snow in a Thermos and set it atop the shack's propane heater. When the water was warm, I poured it over a cup of ramen noodles. Water leaked out the cracks in the crushed Styrofoam.

"So much for a nice hot meal," I said then ate the wet, lukewarm, mostly crispy noodles. I thought about the potential of South America, a true adventure of a scope I wouldn't have even thought about a few months ago. "How cheap is it to live down there, really?" I asked.

"Cheap. Definitely doable. We can live on tortillas, stay in cheap hostels until we find an apartment to rent."

There weren't many people riding the lift, one or two unloading every few minutes. The wind picked up again, first a breeze that made the falling snow twirl and dance, then a violent howl that rattled the shack windows. We went inside. With great effort Bill shut the heavy sliding door. We watched the snow come down, picking up until it was sideways as it changed from flakes to pellets that endlessly tinked against the sides of the shack, so thick we couldn't see more than a few feet out the window. I sat up there with him for a good long time.

With each gust the wind sounded like the Amtrak trains that had passed so close to my house back in Michigan, and the shack felt as if it were about to lift off the mountain. The occasional gusts soon became a steady force.

"Is it like this a lot up here?"

"This is the worst I've seen it," Bill answered.

Although we couldn't see the sky, everything took on a yellow tint I'd never seen before, even during the wild thunderstorms I'd seen out over Lake Michigan.

I thought of Kylie and how I might get back in her good graces. Bill bought Aurelia an international plane ticket, a grand gesture, but no way could I afford something like that for Kylie. "Can't believe you spent that much money, man," I said. "That's true love."

"Money on what?"

"Two tickets to Argentina."

"I didn't actually buy hers," he said. "I offered to. She ended up buying her own."

"It was a bluff?"

"No bluff. I had my debit card out and everything. She said if we were going to share an adventure we might as well share the cost. Worked for me."

The wind-driven snow formed a crust on the shack window. Bill walked out into the gale to clear it with a snow shovel.

"You really should buy your flight soon," he said. "Prices will go up before long."

"It's tempting," I said, not mentioning the lack of money or job. "You ever think about going back to the Midwest?"

"All the damn time, man," he said. "You're thinking about going back, aren't you?"

"I don't know what I'm doing. I may not have a choice."

"You always have a choice."

I crushed my empty ramen cup and tossed it in a hook shot toward the trash can, missing by a foot. Bill tossed it in.

"You know what I miss most about Wisconsin?" he asked. "When the leaves change, the sound of the leaves on the ground when you walk through them. You know that swashy sound? The smells in the air, you know? That's my favorite time of year. I haven't been back there since last summer, but Wisconsin will always be my home, you know?"

I did know—I knew exactly what he meant. I felt an intense pang of homesickness for Michigan. Bill stared out the window into the blizzard for a second and then reached into his backpack and pulled out his wallet.

"But anyway," he said, "don't worry too much about money right now. I don't have tons, but I've got enough to float you." He pulled out a $100 bill and handed it to me.

I didn't know what to say. The gesture made me want to stay, made me feel like this is where I belonged. But I knew I didn't want to owe anyone anything either, not even Bill. "I can't take that, man."

"Don't be stupid. Of course you will. You'll get me back someday, when you've got a real job and I'm still a ski bum in need of a couch to sleep on."

I took the bill and thanked him profusely. He shook if off without a word.

Soon came closing time. I helped shovel the ramp and shut down the lift. As he closed and padlocked the shack door, thunder rumbled—deep, ghostly, and unreal up on the mountaintop.

We skied together, picking our way down in zero visibility. I'd have been scared of skiing off a cliff if I didn't know every pitch of the mountain so well. A few times I opened up my turns, having an eerie feeling of not being able to see, making powder turns in the fine graupel that sprayed it up over my head so that I choked for breath—total white room.

* * *

I dumped my skis back at the Block and walked to Cuddy's through a still raging snowstorm and oppressive cold, the windburn on my face flushing with false warmth. I went in knowing full well that what happened inside might dictate that I cut my season short and go home early with my tail between my legs.

Muppet shouted at me from behind the bar when I walked in. "Lost you in the trees out there. You were really hauling balls."

I waved to him without a word and went straight back into the kitchen. Dex chopped tomatoes, bobbing his head as Sublime blared through the speakers. He didn't even look up when I walked in. "You're not scheduled tonight," he said.

"Truth," I said. "I wanted to talk to you. I don't know if you heard what happened down in New Orleans."

"I heard Derek got arrested."

"That, yeah. I stayed down there to help him out and ended up getting fired from ski school."

He nodded, half listening and half just moving to the music as he prepped for dinner.

"Turns out I need to be working full-time to keep my spot in employee housing."

He said nothing, just kept on with his work, rushing back and forth between prep table and walk-in. He wasn't going to say a word unless I milked it out of him.

"So," I continued, "I'm wondering if I could up my hours here to full-time. Otherwise I won't be able to stay on."

He still said nothing. I didn't know what to do but stand there and wait for a response.

"You just going to stand there?" he asked. "Or you going to help me prep?"

I grabbed an apron and tied it on. "Does that mean yes?"

"Sure," he said. "I've been working my balls off here and need a couple of weeks down in Mexico. I'll get my food orders in before I leave. You can hold down the fort."

I could have hugged him in that moment. I don't know if he was trying to do something nice for me or not, or if it was a mutually beneficial arrangement with good timing, but I got the feeling he kind of liked me. I hustled my ass off during that shift and every one thereafter.

* * *

The snow kept up for three more days. Mesmerized by endless flakes, I kept finding myself just staring at them while on the chairlift and in the room. I skied every day until mid-afternoon when I'd head to the restaurant to prep dinner.

I manned the kitchen alone, and the dinner rushes of those days were crazy. I thought about Kylie often, and about Ryan, but while I worked there wasn't much time to think. For some reason those problems felt distant, like if I ignored them and went on with life, they wouldn't matter too much.

The snow finally stopped falling one morning, revealing a cloudless navy blue sky. A blanket of white softened the contours of the mountain as it glistened in the brilliant sunlight. The blizzard left every pine branch bowed from the weight. Skiing the glades, I purposely ran into the ends of branches to make the snow explode around me as I glided by. The world felt fresh and new.

I worked that night with legs so exhausted from skiing deep snow that they felt wobbly as I walked from fridge to grill to order window. Back at the room after work I took the longest, hottest shower I could handle. Afterwards I felt content, not exactly happy but certainly not sad. Bill was down in Aurelia's room; I was glad to have the place to myself. Then came a knock on the door.

I swung it open to find Kylie standing there. I wasn't sure what to say. She stood there in silence for a long moment too. "Hey," she finally said, her voice soft.

"Hey," I said.

"I brought your keys," she said, holding them out to me.

I took them, her warm, soft hand grazing mine. "Thanks," I said.

She reached out and touched my face, looking closely at my wounded eyebrow.

"It's starting to heal," she said.

"Starting to." I held the door open for her. "Want to come in?"

She stood frozen a moment, as if in deep thought, and then stepped through the threshold.

# 20

I worked every night for three weeks straight. On the slow nights, Kylie came in and sat at the bar sipping old fashioneds while I cooked. I'd make us wings and waffle fries, and when I was caught up on tickets we'd eat together at the order window. We were good, in a blissful period following the fight. The wound above my eye was healed over too, slightly tender still but I hardly even noticed it. We'd talked it over and decided that the season was short, so we might as well make up and just start totally fresh. The blowout fight of New Orleans could stay there and we need not bring it up again. It seemed like an immense thing to sweep under the rug, but I tried not to think about it and soon I didn't.

The overtime of working seven days a week helped my bank account crawl out of its hole to modest respectability. I gave Bill his hundo back never having needed it. On the busier nights, after the kitchen closed, I helped Muppet sling beers for cash under the table plus tips.

I felt flush for the first time ever. A couple of times I looked up flights to Buenos Aires and almost pulled the trigger, but it felt too good to have a $500 bankroll.

When Dex finally returned from Mexico I relished the thought of a couple days off.

Bill found a buyer for Ryan's Toyota on Craigslist so he drove it into Frisco to make the sale on a sunny 40-degree day that felt like springtime. The rest of us piled into the Jeep to pick him up and to have a night in town. Bill did the deal in a Safeway parking lot and handed the keys to a 15-year-old kid, his first car.

"He talked me down to two-fifty from five hundred," Bill said. "But the poor shit is in for a rude awakening. I don't think Ryan ever changed the oil on that thing, and it's going to blow up any minute. I just hope it makes it home for him, because he's got my phone number."

We stopped off at the post office and Bill stuck the envelope of cash into a box with the rest of Ryan's stuff. We added a card on which we all wrote that we better be seeing him next season and shipped it off to Seattle.

For dinner, we stopped at a place called the Portside with a porthole on the door and anchors and crap all over the walls despite there being no significant body of water within a thousand miles. Certainly not fancy by anything but ski bum standards, it did serve a steak dinner. We'd all been working so hard to build up savings, and I at least felt like splurging a little—a double date plus Muppet.

As the waitress led us to our table past the bar, Paul called out from one of the stools. "Goddamn, it's good to see you guys," he yelled, shitfaced, his voice far too loud for the dinner crowd. "I been waiting for some friends to show up all night." He looked like crap, scraggly grey beard and filthy clothes, but most notably a slovenly look about him. He must've gained a good 30 pounds around the middle of his already hulking frame in the few weeks since we'd last seen him.

"Hey buddy," I said, realizing too late that I was speaking to him in a tone you'd use with a child. "How've you been?"

"Honestly, I've been better," he said which seemed like too obvious a statement. "Jen moved out and so did her half of the rent. Unemployment's fine but runs out soon, and any other ski school that'll hire me will make me start over from scratch and won't pay me shit. Fuck 'em. Fuck Silver and fuck 'em all!" He yelled this last bit so loud that everybody within earshot turned to look at him and the bartender stepped over with a look of concern, considering his options.

"Y'all want a shot?" Paul said, calmer now. "Round on me."

"No thanks, man," I said.

"Well fuck y'all then," he said. "More for me." And then he yelled to the bartender, "Two tequilas and a Heineken!"

I was glad to follow the hostess away from him but not before I turned to look at the bartender as he pondered whether or not to grant this request. Thankfully, she sat us in the next room, out of view and earshot of Paul. I felt an odd bit of pity for him and wondered why I'd ever felt jealousy toward him. He seemed like a different person—no longer full of vigor, just a fat slob who looked on the verge of death.

"Is that what I was like at Mardi Gras?" Muppet asked as we sat down. "Because damn, I feel bad for you guys if I was. Shit, I'm embarrassed and I'm sorry."

It made me happy to hear Muppet being self-aware for once and gave me hope that I might be capable of changing for the better too. Bill didn't respond with words but reached up and tussled Muppet's hair playfully.

"You're an asshole eighty percent of the time," Aurelia said to him, smiling. "But the rest you're lovable."

"That's not very nice," Kylie said, turning to Muppet. "I'd give you seventy/thirty at least." She paused, thoughtful. "But Paul, damn, he sure isn't looking too good."

"I hope he's okay," Aurelia said.

"Why shouldn't he be?" Bill asked. "Jimmy got fired from ski school too and is doing just fine."

I tipped my glass to Bill at this in a mock cheers at the half compliment.

"Jimmy's tougher than Paul," Kylie said. "Paul's a big baby. He won't take it on the chin and move on. I bet it's been nonstop Big Macs and Jose Cuervo for him for three weeks straight, and probably harder stuff than that."

We ordered and tried to wipe Paul from our minds. Aurelia talked of their South America plans that were coming together quick and concrete. "We're staying with my parents for a couple of weeks until we can find our own place in the mountains. There's plenty of room if you guys come."

I looked at Kylie and she at me. She scrunched her face in a thinking kind of way that made the freckles on her nose stand out. I decided then that if Kylie wanted to go to Argentina, we'd go together.

Our food arrived. I cut into my thick, rare ribeye with vigor. I'd been getting plenty of deep-fried bar food at Cuddy's, but aside from that it was all ramen noodles, tunafish, and peanut butter jellies. I ate with fury and didn't think about the cost of it. I saved the baked potato for last, using it to sop up every bit of juice from the steak, forcing myself to slow down a bit toward the end to really enjoy it. I asked for extra sour cream and scraped every bit from both ramekins, eating it with the skin and all so that the only things that remained on my plate were tinfoil and garnish.

Kylie'd ordered chicken alfredo and ate half of it when she said she was full and passed it to me. I devoured that as well. After dinner, Aurelia ordered dessert, a huge piece of cheesecake. She took one bite then said she was full. The waitress brought forks for everyone. Kylie fed me a big bite with her fork, and we both laughed at the absurdity of this act.

When the waitress brought our check, Muppet grabbed the check holder, stuck his card in it, and handed it back.

"What the hell, man?" Bill said. "We'll split it."

"Nah," Muppet said. "It's on me. Thanks for taking care of me in New Orleans and for putting up with my shit all the time."

The girls, who flanked him, leaned in with one armed hugs in genuine thanks. "That's very nice of you," Aurelia said. "You just lowered you're a-hole score by a good twenty points."

I thanked him, too, clapping him on the back as we got up to leave, which he took as an invitation to wrap me up a big old bear hug. We walked out, arms around each other, passing the empty barstool where Paul had sat. I wondered if they'd kicked him out or if he'd left on his own free will.

# SKI BUM

We strolled the streets of Frisco without purpose or hurry. The air had turned crisp during our time in the restaurant; it felt like midwinter once again. I reached out and grabbed Kylie's bare hand in mine, her skin cold. Bill did the same with Aurelia. We walked into a t-shirt shop and browsed aimlessly.

"What do you think of this Argentina idea?" I asked Kylie as we looked at dumb tourist tees.

"It would be fun, wouldn't it?" she said.

"We should sit down and look at flights sometime soon, and see about jobs down there."

She wrapped her arm around mine and sort of squeezed, which I took as a sign that she agreed.

We walked out of the shop like that, arm in arm. Kylie led me into a bookstore. The group followed. The rest of us gazed at titles, but Kylie pulled books off the shelf and flipped through them, reading first lines.

"Think of how many words are in this place," she said. "I could spend all my time and money in a bookstore like this, but today I'm only going to buy one."

The rest of us milled about, ready to move on for a good ten minutes before Kylie finally made her choice: *100 Years of Solitude* by Gabriel Garcia Marquez.

"I started reading this one in college once," she said after leaving the register. "But some asshole stole everything out of my backpack that I had padlocked to my bike. It has the best first line of any book, ever."

"What's the first line?" I asked.

"*Many years later, as he faced the firing squad,*" she said from memory, "*Colonel Aureliano Buendia was to remember that distant afternoon when his father took him to discover ice.*"

"Ice," I said, trying to absorb the gravity of the words.

"I know how it starts but not how it ends," she said, "and that's been bothering me for two years now."

"It sounds like it ends with the firing squad."

"Yes, but how does it get there? What happens along the way is the important part—not the outcome."

I thought on this statement as we walked and couldn't wrap my head around it. It seemed simple enough but also seemed too big for total comprehension. Did the future matter more than the present? The future seemed infinite while the present was just one snapshot in time, so to me the future had to be the important part, but Kylie seemed to think otherwise.

The next morning we took off to Steamboat for the day, an idyllic drive in the sunshine where we even opened the windows a bit for the fresh air. As I drove, I leaned my head over into the stream of air rushing through, smiling wide as the wind pushed my cheeks back. In the parking lot we lathered on sunscreen, then we spent most of the day ripping groomers—three of us on skis and Bill and Aurelia snowboarding.

We ventured into aspen glades, cruising follow-the-leader style through the trees, the snow before us striped in shadows of the tall, skinny aspens. Kylie skied her perfect turns, laying down carves like railroad tracks in the corduroy. The morning snow had that ideal consistency, firm to hold an edge but soft enough for buttery carves, and that optimal temperature for pure speed. Any warmer, and it would have slowed us down. Everyone ripped; nobody complained or fell behind. It was the best ski day I could think of save for the very deepest powder day.

We'd brought along a little Weber charcoal grill. At lunch time we went out and cooked brats in the parking lot, sitting around in the sunshine, sipping beers and tossing around a Nerf football. As I ate, I closed my eyes and looked up at the sun. Its light shone through my eyelids as I reveled in the feeling of warmth on my face. After lunch I didn't even feel the need to get back on the hill, though we did for a few more runs on cruisers without that pressing desire to rack up as many runs as possible or make the most of every minute.

# SKI BUM

We called it quits pretty early on and spent the rest of the afternoon on the main street of Steamboat Springs, wandering shops again with no desire to spend any money. It felt good to be the gapers for once. In a Western store, Kylie and I tried on cowboy hats in front of a vintage mirror while Bill and Aurelia ogled tooled leather cowboy boots.

"How cool would these be for Argentina?" she asked.

"Let's get them," Bill said, turning the price tag over to read it. He whistled. "Never mind. Maybe we can find some nice ones down there."

Antique framed photographs of horses pulling skiers down the snow-covered main drag of Steamboat Springs lined the walls.

"Dang," Muppet said. "We have *got* to give that a try."

"Darn tootin'," Aurelia said in her best impersonation of a twangy American accent.

We crossed the street and looked through a window at more old-timey photos. It took me a second to notice a couple of sepia toned dudes wearing ski goggles. These weren't old photos but were just made to look old. Aurelia dragged us into the place before I even knew it. Kylie threw me a buckskin vest, chaps, a cowboy hat, and an old flintlock rifle. I put on the buckskin with no shirt underneath so that my chest hair spilled out. She went into a dressing room and came out in a skimpy frilly dress and a garter with a pistol sticking out of it, and a big elaborate feather in her hair. She looked sexy as hell.

Aurelia put on a similar dress to Kylie's. Then Bill came out of the changing room naked, covering his junk with a ten-gallon hat. Kylie and Aurelia both squealed in laughter.

"You're disgusting!" Aurelia shouted at him. "Put on some clothes." She tossed him a vest and tie like a Wild West barkeep would wear.

Muppet wasn't going to join until I dug through the costume trunk and threw him a massive fur robe. He put it on and looked like some kind of grizzled, red bearded, mountain man. His wounds, like mine, were mostly healed, but his face still had a mushy swollen look in places, with a few purplish spots and scabs. This made his costume look all the more intense.

We posed for the photos, us guys trying to look tough and the girls showing off their legs. Muppet sat in the middle holding a fake whiskey bottle in each hand. "Can't we get some real whiskey up in here?" he asked.

Aurelia bought the expensive package with all different sizes of sepia-toned prints. We were all-in as tourists, but in that moment it also felt like the start of an end of something, a deliberate attempt to lock down some memories of the season on a mild and sunny day in which the air had a distinct whiff of spring.

At dusk we drove up some dirt roads toward a hot springs somebody'd told Bill about. As the road climbed into the mountains, it narrowed then became an unplowed fire road covered in packed icy slush. I shifted the Jeep into four-wheel drive and kept on the gas for fear of getting stuck.

We parked in a dirt lot with a few other cars. The pungent smell of sulfur hit us as soon as we opened the doors. We followed a well-trodden path in the snow, lit by moonlight, with the sound of a rushing river drifting through the trees. Previous footsteps had hardened the snow; what melted in the daytime was refreezing now. Kylie and I held onto each other for balance, the trail slick and also the idea of going into freezing wintertime woods to strip down and jump into unknown water leaving us jittery.

We arrived at the spring: a large, natural moonlit pool cloaked in thick steam. The silhouettes of a few people shone through, their voices blending with the murmur of the river current beyond. An old couple darted past us from the trees, bare-ass naked, and waded quickly into the water before disappearing in the mist.

Us guys stripped down to boxers in the cold, piling our clothes on a log. The packed ice felt cold on my feet and the air exhilarating against my bare skin. I felt goosebumps pop up on my arms and my nipples harden. The girls shed their clothes with more modesty, sharing a

woven blanket they'd wrapped around themselves as they stripped down to boy shorts and bras. They hurried toward the water, Kylie's miniscule white bra and shorts glowing in the moonlight. Watching her, more than the cold, made me shiver.

"Hurry up!" she yelled to me. "You're going to freeze."

But I stood there in my boxers a while, embracing the cold until I no longer felt freezing but instead felt warm. I slid down the ice toward the edge of the pool, trying not to fall on my ass.

Moonlight lit the path to the water and gave the steam a bluish glow. My skin burned as I stepped into the pool, even hotter than a hot tub. I stepped down the crude stone steps into Kylie's awaiting arms. The pool seemed to be part natural and part manmade, like people had shaped it over the years out of the existing rock. The smell seemed to fade, or we just got used to it after a while. We waded toward the middle.

The steam thickened so that Kylie was the only person I could see, though I heard Muppet and Bill's voices as they wrestled in the water behind us. The middle of the pool was deep enough that I couldn't touch bottom. Dunking my head, I felt the sting of the nearly healed wound above my eyebrow, the first time I'd even noticed it today. I treaded water for a minute then swam to a spot where I could stand on my toes with just my head from my chin up sticking out. I felt myself sweating in the profound heat. I took long, slow, deep breaths. Kylie jumped on my back and latched on piggyback. I spun us around in the water while we looked up through a break in the steam at the stars above. On this clear, silent night, they looked bright and close in the sky.

"Carry me around," she said, and I did, walking a wide loop around the perimeter of the pool, avoiding getting too close to any of the other bathers, wanting to feel like this place was our private secret.

Separated from the hot spring by a wall of rock, an icy river rushed through the night. We couldn't see it, but its whooshing sound grew as we neared it. Some teenage kids up on the ledge screamed in the night as they jumped off into the river where there must have been a pool. Their high-pitched cries echoed through the darkness as they leapt, each scream cut short by a splash.

Breathing heavy in the oppressive heat of the pool, the rush of the river sounded refreshing. I climbed up onto the rock with Bill and Muppet. We walked to the edge, the frigid air feeling great after the intense heat. It felt good to stand there and breathe easily as we peered over into an eddy of swirling water the size of a hotel pool ten feet below us. The water looked cold even from this height. Across the river, pine trees lined the snowy bank.

Bill ran up behind Muppet without warning and pushed him. I, in turn, pushed Bill. But as he fell, Bill grabbed onto my arm and pulled me off with him. The drop took longer than I thought. I braced myself for the cold. As I landed, it felt like icy water pushed all the air from my lungs. I couldn't get back to the surface fast enough.

We gasped for air as we resurfaced, swimming furiously to get to the rock and then climbing back up and over it. I dropped into the hot spring with a splash and sunk down to envelop myself in the heat. I knelt so that my eyes and nose were all that stuck out.

"How was it?" Aurelia asked.

"Exhilarating," Bill said, "until the hypothermia sets in."

"You guys are all crazy."

Kylie swam over and latched onto me. "Will you do it again?" she asked. "I want to do it with you."

"Hell yes."

We climbed up onto the rock, moonlight glinting on Kylie's wet skin. As I climbed up behind her, my heart about stopped at the sight of the tiny goosebumps on the backs of her thighs. She stood atop the rock, seemingly comfortable in the cold, but I could hardly breathe. I squeezed her from behind.

"Push me, you die," she said, leaning into me. She grabbed my hand. "You ready?"

"Just a second," I said. Then I dropped my boxers and tossed them down on the rock. She looked at me with the biggest grin possible, and without hesitation, unclasped her bra. She peeled it off and held it out to me on one finger. Totally engrossed in everything about this girl, I snatched her bra and threw it down with my boxers. Then she shimmied out of her shorts in a few tiny elegant motions, never losing eye contact with me. She tossed the shorts down as well. I forced myself to breathe.

The guys down below hooted and hollered. I could hear Aurelia's giggle. "You get it, girl!" Aurelia yelled.

"Jump already, you gross silly ass," Bill shouted.

Naked in the moonlight, we peered over the edge. I grabbed her hand and we swung our arms back and forth. With the third swing, we jumped together—a frozen ephemeral moment, suspended in air, the world felt perfect. I'd have paused gravity and time right there to take it all in if I could've.

Still holding hands, we hit the water, my other hand cupped over my balls for protection. As we sunk, my foot touched hard, slippery river rock, and I pushed off back to the surface.

"Cold, cold, cold, cold, cold," Kylie said over and over as we swam. I climbed onto the rock then reached out a hand to help her up. I grabbed our clothes then flopped back into the steaming pool, sinking every part of myself and ignoring the burn.

Muppet and Bill scrambled up for another jump, getting naked themselves.

"Woo," Aurelia yelled up to them. "Look at that sexy ass."

"You're the only one still clothed, you prude," Bill shouted down, blowing a raspberry at her.

She unclasped her bra, pulled it off, and held it up for all to see. We all cheered.

I waded over to Kylie and picked her up, her naked body weightless as she floated in my arms. As Aurelia watched the guys jump, I carried Kylie along the edge of the pool to a spot where the rock overlapped itself, forming a tiny cavern. Inside, a small stream of icy water trickled from the river above. Hissing steam billowed where cold and hot met. I sat down in the pool under this waterfall on a seat formed of rock.

I guided Kylie's slick perfect body onto my lap. She leaned into me—pure energy like grabbing hold of an electric fence and refusing to let go. She rotated her hips. We moved barely, gently, letting the ice water fall upon us until it froze solid in our hair.

# 21

Speeding west on I70 toward Silver, Bill and I gazed at the traffic backed up in the eastbound lane, cars and cars of skiers heading back down to Denver.

"Jesus H. Christ," Bill said. "Look at all these damned people. Can you imagine how much better the skiing would be if they all just stayed home? No lift lines, nobody tracking up all our snow."

"True, but neither of us would have jobs."

Bill shrugged at this. We'd been in Frisco for a grocery and beer run between a ski morning and my dinner shift at McGillycuddy's. I felt damn proud of my bank account. I hadn't even checked my balance before buying food.

He munched fast food cheese curds in the passenger seat. "These things suck," he said. "Damn near inedible. Stop at any gas station in Wisconsin, and you'll find better curds than this."

"Why eat them?"

"Cheese curd's a cheese curd."

I reached over and grabbed a few, popping them in my mouth. As I chewed, something under the hood of the Jeep shuddered, and the dash lit up like a Christmas tree. I looked down at the temperature gauge as it rose up into the red.

"Mother fucker," I said, mouth full of curds, feeling a trembling in the gas pedal beneath my foot. For a second I questioned whether to pull over or try to limp back to Silver. But as I pressed the gas, the temp needle pinned itself as high as it could go and a terrible noise came from the engine bay. A belt or some shit shot out onto the highway. I watched it in the rearview as it flopped dead on the pavement. I closed my eyes and took a deep breath before pulling over to the side.

I popped the hood. It coughed out a smoke cloud when Bill opened it.

"Fuck, man," he said. "This is going to be spendy."

I nodded, already thinking it. Kneeling down on the shoulder I watched liquid drip down into a puddle on the asphalt. Bill stuck his finger in and rubbed the stuff between thumb and forefinger.

"Coolant," he said. "Radiator took a shit, if you're lucky. More likely it's a blown head gasket."

I opened the tailgate and sat there. Bill dumped out our fast food cups, cracked two beers from a fresh 30-pack, and poured them in. He sat down next to me and we drank.

"What do you think?" he asked.

"I think I'm fucked."

"Cherokee's fucked," he said. "You'll be fine."

"Thanks," I said.

"Option one, we get Muppet to haul us out some tools and we try to figure it out ourselves. But I don't have tools here and this fix is probably above my pay grade anyway."

"And option two?"

"You pony up for a tow."

Two hours later, with the Jeep sitting in the lot of some mechanic in Silverthorne, the tow driver dropped me off way late for my night shift.

* * *

The next day, as Kylie and I skied the bumps of Union Peak, the shop called. Without a cell phone of my own, I'd given them hers. I called back from the chairlift. Bill had been spot-on with the head gasket guess, a four-figure repair—borderline not worth it on a rusted, 15-year-old Cherokee with 150,000 miles on the odometer. But I had no

choice. The thing belonged to my parents and was still worth a few grand. I told the shop to go ahead with it.

I felt nothing, not anger or frustration, just an emptiness in the pit of my stomach—right when things were looking up.

"So much for trying to save money," I said. I'd been flat broke before and knew I could climb out of it, but with the uncertainty of the end of the season fast approaching, it was hard to take. That thousand plus dollars was my ticket to whatever came next.

South America was still on the table if I truly wanted it to be. I could put the flight on a credit card, and the rest would fall into place. If that's what we were going to do, I wanted to make the decision now.

"You'll get your savings back up in no time," Kylie said. "Still a month to go in the season."

"It's time we make up our minds on South America. Time to shit or get off the pot."

She nodded as if she understood. I knew she'd been thinking the same thing.

We skied another run, fast and nimble, picking separate lines through the Enchanted Forest, dodging rocks and stumps the warmer weather exposed. It hadn't snowed in a while. In the trees the tracked-out ruts and heavy piles made for thigh-burning turns. It felt good to ski this stuff fast—pick a line and commit—and while I felt borderline out of control at times, I never full-on ran into a tree.

Back on the chair I picked up our conversation right where we'd left off. "I say we do it. Let's quit being wishy washy and dive in together, buy our flights tonight and commit."

I was sure she'd agree with an enthusiastic *hell yes!*

"Your Jeep," she said, not the response I'd hoped for or expected. "That's so much money. It seems irresponsible to commit to something so big without a buffer of savings. I don't exactly have a trust fund either."

I winced at the phrase *buffer of savings*. It sounded gross, corporate, not the type of phrase that fit Kylie's personality—at least not the Kylie I knew.

"It's just money," I said. "Money doesn't even matter."

"It matters when it's the thing that buys plane tickets, and food, and a bed to sleep on."

We sat there, two of us together on the middle of a quad chair, in silence for a minute with just the hum of the haul rope and the clunking as we passed over the rollers of a tower.

"I've been thinking," she said, "the end of the season is only a month away."

"Yeah?" I prompted, trying to sound as calm and understanding as possible, realizing that I *really* wanted this trip to happen. We'd all of us been talking about it all season long, and now in the midst of spring, it felt close, real.

"I just don't think we can pull this off—you and your Jeep, me and my student loans. Maybe we can save enough for plane tickets, but what will we do when we get down there? It could be a while before we find jobs—neither of us speak the language—and we'll need money to live off of."

I could've argued against these points with the same arguments Bill laid on me all season. We could live cheap, be scrappy, trust that everything works out, rely on the kindness that Aurelia had already offered. But I knew from the way Kylie said it that she wouldn't be persuaded. I'd felt a sick emptiness since the breakdown, but now the feeling grew.

She was using my Jeep as an excuse. I wondered how long we would have waffled around with talk of South America if that engine hadn't blown up. I didn't call her out for it. We were happy; I didn't want to disturb that with another fight despite the immense letdown I felt knowing the adventure we'd talked about wasn't going to come to fruition. Yet it was also a relief of sorts having a concrete decision made. I could have gone to South America without her, of course, but I

was too *something* to do it without her; maybe that something was afraid—maybe it was something else.

"So you don't want to go?" I asked, just to make sure the nail was flush with the board.

"I'd like to," she said. "But what if we waited?"

I thought what Bill's reaction to this would be. Waiting is the same as no. You either dive into something or you do nothing at all.

"Waited until when?"

"Until we can save up some money. After the season ends, I could come back to Michigan with you and we could get jobs. I could waitress somewhere."

This caught me off guard. We'd never talked about what was to come after the season, beyond the possibility of Argentina, much less about the idea of her coming home with me. The disappointment about South America lightened at the thought of Kylie in Michigan. We'd reached the top of the mountain. We unloaded the lift and stood there in the stiff mountaintop breeze, not immediately skiing down as usual.

"You'd come to Michigan?" I asked.

"If you wanted me to, I mean," she said. "I'm asking whether you'd want me to."

I grabbed her up in a hug and lifted her, in her skis, up off the snow. I'd thought about this possibility but hadn't said anything to anyone for fear of her thinking I was rushing things. "Of course," I said. "I'd love you to come. We could find a cheap apartment somewhere, maybe stay with my parents for a bit."

"I figure we could work for a few months," she said, "save up some money. Then do whatever we want. Maybe fly down to Argentina—it will still be ski season down there in July. Or, if we want, we could stay in Michigan a while. You could do your fall semester, and I could start taking classes again, work toward an art degree. Maybe come back out here next winter."

"What about your family?" I asked. "They're expecting you to come home, aren't they?"

"I don't mean that I'd stay in Michigan forever. Maybe. But for a year or two while you finish school. Then we could go somewhere else—maybe New Hampshire, maybe here. I don't know. Michigan seems nice. Lots of water and trees."

We skied off into Union Meadows, taking turns following each other and then ducking a rope into our secret spot. Rocks poked through the slushy snow and our skis took hits, each rock making me wince at the potential core shot. We ducked out of there and spent the rest of the afternoon bombing soft cruisers, talking on each lift ride about the future. The way to Michigan we'd turn into an adventure, taking a long and winding route home, west to California and north up the coast, maybe see Ryan in Seattle before turning back east toward the Great Lakes. We'd take a few weeks, camp along the way.

I left for my shift at Cuddy's totally happy—the bullshit expense of my Jeep mattering not and the thought of Kylie coming home with me superseding any disappointment in the South America decision. It was a slow night so I spent a good chunk of it leaning against the bar as Kylie sat there sketching on cocktail napkins.

We talked of a dreamy future beyond our road trip to Michigan—these vague distant plans including a cabin up in the mountains, a dog, an art studio for Kylie out back. She drew this little log cabin in blue ballpoint ink, smoke pouring from the chimney. I'd spend the summer and fall chopping wood for the woodstove, waiting for the first flakes of winter.

Aurelia and Bill joined us when I got off. Bill slapped me on the back lovingly. "You two look pretty damned happy," he said. "News on the Jeep couldn't have been that bad, eh? I've been waiting all day to hear the diagnosis."

That familiar sick feeling in my stomach returned. I hadn't thought about Bill's reaction to our news. I knew he'd be disappointed. I told him about the head gasket and its estimated $1,200 price tag but not about the other.

"Ooo." He pursed his lips with a look of pain on his face. "Your next drink's on me."

"In that case, make it a double Grey Goose," I said.

"You'll have PBR, and you'll like it."

I went back behind the bar and poured us a round.

"You don't seem that bummed," he said.

I sipped long and hard. I didn't want to tell him. After an awkward silent moment, Kylie said it for me. "Great news," she said. "We've decided to road trip once the season ends, and to wind up in Michigan."

Aurelia squealed in delight, happy Ky and I had decided on this next step together. Bill stood there and said nothing, suddenly very interested in a hockey game on TV.

"We really did think hard about South America," I told him. "Damn near pulled the trigger."

"Maybe we'll come in a couple months," Kylie added, "after we save some money."

Bill shook his head as he continued gazing in the direction of the television.

"What's wrong?" Aurelia asked him.

"Everyone talks about going on big adventures," he said. "But nobody ever does it. Money's not a reason. It's an excuse."

"We said maybe," I told him.

"Maybe means no."

"Maybe means maybe," Kylie said. "Maybe in June or July."

"That's fine," he said. "Happy for you guys. Michigan will be fun."

For the next few days he was pretty cold with me—not hostile or anything, but he spent his spare time with Aurelia in the girls' room, and I spent mine with Kylie in ours—planning our separate adventures. In a way, I wished I could be more like him, willing to go anywhere and do anything without a second thought, willing to trust in the world to work things out. It didn't matter now anyway, not as long as Kylie and I were making our plans together.

Those plans included a return to Colorado next winter, especially once the ski school told Kylie they'd be hiring a new Youth Director for next season to replace Paul, and they wanted her to interview. She was ecstatic about the prospect and what it could mean for us next season. With her working a real job like that, maybe we could get a place in Frisco together instead of living in the Block. The night before the interview, in my bed half-heartedly watching a movie, I helped her prep, asking mock questions so she could practice. "Why do you want this job, Miss Harris?"

"I love teaching, I love kids, and most of all, I love skiing," she said. "At ski school I think we have the opportunity to foster a love of skiing in these kids and to make them into life-long skiers."

"Damn," I said, propping myself up on my elbow to look at her. "That's a great freaking answer. You're a shoe-in."

All her answers sounded spot-on to me, though I'd never interviewed for a real job that carried with it any modicum of responsibility.

"What would you say is your biggest weakness?"

She thought for a long time. "Now this one is the big stumper," she said. "It's a bullshit question, but they'll probably ask it anyway. Do you say something nonsensical like *sometimes I'm just too darn committed to my job*? Or do you get overly personal with it? *I can't commit to anything because I can't decide what, or where, I want my life to go—oh, and sometimes I drink too much*."

"I think you're supposed to talk about a weakness that you've already fixed," I said, "a weakness that isn't really a weakness anymore, and how you've worked hard to overcome it. *I wasn't always good at dealing with kids that pee their pants in the middle of a lesson, but I've learned to remain calm and not get disgusted by it anymore.* That kind of thing."

"I think I'm just going to call it out as a bullshit question. Tell them a question like that is a waste of time that teaches them nothing of

value about me. Tell them to ask another one where I can provide a useful answer."

"Really? That's what you're going to do?"

She thought on it for a second. "Yep."

I sat upright and clapped my hands in applause for her. "That's a goddamned power move. Show them you're no pushover. That takes balls."

"Nope," she said. "No balls."

She kissed me goodnight. "Wish me luck," she said, then crawled out of my bed, heading down to her own room for a good night's sleep before the big day.

"Break a leg, my dear," I said, the apple scent of her shampoo lingering on my pillow.

* * *

I waited on a big plush couch in the lobby to hear how the interview went, after which our plan was to take the bus into town to pick up the Jeep. She leaned over and wrapped me in a hug from behind before I even knew she was there, then climbed over to sit next to me, more or less on my lap with a huge grin spread across her face. She wore a sweater and skirt, her curly hair done up nice—gorgeous without sacrificing the goggle-tanned ski bum look that I loved.

"So?" I asked.

"I. Fucking. Nailed it. They're interviewing a few more people and will let me know next week, but I can't imagine anybody giving better answers to those questions."

This news felt good. I knew I was smiling as big as she was. It seemed like real things were happening to us. Real life.

"Did they ask the weakness question?" I asked.

"Yep."

"And?"

She sat upright and delivered her answer just as she had in the interview. "I feel that's a nonsense question, and it tells you more about my interview skills than about me as a person and as a candidate for this job, so let me tell you a bit more about why I'd be great for this position..."

"Ahhh!" I yelled, excited. "And they liked it?"

"They seemed to eat it up."

"Big, brass balls," I said.

"Nope. No balls." She smiled wide and squeezed me in a hug.

She was giddy the whole ride into town. We strolled the few blocks from the bus stop to the mechanic's in warm March sunshine. At the shop I didn't think twice about giving them my debit card to let them drain my account. It felt good to have a fresh Jeep ready for another hundred thousand miles. A few thousand of that would come on our grand, post-season adventure together.

The world felt full of possibility.

# 22

St. Patrick's Day brought dumping snow and, for me, an eight a.m. shift at McGillycuddy's. The drink specials started early with fifty-cent green beers, and with everybody there to drink I didn't do much cooking. I helped Muppet behind the bar for a while before prepping dinner. Back in the kitchen, I drank Irish coffees and had a little buzz on by the time the lunch rush hit.

Come early afternoon a rowdy crowd packed the place, as busy as I'd ever seen it. When the food orders started coming, they seemed to hit all at once. Sweating over ticket after ticket sobered me.

Muppet kept setting fresh pints of Guinness in the kitchen window for me. "Poured an extra by mistake," he'd say with each one, which was pure bullshit. "Can't let it go to waste."

When I finally did get a break, I went out the back door buzzed and sweaty and stood out in the falling snow for a minute letting the fat flakes land and melt on my forearms.

Things got even rowdier once the lifts closed, everyone either in ski gear or wearing green. Lifties we knew from the Block made out with random tourists. The Aussies commandeered the Irish music and belted out their own drinking songs. Kylie and Bill showed up right as Dex took over for me, and we joined the party in earnest. I was over-the-top nice to Bill, who was still acting a little somber. I knew if I kept it up he'd drop the act—it wasn't like him to hold a grudge. We did car bombs then went to see Aurelia at the umbrella bar.

As we walked, Bill's phone buzzed. He looked at it, stopped in his tracks, and answered. "Dude!" he yelled into the phone. "What the hell is up, my friend?" He put the phone on speaker, and while the voice on the other end was drunk too and kept cutting out, it was obviously Ryan.

"I freakin' love you guys!" Ryan yelled, having called from a loud bar where bass thumped behind him. "Everybody here is a bunch of posers pretending to be cool."

We heard a clunk and then indecipherable crowd noise backed by the beat of music.

"Get your ass back here!" Kylie yelled at the phone.

"I'm back. I'm back," he said. "Dropped my phone on the ground."

"I mean come back to Colorado."

"Next winter," he said. "For now, I gotta wear a tie to work. A freaking tie!"

"Your dad's trying to turn you into a respectable young man," Bill said.

"He's got a long time to wait then."

"Don't let the assholes get you down, buddy," I said.

"Amen!" he yelled. "Drink a green beer for me, and smoke some of that green too if you have it. Love you guys."

"We love you, man," I yelled.

"Miss you, buddy," Bill said

The call ended, a minute or so of mostly gibberish, but something we'd all needed. I nearly choked up hearing his voice for some reason, way more emotion than I thought I'd feel though it could have been the Guinness. We stood there staring at Bill's now silent phone as the wet snow fell on us. I felt happy knowing Ryan was okay and thinking about us just as we'd been thinking about him. Right then I was sure I'd see him again, if not on our road trip, then next season for sure.

Bill put his phone away and then form tackled me into the snowbank, giggling. I grabbed the back of his bald head and whitewashed his face. I don't know if it was Ryan's drunk dial that ended Bill's animosity, but maybe. The rest of the night we wandered back and forth between Aurelia happily tending the umbrella bar and Muppet on a marathon shift at McGillycuddy's, drunk and laughing along the way as

the snow fell. When we finally did close Cuddy's down, we walked back to the Block, arms around each other, making meandering tracks in a fresh layer of white.

* * *

Booms of distant avalanche blasting echoed through the village. Muppet and I skied together in fresh but heavy snow. With spring break season in full force, the lift line on the Flyer stretched far beyond its steel maze. Even further up the mountain we had to wait in line. We ended up on Mountain Chief and, trying to ditch the crowds, got off and hiked the ridge toward Tucker Mountain.

The storm let up, exposing the sun. We moved at a clip. Soon sweat drenched us. I stopped to take off my jacket and tie it around my waist. I hoisted my skis back onto my shoulder and kept marching on in just a t-shirt. We reached the Tucker Mountain gate where people stood taking pictures in front of the double black sign. Muppet and I passed them without stopping.

Our steps fell into a steady rhythm, the sound of our boots kicking into the packed snow staircase in unison, with Muppet just a couple paces behind me. We left the trail to pass some other hikers who moved slowly up the ridge.

"Three weeks, man," I said, shouting it so I could keep on moving forward without turning my head.

"Three weeks?"

"Until we're out of here, 'til this place closes."

"You're right."

"What's your plan?" I asked him. "You going back to Michigan?"

"Nah," he said. "Maybe eventually. I'm headed to Cabo for a couple weeks on the beach. Let somebody else pour me drinks for a while. Then I'm back here for the summer. The tips won't be great once the season ends, but bartending will at least keep me afloat."

"I'm going to miss this place," I said.

"Miss what?"

I stopped hiking for a moment. Muppet was following so close that he almost ran into me. "Miss this," I said, motioning to the jagged distant peaks, their white tops jutting into clouds. The sun was now out in full backed by a deep blue sky.

"Those mountains," Muppet said, nodding to them as he stepped around me and continued to climb the slushy ridgeline staircase, "those mountains aren't going anywhere."

"I know the mountains aren't going anywhere, but look at it. The snow is melting. Spring is here."

"It'll be back. Just when you start to get sick of summertime, the snow will start flying again. By Thanksgiving, we'll be skiing again."

"You'll for sure be here next season?"

"Yeah," he said. "I think so. I do think Tahoe would be fun, or maybe Utah where they get pounded every night. But I've got a good thing going here. So yeah, I'll probably be here."

We kept on hiking and topped the ridge onto a rounded stretch toward the top. In this windblown spot, there was no snow and we hiked on rocks. A breeze blew out of the east and chilled my sweaty back. We passed a cairn that marked the Tucker Mountain summit and kept hiking to the top of a chute called the Taco. We stopped here and put jackets back on.

"You'll be back next winter," Muppet said, a statement more than a question.

I dropped my skis to the snow, buckled my boots, and scraped the packed snow from the bottoms with the tip of my pole. "You're probably right."

Muppet nodded and without a word, skated up to the edge of the chute and dropped in. I watched him make four smooth jump turns in the heavy but soft snow, sluff falling alongside him as he opened it up into wide, surfy turns.

I dropped in after him and made a few quick turns to get a feel for the snow, and then with the steepest part of the chute behind me and

without a thought, I pointed my skis downhill and straightlined, leaning back a bit to keep my tips from digging into the heavy snow and death cookies. I absorbed the bumps with my knees and felt right on the edge of losing it, picking up more and more speed as I cruised past Muppet and heard him *whoop* with glee at watching me. I stood upright and stuck my arms out to feel the wind buffeting against my jacket. I was hauling so fast that I felt my jacket parachuting to slow me down. As the slope flattened toward the bottom of Tucker, I felt adrenaline coursing through me and made a few carvy turns as we skied back toward Mountain Chief.

We worked our way back across the mountain and ended up on Resolution where Bill stood outside the top shack leaning on a shovel. He complained of a car bomb hangover when we stopped to see him.

"Shoot me now," he said. "I feel like shit and the season's ending anyway."

"Season's not ending anyway," Muppet said. "We've got damn near a month left."

"We've got a couple weeks of shitty skiing. They're closing down Resolution next week and cutting hours across the board."

"Closing already?" I asked. "Even with all this new snow?"

"Half this new snow will melt today," he said. "It's just dust on top of rocks down there. Good way to fuck up a nice pair of skis." He picked up a chunk of snow and rubbed it across his forehead, above his goggles. "Good God, this headache. Car bombs, man. Can't be mixing like that."

"I don't know what the big deal is," I said. "I drank the same as you, and I feel fine."

"Just you wait five years until you're my age. Live it up now while you can." He pressed what was left of the snow to his head, letting it melt there. "And you," he said to Muppet. "How aren't you hungover? You're as old as I am, and you drink all day long."

"I'm always hungover," Muppet said. "I'm just used to it."

Chair after chair of people unloaded the lift, nearly every seat full on this slow, back bowl triple that was usually downright empty. Bill half-assed some shovel work. I wondered why he didn't just go sit in the shack and rest. He was probably scared of falling asleep or of the propane heater fumes making him vomit.

A chair of kids unloaded, three children awkwardly snowplowing down the ramp before one of them fell over. Bill walked out and picked him up by the back of the jacket to get him out of the way. The two kids who'd remained standing turned around to see the next chair, with their parents on it, approaching the ramp. The mom yelled, a squawk like an eagle as Bill hauled her fallen kid off to the side. She fell as well when she tried to get off the lift, spread eagling on the ramp. Her husband didn't get off at all, riding around the bullwheel. With Bill still tending to the first fallen kid, he was out of reach of the stop button, so the chair didn't shut off until the dad's skis clipped the emergency stop cable on the other side of the bullwheel, sending him tumbling into the snow enclosure. He let out a grunting *oof* sound as he fell. Neither he nor his wife could figure out how to get up.

Bill ran around trying to get the situation under control, first getting the mom unclipped from her skis so she could stand. She just lay there, deadweight like a frozen fish. Muppet and I stood watching the situation like you'd ogle an overturned tractor trailer on the highway, though I suppose we could have jumped in to help. The kids watched on in horror, the youngest one bursting into tears. Though they were decked out in fancy gear, the family obviously couldn't ski for shit.

Bill finally got the mom sorted out and her gear off the ramp before going to work on the flabby dad, who just floundered there on his back with limbs moving aimlessly in the air like an upturned beetle. When Bill went to pick him up, the guy pushed Bill away as he yelled and huffed things like, "I can't believe this." In his panic, he couldn't even get his feet beneath him. Bill finally manhandled him to his feet and the guy trudged off toward his family leaving his skis behind for Bill to clean up.

"Oh, honey," the wife said.

"Are you okay, Dad?" one of the kids asked.

Bill dropped the guys skis at his feet and ran back to get the lift restarted.

"That was your fault," the guy said to Bill. "I can't believe it. The incompetence."

"My fault you forgot to stand up?"

The guy huffed at this. "The lane was unclear. You didn't clear the lane!"

The family kept standing there, clogging up the way so the other skiers now unloading the lift had to skate around them, just begging for another pileup.

"The lane?" Bill said. "Give me a break. Get the hell out of here."

"Get the hell out of here? Do you know how much I pay for this vacation? You're nothing but a bum. What's your name?"

Bill puffed out his chest to emphasize the nametag pinned there. He stuck out both middle fingers, pointing them at the tag. "Bill Larson of Whitewater, Wisconsin," he said. "What's yours, douchebag?"

The man opened his mouth to yell, but I interrupted him. "Just get out of here, asshole. You're blocking the way."

"You shut your mouth, hippie," he said, his face red.

The kids and wife, embarrassed, skied away. The guy finally clicked into his skis and struggled to follow but not before turning around and yelling, "I'll be speaking to your supervisor, and it will not be good for you, you dirty little punk."

"You can speak to my ass!" Muppet yelled after him.

A little crowd of onlookers had built up. Now it dispersed, many of them giving Bill sympathetic smiles.

"You guys better get out of here," he told us. "He's going to complain and somebody will be up here to yell at me soon. Don't want you getting in trouble too."

I patted him on the shoulder. "Good luck, buddy."

"Don't let them give you too much shit," Muppet said as we skied away.

It had been an ugly interaction. Not that Bill had been the one in the wrong, but I knew if he'd been in a better frame of mind he'd have deescalated things before it became a scene. I'd seen him do it before. That cheesedick gaper just wanted an apology whether it was deserved or not. Bill typically would have just given it to him and let him go on his way.

I felt sick again, for Bill this time, and didn't feel much like skiing after that. Muppet and I headed down, needing to get ready for evening shifts at Cuddy's anyway, cruising blues and dodging gapers stopped mid-hill like slalom gates.

* * *

After a busy shift and smelling like fryer grease, Muppet and I met up with the rest of the crew at a bar in the village called the Matrix. Walls painted black and glowing blacklights; it was a tourist kind of place that thumped techno music too loud to carry on a conversation. Not my jam, nor did anybody else seem to love it, but that's where they'd decided to hang out—maybe for a change of pace.

I pushed my way across a full dance floor when I got there and grabbed a stool at the bar between Kylie and Bill.

"Any news on the job front?" I asked Kylie, yelling to make myself heard. I knew she would have been bubbling with excitement had she heard about the job, but I had to ask.

"Nope," she said. "Checking my damn phone all day long, but nothing."

"Damn."

"Why this place?" I asked.

"Didn't want to run the risk of seeing that guy from today," Bill said. "Figured this is the last place he'd be."

"How's the hangover?"

"I'm getting over it," he said, raising his Jack and Coke.

"What the hell ended up happening with him?"

Bill grabbed his pack of American Spirits from the bar top and gestured to the door of the place. "Come outside and I'll tell you."

Out on the patio, we stood around a propane heater though we almost didn't need it, and smoked. I'd grabbed one for the hell of it when Bill offered. I took a couple of puffs and then passed it to Kylie. She took one drag, passed it back. The quiet out here felt immense after the noise inside the bar. The wall seemed to bump with bass while sound poured out the door every time another smoker opened it to go in or out.

"So the guy complains to guest services," Bill said. "Says I *disrespected* him." He made air quotes with his fingers at this part. "They sent the goddamn Vice President of the mountain and my boss up to talk to me. The guy told them that he wanted me fired or that he'd be vacationing at Vail in the future."

"They didn't fire you."

"No, they didn't fire me." He took a long drag and then fired up another cigarette. "My boss vouched for me, talked about my *superior track record*." He used the air quotes again. "That's the only thing that saved my job. They suspended me, though, for the rest of the week, until the asshole goes home."

"Did you tell them how big of an asshole the guy was?" I asked.

"Doesn't matter. *The customer's always right*," he said in a 1950s film reel voice.

Aurelia grabbed his hand and held it. "And get this," she said, "they're giving the jackass and his family free lift tickets next year, so we get to see him again."

"At least you've got a week off so you can just get out and ride," I said, trying to cheer him up.

"Can't even do that," he said. "I'm not allowed on the mountain at all. Got to be out of sight."

I couldn't think of anything to say to him, so I patted him on the back. The punishment seemed excessive, even though he had lost his cool and called the guy a douchebag. Money always won, and that was a bummer.

The tobacco wasn't half bad. When Kylie and I finished our cigarette, I grabbed another from Bill's pack, lit it, and quickly smoked it down in silence.

Back in the bar, our seats had been taken, so we stood along the dance floor, nobody in the mood to dance to this shitass music. I stood in line to buy a round of Jack and Cokes. A group left, and we snagged their sticky booth in the corner—a quieter part of the bar but not by much.

Kylie's phone buzzed and she looked at it, lightning quick. "Ski school," she said and jumped up and out the door.

It seemed late for them to call but I didn't think much about it. A cocktail waitress I recognized from the Block walked around selling glowing neon Jell-O shots from a tray. We bought a round to celebrate Kylie's big new job, but when she came back in she looked stunned. It clearly hadn't been good news.

"Oh, Ky," Aurelia said. "I was sure you'd get the job."

Kylie shook her head. "It wasn't that," she said.

"It wasn't ski school calling?" I asked.

"It was." She paused, a blank stare on her face that made her look like she was about to be sick. "They called about Paul. He left a bar in Silverthorne hammered drunk and wrapped his truck around a tree."

"Jesus," Bill said. "Is he alive?"

"He's alive but barely," she said. "Alive for now, but who knows. He's unconscious I guess."

"Anybody else involved?" I asked.

"Didn't sound like it," Kylie said. "He could have killed somebody. If he ends up dying, at least he didn't take anybody else with him."

I didn't know what to think or feel other than speechless. It felt weird to just keep sitting at this shitty bar but also would have felt weird to leave.

"How'd the ski school find out?" Aurelia asked.

"I guess he had a business card in his wallet. Didn't have a cell phone on him or anything else. They tracked down his family and were notifying a few people they knew he'd been close with I guess."

"Should we do something?" Aurelia asked.

"Nothing we can do," Bill said.

We all sat there, not talking much, the mood somber and our shots sitting there undrunk, glowing neon. I held Kylie's hand and she sort of held mine back. I don't know if we were quiet because we were sad or if we were just stunned by the concept of mortality.

Bill and I went back out to the patio for another cigarette. The storm let up completely, bright stars in a crystal clear sky, and a crescent moon illuminating the village in pale light. This night was my first at Silver in which the air lacked the bite of winter. I dragged deep on the cigarette, its tobacco taste no longer acrid but now earthy and good. I blew out a mouthful of smoke and watched the tendril float upwards into the night sky.

"Seems like this was bound to happen," I said.

"Bound to happen, my ass," Bill said.

"What do you mean?"

"You saw him at the bar the other week. The guy became a lunatic. He made a choice, a series of choices, to get piss ass drunk time and time again and wind up so belligerent that he just gets in his truck and drives off. Nothing's ever bound to happen. This was a dumbass being a dumbass."

I took a long drag, pondering what Bill said. It seemed harsh but not wrong.

"Don't give me that look," he said. "We all get as drunk as the next guy, but then we walk our asses home."

"You're right," I said. "But it's still sad."

"It's sad for sure," he said. "Never said it wasn't. I like the guy—or at least I liked him at one point. I hope he ends up being okay."

I snubbed out my cigarette butt on the metal railing before tossing it into the giant ashtray by the door with a thousand others.

"It is sad, though," he said. "You're right as rain about that."

Back in the bar, the girls had their coats on.

"You guys leaving?" I asked.

"We don't feel like being out right now," Aurelia said. "It's not fun. You guys should stay out though if you want to."

I reached out and grabbed Kylie's hand and squeezed. She looked at me without saying anything. "You want me to come back with you?"

"Stay out," she said. "That's fine."

I couldn't quite read her tone, but I took her at her word and stayed out with Muppet and Bill. The girls took off and us guys sat in silence for a minute. I reached into my pocket and pulled out the napkin on which Kylie had drawn our cabin the other night. I'd forgotten that I'd kept it. I unfolded it and looked at the blue ballpoint ink embossed into the thin paper in Kylie's intricate perfect strokes, the dog that looked like a lab and the smoke pouring from the chimney into the sky. Then I neatly refolded it and put it back.

"Jesus, man," Muppet said. "Think he'll live?"

"Who knows?" I said. "Hopefully." It sunk in a bit for me here that Paul might actually die. I'd never known a young person that died, never somebody where death didn't already seem inescapable.

"Are you afraid to die?" Muppet asked, not so much directed at me or at Bill, but just sort of asked of the ether. I didn't really have an answer, though I hadn't ever thought all that much about it.

"I'm afraid of having a boring life and a boring death," Bill said.

Muppet nodded in agreement. "When I die," he said, "I hope it's a helicopter crash, or I get eaten by a shark or something." He got up for another round of drinks.

I didn't much feel like drinking, didn't much feel like being here, but didn't feel like going home either. "What I'm most afraid of," I said, "is

taking up space in a cemetery for the rest of time. Or being stuck in some urn up on the mantle. Burn me up and dump me on a mountain, or into a lake."

"Noted," Bill said. "I'm right there with you. Ashes to ashes."

Bad music thumped as we sat there with fresh drinks—well-whiskey and Cokes from chintzy little plastic cups. I took a few sips, but it mostly sat there as the ice melted. With the dance floor crowded as ever, we three watched the spring breaker girls dance in their tube tops and heels and skirts. We watched frat dudes with popped collars try to dance up on them and take them home. None of them looked like skiers.

"What do you say we get the hell out of here?" I asked. The boys nodded.

We walked the path back to the Block without a word, string lights reflecting off the flagstone sidewalks wet with snowmelt. Back home I thought about knocking on Kylie's door but didn't. She was probably asleep anyway.

# 23

It had been a tense few days with no real news of Paul; no improvement, no decline. He'd broken about a dozen bones and was in and out of surgery. His head was too swollen to comprehend the damage. Everybody seemed a bit on edge, especially Kylie who played it down though I could tell it was on her mind. I didn't blame her. Rumors spread around the Block—speculation about how drunk Paul had been, nonsense like he'd been running from the cops when he crashed, or that he'd done it on purpose. And I felt guilty for talking about death the other night after the girls left the bar, like it had been bad karma.

With Bill still banned from the mountain, he and I drove an hour south to a little mom and pop ski hill down by Leadville. Compared to Silver it seemed tiny, with only two lifts and none of the hotels or condos or restaurants that came with the term *resort*. It reminded me of the ski hills back home, save for the vert that dwarfed any hill in Michigan. It had one lodge that held the ticket window, rental shop, ski patrol, cafeteria, and bar. The whole building had the dank smell of drying socks. A fire burned in a big stone fireplace right in the middle of the lodge even though it was damn near 60 degrees outside.

Standing there in the ticket line made me nostalgic for Michigan where the Hoosiers from Indiana would show up in church busses on the weekends to ski in jeans and rear-entry boots. They had none of the pretenses of skiers in Colorado and didn't feel the need to try to prove something with fancy clothes and equipment.

We skied groomers all morning without talking much, full on spring slush in hoodies and sunscreen, avoiding thawed patches of grass, rocks, and dirt—most of the steeper stuff closed for the season. I tried to enjoy the feeling of sun on my cheeks and warmth on the chair after feeling the breeze through cotton while cruising groomers, but thoughts of Paul hung like a cloud.

I was glad to be away from Silver for the day.

Early in the afternoon, Kylie left Bill a voicemail. I called her back from the chairlift. "Any news?"

"Good news," she said. "He's not out of the woods yet, but he's conscious at least and doing well. Swelling's down and they don't think there's internal bleeding. Mostly just a shit ton of broken bones, a face all banged up, and a bunch of legal trouble."

At hearing this, I took the kind of deep, satisfying breath I hadn't taken in a few days. "Good things?"

"Good things," she said back. "He looks like absolute shit though, black eyes and busted nose and his face swollen-up like a football."

"You went to see him?"

"No, I didn't go to see him," she said. "His parents texted a pic of him giving a thumbs up to the ski school and they sent it around."

"Oh."

"He'll be in the hospital for weeks, but they're pretty sure he'll live."

I shared the good news with Bill. Our ski day improved. On the chair I leaned my head back, eyes closed, and let the sun warm my face and the pleasant breeze cool my body. It felt damn good, like summertime.

I laid down turns in slush on steep groomer pitches in the fluid way of carving behind a speedboat on a glass lake in some muggy August twilight. We dropped onto a trail where a pair of bikinied girls, a skier in yellow and a boarder in American stars and stripes, wove gorgeous turns ahead of us. I skied behind them, tempted to follow when they veered right at a fork in the trail. But Bill turned left instead, so with him I went.

The wet snow held an edge but barely. Bill surfed big wide carves, his board totally on edge so that with each turn his gloved hand nearly brushed the snow's surface. He carved wide in front of me, slush roostertailing behind like a Mackinac Island ferry, raining down on me in a refreshing shock of cold on exposed forearms. I straightlined to pass him and then made huge, fast carves gaining speed with each one until an edge gave way and I fell onto my ass, sliding 50 yards down the slushy pitch before finally coming to a stop soaked head to toe. Bill stopped next to me, laughing like a madman, and offered a hand to help me up.

"What do you say we grab a beer in the sunshine and dry out?" I said.

"I don't need to dry out—you do," he said, "but a beer sounds good."

From the patio we watched the cheery spring ski crowd, many decked in costumes, Hawaiian shirts, and bikini tops. This crowd had more of a locals vibe than you'd see at Silver, well-worn gear and goggle tans.

I took off my hoodie, draped it over the railing to dry, and could damn near feel the sun evaporating the moisture from my t-shirt. Bill globbed SPF 50 onto his head, the coconut smell of it pleasant and thick in the air.

"Your nose is burnt as hell," he said, and reached out to smear a glob on my face. I let him do it then sipped a satisfying sip of fruity beer that tasted like summer.

* * *

Back at Silver, closing day fast approached, the spring party vibes strong. Still no word, though, on Kylie's job prospect. More bare runs with each passing day caused chairlift after chairlift to shut down for the season, each closure leaving a crew of lifties out of work. A revolving pile of luggage filled the Block lobby as more and more people left every

day. By the time Bill returned from his suspension, Resolution Bowl had closed, though they let him fill in on another crew. It was weird seeing him bump chairs on green runs over by the schoolhouse.

On the thawed pond outside McGillycuddy's, usually occupied by ice skaters, a fountain replaced the Christmas tree that had stood lit up at center ice all winter. Behind the Block a creek flowed freely, having been ice-bound and snow-covered all winter. I hadn't even known it was there.

That last week of the season, though, the temps dropped again and a sleeper storm rolled in overnight bringing with it April powder. Kylie had the day off, so I called in sick to ski with her, knowing it would be our last powder day. We tracked up the eight inches of perfect blower fluff, an enigma this late in the year when even the fresh snow usually had a springtime heft.

In the lift lines, she'd hand me an earbud and we'd listen to bluegrass together—an intimacy in being the only people in a crowded maze listening to the same song. On the chair we talked about vague plans for our road trip and upcoming summer in Michigan. I threw out places I wanted to hit on the drive—Moab, Yosemite, the California coast all the way up through the redwood forest. Getting antsy and excited to hit the road with her, I tried to piece together the itinerary in my head, guessing at driving times based on inches on the map. Kylie wanted more spontaneity.

"I don't want to have a plan," she said. "I want to just drive, just have the freedom to see what we see and go where we go."

"You don't want to have a destination in mind? Or at least decide on a way to go?"

She thought for a second. "That way," she said, nodding her head toward the west, toward the 170 ribbon unfurled far below us. "Let's drive that way."

"West," I said, and that was good enough for me.

She turned the topic back to the ski school job, which she discussed with an almost nervous panic. Every day that passed without news had her more and more on edge. "Them taking this long to decide is not a good sign," she said several times in different ways.

"They're in no rush," I assured her. "They're just focused on the end of this season before worrying about next. I'm certain you'll get it."

"You can't be certain of that. You don't know that."

I left it at that, wanting her to just enjoy this last deep day. On the next lift we rode in silence, sitting close together with the chair tilting in the direction of our weight. Kylie leaned her head on my shoulder in a melancholic way that I took as a bittersweet feeling about the ending season.

With most of the mountain now closed, we tracked up all the open runs by mid-morning, even with the dumping storm providing refills. We stopped at a bumblebee rope blocking off Looking Glass and glanced around for ski patrol.

"Let's make tracks," I said, pulling up the rope for Kylie.

She ducked it and skated off to paint turns in the forbidden pow. I chased her, reveling in face shots and not giving a damn about the rocks blasting against P-tex and steel at the trough of each burrowed turn. We ducked into every closed glade we could find all morning until a couple of patrollers doing the very same thing caught us red handed. They shouted at us to stop; we fled, a rush of adrenaline hit as we straightlined in racing tucks. I don't think they actually chased us—we never turned back to look—but they'd never have caught us anyway.

The storm broke by noon. As the sun pierced the clouds, it returned our world to springtime. As fast as this fresh pow had piled up, it began melting away again. With the whole mountain tracked out, we moved on to mogul runs, making rhythmic metronome lines in the softening bumps. Kylie skied them fast, with seemingly minimal effort, her upper body hardly moving at all as she absorbed each bump with her legs. I skied the same as she did, always looking two or three turns ahead, and I thought back to the beginning of the season when I had to stop after every few mogul turns to scout a new line. When the bump runs dumped onto groomers we bombed the chewed-up crud that just hours ago had been fresh and new.

The last ski school torchlight parade of the season was that night. Aurelia and I hung out on the umbrella bar deck waiting for Bill. Kylie, the only one of us still part of the ski school, headed up the lift with the other instructors. We drank free keg beer from red Solo cups as part of an employee appreciation thing. Aurelia had just gotten off a long shift and gulped hers with vigor.

"I thought Bill was really annoying at first," she said.

I laughed at this. "Don't tell him that," I said.

"Oh, he knows it. I've told him."

"And now look at you," I said. "Making the move to another country together. Another continent."

"He won't stay there for more than a few months. Will he?"

I shrugged. "I don't see why not. He seems to want to be wherever you are."

"If he stays long enough for me to get my degree, then he and I can pack up and travel together."

"Where to?"

She shrugged. "Anywhere, I guess."

I admired her ability to embrace this uncertain future, and I told her so.

"I'm serious about you coming down with us, if you ever decide you want to, whether Kylie comes or not," she said as we replenished our keg cups. "You'll have a bed to sleep on and all the meals you need until you're on your feet."

It made me happy to know that it was more than just Bill who would greet me with open arms.

As we waited for the parade to start, I wondered what the mood was like amongst the ski school crowd at the top of the hill. The one I'd been part of had been a big party, but Paul had been up there handing out beers and egging people on to a good time. Down here, things felt festive and warm, and from the bar deck I people-watched as crowds gathered around the bonfires of the village.

Bill showed up as darkness fell, just in time to see the tiny torchlights appear high on the mountain. We leaned against the railing to watch as the snake of light started its wide, slow turns. The crowd around us cheered at the sight. It *was* quite pretty. As the snake neared the halfway point, it became no longer one rope of light but many individual ones. One of the instructors ate shit, kicking up a cloud of snow before coming to a skidding stop, but managed to keep his torches lit. We joined in the cheering. He got up quickly and sped to reunite with the group.

With a few turns left, the crowd's cheering peaked. As soon as the skiers were close enough to be distinct, I picked out Kylie toward the back of the line, her skiing stronger and prettier than the rest. When I could make out her face, though, I saw that something was wrong. She looked on the verge of tears and while she kept her cool as the parade came to a stop and all the instructors extinguished their flames with a bow, she skated away from the group as fast as she could once the thing had ended.

She came toward us holding back tears, leaning her skis against the deck railing. I'd poured her a beer and offered it as I asked what was wrong. She shook her head no at the cup. "I didn't get the job."

I wanted to console her, but standing there with a beer in each hand I froze, it never crossing my mind to put the damned cups down and hug her.

Aurelia rushed in for the embrace instead. "Oh, Kylie," she said. "I'm so sorry."

We followed Kylie to a back corner of the deck, away from the other instructors who'd joined the party. She slumped into a chair and we sat with her. I reached out to hold her hand, which she just kind of held there, limp.

"Turns out I was never much in the running," she said. "They interviewed half the ski school."

"They thought the torchlight parade would be the best time to tell you you didn't get it?" I asked.

"They didn't bother to tell me anything. They introduced that bitch Sheri as the new director. Had her lead the damn parade."

"Idiots," I said. "Bunch of idiots."

"It was all pointless, planning for next season, getting my hopes up, trying to impress them."

"It wasn't pointless," I said. "It's all life experience."

"It's all bullshit."

"It's their loss," Aurelia said. "You're destined for better things."

Kylie managed a weak smile toward Aurelia.

"You need a drink," I said. "Can I get you a drink?"

"Sure," she said.

"What do you want?"

"Whatever."

"Rum and Coke?"

"Sure."

I felt a burden lift getting up from the table. I didn't know how to comfort her—Aurelia seemed better at it than I—but I could sure get her a drink. Bill followed me, eager to leave the girls alone. We milked our time waiting for the bartender, and when we did get back to the table where the girls sat close together but silent, I set her glass in front of her and tried to change the subject to a cheerier topic.

"I was thinking on our trip we could stop and ski Mammoth for a few days," I said. "They stay open clear into summertime. Conditions could be great for the next week or two."

"I can't talk about this right now."

I nodded and sat with her in silence, interrupted by the first whistle, pop of the season's last firework show. Aurelia and Bill went to the railing to watch as I craned my neck to see the first few blasts before turning back to face Kylie. In the flashing reflections of red and blue light, she chased an ice cube around her glass with a tiny plastic straw.

# 24

Bill and I cut our jeans into short shorts for closing weekend and skied with Aurelia in her pale blue bikini top and a shirtless Muppet in denim overalls. Only Kylie was missing, who despite being pissed as hell at the ski school, still took her job seriously enough to show up to teach the few remaining kids in lessons.

I'd told her there was no reason to be loyal to the ski school when they hadn't been loyal to her, and that nobody'd hold it against her if she bailed on teaching for the day and joined the party. Maybe that was insensitive of me, but damn, this was our last chance to all ski together and if we weren't out here to ski then what the hell was the point of it all?

Perfect spring sun reflected off the slopes, making it warm enough for comfort on exposed skin, but cold enough to keep the snow in decent shape and give the air a crispy bite. I imagined Kylie skiing with us, carefree in that white bikini from our first poached hot tub, the pale fabric against milky, goose-bumped skin.

We rode fast, follow the leader style on sherbet slopes, enjoying the celebration: random breakout slushball fights with other employees, live music thumping from the village, tipping lifties in beers from our backpacks. We passed by the schoolhouse and saw Kylie out there teaching a depressing lesson to just a couple of tiny kids. Though Kylie wore a tank top, the kids looked bundled for the coldest day of January in coats, mittens, and bobble head helmets. We called out and waved. She looked up and waved without her usual smile. It had to suck being stuck there teaching three-year-olds with the rest of us out party shredding.

# SKI BUM

From up on Carefree we looked down at the base of the Eagle where a crowd surrounded a pond skim. We waited our turn. From a few hundred yards above, I sped toward the pool, hitting the little jump that launched me out over the water. I hit the surface, leaning back to help me glide across to the other side, then turned to watch Bill. He slashed a turn in the middle of the pool, spraying a wave up into the howling crowd. Then came Aurelia, speed checking a bit too much into the jump so that she stalled toward the middle of the pond and barely eked her way across without sinking. Finally, Muppet launched from the jump with his typical overzealous speed and tried to spin a 360. He under-rotated it and landed edges first, throwing him down with a massive splash that rained on us with a shocking chill. The crowd went nuts. He emerged from the water with a bow. He got out shivering so a ski patroller threw him an old dog blanket to dry off.

We passed around chairlift beers, getting a good buzz on in the afternoon sunshine. Muppet and I both had night shifts to work at Cuddy's but knew nobody would care too much if we showed up tipsy as long as we weren't shitfaced. I tried to take it all in; the weightless, gut dropping, flying sensation of carving that I knew I'd have to go seven months without—the way the afternoon sun made the peaks of the Ten Mile Range glow golden as if the light came from within them. We mobbed every open run on the mountain, turning like a flock of birds with nobody really in the lead and nobody falling behind. An hour before lifts closed it was damn hard to peel ourselves away from the party to go into work.

When I punched in, I went straight through the kitchen to stand in the walk-in for a minute. I felt my skin harden into goosebumps as I took a few deep breaths to sober up, which worked surprisingly well.

"Surprised you showed up at all," Dex said when I came out of the fridge as he called out the first ticket of the evening.

I stood over the deep fryer, feeling the heat and the greasy smell as I worked up a sweat cooking and plating apps for the rowdier-than-normal après crowd. By mid-shift we'd pretty much run out of food,

Dex having placed his food orders with the intention of ending the season with an empty fridge. Down to the dregs of our frozen deep fryer stuff, I'd just dumped the last of an industrial-sized bag of mozz sticks into a fryer basket when Kylie showed up at the window. Looking morose, bundled up in her puffy coat with fur-lined hood pulled up, she seemed out of place with the jovial closing weekend crowd behind her.

"Can we talk?" she said.

"I'm busy here," I said, or yelled, maybe too irritably. *What the hell? I'm in the middle of a shift.*

When we caught up on tickets I took off my apron and found her at a corner table, sitting there alone in her jacket with an ice water in front of her. People kept on filing into the bar. The place smelled dank and funky like sweaty ski clothes and sour wash rags. The lull in the kitchen wouldn't last long.

"I'm sorry for yelling," I said. "We were busy." She shook her head. "What's wrong?" I asked.

She said nothing—just looked down at the table.

"I can't sit here all night," I said. "I'm still on the clock."

"I'm not going to Michigan," she said.

I didn't fully comprehend what she'd said at first. When I did, my first temptation was to get pissed off, but I knew that would just send things downhill. "What do you mean?" I asked, trying to get a grasp on it. "Like you want to go to New Hampshire to see your family first? We can totally do that. It'll add some time to the trip, but we have nowhere to be. No rush to get home."

"Home?" Her words turned harsh, almost mean. "Michigan isn't my home."

The way she said it caught me off guard. "I didn't mean it like that," I said. "I just mean the place we planned on going; my home."

"I don't know how it got decided that's where we were going. I have a home too, you know? I have a family and a life in New Hampshire. It's not fair that I'm the one that has to make all the sacrifices to accommodate you."

I thought she'd been excited about it. I thought the decision to go to Michigan had been mutual—had even been her idea. "I never asked you to come to Michigan."

"You don't even want me to come?"

"That's not what I said. Not if you're going to be like this. Not if you don't want to."

"It's like you coming home with me was never an option."

I glanced up at the bar where Muppet poured a shotski for a group of girls in ski boots and tank tops. One of them shouted a cheers and they raised the ski, glasses to lips. The crowd around them laughed and shouted, nobody sad or mad or dealing with bullshit.

I turned back to Kylie. "I'm the one that's almost done with school," I said. "It's easier for you to come with me than for me to transfer to a whole other place."

"So I'm just supposed to change my entire life to fit what's easier for you?"

That's not what I'd meant at all, but I knew that's how it sounded. I looked over toward the kitchen and saw that a new load of tickets had come in. I saw Dex's bald head, gleaning with sweat, through the window as he moved quickly around the kitchen.

"Well don't come to Michigan then," I said. "I don't care where we are. I'll come with you."

"I don't want that either," she said.

"Then what do you want?" I asked. "Where are we road tripping to?"

She didn't answer. The growing mass of people pushed in on us a bit. The end of season rowdiness made it hard to hear, hard to think. I felt like there was some writing on the wall, felt a bit like I was melting. I sensed something slipping away from me but also a burden starting to lift. Knowing what was coming gave me a feeling of impending relief, impending freedom. I knew I ought to get back to work but also that I'd be worthless if I went back in there now before finding a resolution here. "Can we go outside?" I asked.

"Sure," she said.

As we got up to leave, I noticed Muppet behind the bar, watching us with a look of concern. And Dex through the window stressing over tickets, having been deserted by his partner. Out in the crisp nighttime air, I shivered in my dishwater and sweat-soaked t-shirt. Breath spilled out in clouds. "So where are we going?"

"We're not," she said, a tear rolling.

"What does that mean?" I asked, knowing perfectly well what it meant yet needing to make her say it, needing to hear it in its finality without any beating around the bush. I wasn't going to let her off the hook without coming out and saying it, but she was sure taking her sweet ass time about it and I wanted her to hurry the fuck up. She cried but said nothing.

"Well?"

"I can't do this anymore," she finally said.

"Can't do what?"

"This," she said. "Us."

Out on the sidewalk, people passed us heading into the bar—some we knew and others we didn't. Every one of them gaped at us, and I didn't much blame them. I wanted to rip the bandage in one quick pull and go our separate ways, yet in the same moment I wanted to prolong things as long as I could. Either way, I didn't like us being a spectacle to all these people.

"Can't we talk about this later?" I asked. "I need to get back to work."

She shook her head. "There is no later."

"What's that mean?"

"I'm leaving tonight," she said. "I have a flight out of Denver first thing in the morning. Shuttle's taking me to a hotel down there tonight."

"You had this planned?" I asked, pushing the words out with stomach muscles clenched, pissed at the idea she'd been leading me on

for weeks, letting me pour over maps and look up campsites with no intention of ever being there with me.

"No."

"Then how are you packed and ready? You have a flight. You have a hotel by the airport."

"I had it planned before I came here," she said. "But not before today."

This end of something had me on the verge of crying, but instead I just steadied myself into a resolute calm, feeling a sore kind of pressure in my throat from holding back tears. I knew then that I'd never see her again. With the warm sunshine of this afternoon gone, the wet hemline of my t-shirt had frozen hard. The chill made it a bit hard to breathe.

"Does this have something to do with Paul?" I asked. I knew it didn't but I had to ask it for some reason because I knew the question would piss her off a bit.

"Of course not," she said.

"Why then?"

She thought on it for a minute and just stood there sniffling, which annoyed me. "It's too big a thing," she finally said. "Too big a thing to move somewhere together."

"I thought you were somebody who wanted to do big things."

"I just want normal," she said.

"Normal?"

"And the fights," she said. "I can't do it. Don't want to do that all the time."

I couldn't argue with her there. A tension in me loosened as I started to realize she was right. Maybe I'd already known that, known that whatever we had was meant to be fun for a season but was never destined to last beyond closing day. Maybe that's what I'd wanted all along, not that it made it all that much easier.

"Okay," I said, turning back toward the door, trying not to think about the fact that this would be our last interaction.

"Can I have a hug at least?" she asked.

I shook my head no. "Safe travels," I said, knowing what a dumb, dicky thing to say it was. I said it anyway.

I left her standing there as I went inside. I rounded the corner from the entryway into the bar and looked back to see her. She just stood there for a long moment, then turned and headed off toward the Block with hands in pockets and hood up. As she walked she leaned forward a bit, like she couldn't get away fast enough. I knew I was supposed to run after her and wrap her in a hug and tell her I'd go anywhere she wanted to go, tell her I loved her and beg her to reconsider. I knew that's what I was supposed to do but not if that's what I should do. And I knew if I wanted this job to take me back next year—which seemed in the moment a far more significant consideration than dealing with my now ex-girlfriend—ditching the chef on the last night of the season was not the right move. The unknown future more important than the immediate past, I went back inside and headed back toward the kitchen.

Muppet looked up from the bar and shouted over the crowd, "You alright, buddy?"

I gave him a thumbs up, grabbed my apron off the kitchen hook, and tied it back on, sure I'd get some snarky comment from Dex. Instead, he said nothing and moved down the line to make space for me. I felt tears streaming down my cheeks before they fell into the fryer grease as I dropped chicken fingers to sizzle. I knew Dex could tell I was crying, but he didn't say anything. I worked my ass off, trying to occupy my mind with hot wings and dishrags, my last time in this kitchen for a while.

Once my shift ended I headed out the back door hauling the night's trash bags with me, skipping the typical shooting the shit over a beer up at the bar with Muppet. I totally Irish goodbyed, not wanting to deal with any end of season nostalgia just now or talk to anybody about what just happened. Lifting the lid of the greasy-ass dumpster, I hoisted the huge bag up over the edge, a now familiar rotten stink spilling out even in the freezing cold.

# SKI BUM

I thought if I could catch Kylie, there'd be something I could say to her to fix things, though I didn't know what I would even say, and I didn't even know what *fix things* would look like or even if that's what I wanted. I just thought I'd figure that all out in the moment.

I walked toward the Block along the raging creek of snowmelt and, without thinking about it, slowed and slowed my pace as I got closer. I felt a bit stunned, a bit sick, a bit glad, and a bit free. I looked up at the moon, glowing light mostly shrouded in cloud cover. Tomorrow would be a ski day, the last of the season.

At the Block I went straight up to Kylie's room and didn't even have to knock on the door because it was propped open with a trash bag.

Aurelia sat on her bed and looked up at me with a frown, the other side of the room a sad kind of empty: bare cinder block walls and a cheap dorm mattress with no sheets on it.

# 25

The last day of the season I skied alone in a constant drizzle, the snow grey and dreary as it melted away. Rivulets streaked across my goggle lenses like rain on a car window. As water soaked through my layers, I felt nauseous and empty in addition to the cold.

The crowds must have gotten their fill of the perfect spring conditions of yesterday. I skied the mostly vacant mountain without turning, the damp cement snow providing little glide—like wet panes of glass stuck together. The constant patter of rain against my Gore-Tex hood gave me something on which to concentrate other than Kylie. It made me somewhat numb to her, like my time with her had never really happened.

Hunkered down and sodden, the lifties looked miserable as I loaded solo lap after lap. I didn't so much mind being wet. From the chair I looked down at the dirt patches below. Thin rivers of melt coursed in zigzag streams cutting roughly down the fall line. On the chair I shivered and couldn't help but think of her. I considered what we'd had and questioned if it had been real or imagined. The initial attraction had been there, no doubt, but after that I couldn't say. Now that it was over, everything with her felt as if we'd faked it. I wondered if I'd been dumb for thinking it true. I wondered how long she'd known it was over, and it pissed me off thinking she knew what was coming as we skied together and made our plans for the future. I wondered if I'd known it and had just suppressed the thought—maybe, probably. I was glad I no longer had a cell phone because I'd have called her in that moment.

# SKI BUM

I looked for steeper lines, searching for speed, gravitating toward the silvery clear icy patches rather than the dull grey slushy ones. Skiing faster felt good, but each run lasted only so long. I found Bill at the bottom of Sierra, sitting there bored and wet with three other lifties. When he saw me he asked the crew boss, "You don't need me here, do you?" then grabbed his board in his arms and loaded a chair with me before he'd really gotten an answer.

"Another season in the books," he said as we rattled under the first tower. "Unemployed once again."

He didn't mention Kylie or ask how I was doing, and I was glad we had a real friendship where we could just leave things be without having to talk about them. He offered an American Spirit. I tucked my chin into my shoulder to block the weather as I lit it. The rain turned to sleety clumps that melted on our clothes just as soon as they landed.

"This time tomorrow, you guys'll be long gone," I said, a bit guilty that this bummed me out almost as much as getting dumped.

"Wheels up at the butt crack of dawn," he said like a mantra. "A few hours shuteye at the airport tonight, redeye to Mexico City, then on to Buenos Aires. Long travel day tomorrow."

I nodded, blowing smoke into the abyss as our chair zoomed ahead. I'd known their travel plans for weeks now, but he didn't seem to be announcing them for my benefit—more like he was psyching himself up.

"One-way flights still $600," he said. "Checked this morning."

"How much for round trip?"

"I didn't look at round trip."

I thought about it hard as I finished my cigarette, pinched it out with wet leather gloves, and zipped the butt into my shell pocket. I tilted my head to let the pooled water spill from my hood.

"Could ski the Andes all summer, then head off to the Alps come September or October," he said. "Come back and bum around here next winter. Then maybe head down to New Zealand next summer."

I smiled at the thought. "That'd be awesome."

"I bet we could get Ryan to come. Just carry our gear in our backpacks and stay in hostels or crash on people's floors. Ski the world."

People always talked about doing things like this, but I knew Bill would really do it—some of it at least.

"Maybe," I said, meaning it. "I'm going to bum around solo for a bit first and see what happens."

For the first time I could see that Bill believed that I might come, that my reasoning resonated with him. For the first time, I believed myself.

Each run became a choose your own adventure of flat light, slush, puddles, wet sideways-falling flakes, fogged goggles, exposed rocks, mud patches, and bits of gravel mixed into what was left of the snowpack that clicked against bases with every turn. I took the lead, bombing, a little in the back seat to plow through whatever slop I came upon.

After a couple of runs, Muppet joined us. And then Aurelia, the rain having squashed the potential of a busy closing day on the umbrella bar deck. Nobody would have called it good skiing, but it was skiing and therefore worth it. Despite a deserted mountain, a few diehard costumed revelers and lift maze slushball fights gave the proper closing day feel. The four of us rode together—two skiers, two boarders—soaked to the bone, trying for some speed, some momentum in the sticky slush as the nasty sleet fell and fell and fell.

Close to 4 o'clock we worked our way to the top of Rendezvous, as high up the mountain as was still open. Maybe out of superstition nobody mentioned last run, but we all knew this was it. I looked off in every direction for one last view from the top, but a grey fog obscured everything. Muppet and I gave Aurelia and Bill a push and then skated off to straightline the first pitch, gathering all the speed we could. With goggles too fogged up to see, I pulled mine up and squinted as I rode, sleet stinging as it pelted my face. We four made sweeping turns, weaving between each other, yelling and laughing in a party mob that reminded me of how I'd skied with friends as an eighth grader—it felt

more like recess, a frenzied game of playground tag, than it did a serious pursuit.

I wondered if we hurried, if we could grab one more ride up the Flyer but knew that was nothing more than wishful thinking. The empty lift overhead meant they'd already loaded last chair. Toward the bottom we slowed, not wanting it to be over. No longer carving, I tightened my turns, letting my tails slide just a split second too long with each one to savor that very last instant in the apex before changing direction, no more hooting and hollering but just trying to embrace that fleeting feeling of perfection.

I reached the base first, passing grey puddles of snowmelt and the roped off maze to the Flyer where the lifties struggled to roll up orange snow fencing for the season. Hockey stopping, I let myself topple over in the slush and laid there, muscles relaxed. The others ended their own runs, falling over as well into the snow beside me. I took off my dank, sopping gloves and with a clammy hand wiped the moisture from my face, relishing the wind and wet burn on my cheeks. We sat there, soggy and silent for a sweet long time before unclicking our gear and getting up.

People filled the lobby of the Block, packed luggage and ski bags piled everywhere, a hum of goodbyes. Cars jammed the driveway out front, license plates from all over. People crammed bags into trunks and strapped gear to roof racks.

Up in the room with our musty wet clothes hanging in the shower to dry, Bill finished packing. He rolled each piece of clothing like an ounce-counting backpacker. Outside the window, the buzzing of the last few ski patrol snowmobiles finishing their daily routines went silent as the last traces of light disappeared behind the mountains. Aurelia came in just as Bill closed the drawstring of his vintage Boy Scout pack. He'd managed to fit everything he owned into a backpack and a snowboard bag.

"Ready to go?" he asked.

"Room empty," she said. "Key turned in."

I walked them down to the lobby, stopping outside Aurelia's room to help roll her wheelie luggage downstairs. We loaded their stuff into the bed of an idling Ford pickup with New Hampshire plates that, of course, reminded me of Kylie and made me wonder exactly where she was in that moment. The liftie who owned it would be dropping them at the airport on his way east.

Aurelia grabbed me in a hug and kissed both my cheeks. "Goodbye, Jimmy," she said. "Hoping to see you real soon."

I reached out a hand to shake Bill's, but he grabbed me into a big bear hug instead, lifting me off the ground for a good few seconds before putting me down. "I'll see you later, man," he said just like he was leaving for work and I'd see him that evening. They got into the back seat and clapped the doors shut. Aurelia waved as they pulled away.

The room didn't look lived in without Bill's stuff and my own strewn about the floor half-packed. I flopped onto the bed, laying there supine but not sleeping for a good hour or so before getting up to finish packing. I stayed up late, alone but not necessarily lonely, putting my piles of stuff together, envious of Bill's ability to go so fast and light. When I came across Kylie's drawing of our cabin and dog, I pondered it long and hard before wadding up the fragile napkin and tossing it in the bathroom trash.

In the mirror I admired the crisp tan lines on my cheeks—pale skin under my eyes where my goggles usually covered, the rest a deep stubbled bronze. I couldn't help but crack a grin before flipping off the light for the night.

Late in the morning when I woke, bright sun streamed in through the window. I looked out at the mountain, chairlifts idle like great dormant monsters—no lift lines, no snowmobiles wailing. Sparse tiny flakes fell, glistening along their earthbound paths.

It took me three trips to empty the room. I looked out the window at the empty hill one last time, turned in my key, and left the Block, stopping at an ATM to drain my bank account.

At McGillycuddy's the windows were dark but the door unlocked. Behind the bar, Muppet loaded liquor bottles into a cardboard box.

"I thought you forgot your check," he said, handing over an envelope from next to the register.

"No way," I said. "I need every penny I can get."

"I'll see you next season," he said, then came out from behind the bar for a handshake turned lingering hug.

Leaving Silver with a chirp of tires on blacktop, I hit the westbound I70 on-ramp and mashed the gas pedal to the floorboard—six cylinders chug, chug, chugging up to speed. I rolled down the window and let the cold air howl against the side of my face. It smelled of road salt and freedom. The highway curved around some mountains and headed up toward Vail Pass. In the rearview I watched the rounded top of Silver Mountain disappear from view.

Bill and Aurelia were in the air now on their way to Argentina, and I knew they'd welcome me if I decided to go. Probably I would. There was Michigan too. I missed it and took comfort knowing I could go back whenever I wanted.

But now, I had almost a grand in cash in my pocket and a full tank of gas, and with each moment of driving, that was the furthest from home I'd ever been.

# About the Author

Still a Michigander at heart, Colin Clancy lives in the mountains of Utah with his wife Amy, toddler son Jackson, and dogs Daisy and Matilda. Baby brother is due to arrive here on Earth shortly. Colin spends his free time outside—skiing, fly fishing, and hunting—and drawing and painting in India ink. *Ski Bum* is his first book. Find more of his work at colinclancy.net.

# Acknowledgements

First and foremost, thanks to my wife Amy, parents Tim and Stacey Clancy, and in-laws Roger and Cathy Bullock for your love and unwavering support. Thanks to my son and the greatest joy of my life, Jackson. And to baby brother on the way: I can't wait to meet you, bud! Thanks to the English departments at Western Michigan University and Northern Michigan University and to the teachers and friends who've encouraged my writing over the years—there are too many to list, but I'd particularly like to thank Cynthia Brandon-Slocum, Roy Buck, Cam Contois, Andy Hilleman, Tim Johnston, Liz Monske, Omar Muhyar, Adam Schuitema, Joe Slocum, and Rob Ware. Also to Jeff Galbraith, Colin Wiseman, and the rest of the crew at Funny Feelings LLC—The Ski Journal, the Snowboarder's Journal, and The Flyfish Journal—for giving my work a home I'm proud of. To my Copper Mountain crew for endless inspiration—you'll no doubt see glimmers of yourselves in these pages: Claire Adams, Laura Burke, Sarah Dawson Shepard, Sara Mason, Mike McNett, Travis Meyer, Jack Sanders, and Adam Watson. To my original ski buds—frigid nights skiing Bittersweet ice with you guys was my first taste of teenage freedom: Nick Beimer, Derek Clarkson, Matt Lafond, Geoff Lindenberg, Jason Lindenberg, Brad Russell, Maggie Walters, and Trevor Zielinski. And finally, a huge thanks to Trisha Lewis at Van Velzer Press for your enthusiasm, knowledge, and support in bringing this book to life.